Delilah

Delilah

Shelia M. Goss

www.urbanchristianonline.net

Urban Books, LLC
78 East Industry Court
Deer Park, NY 11729

ISBN 13: 978-1-60162-885-5
ISBN 10: 1-60162-885-4

First Printing January 2011
Printed in the United States of America

10 9 8 7 6 5 4 3 2 1

This is a work of fiction. Any references or similarities to actual events, real people, living, or dead, or to real locales are intended to give the novel a sense of reality. Any similarity in other names, characters, places, and incidents is entirely coincidental.

Distributed by Kensington Corp.
Submit Wholesale Orders to:
Kensington Publishing Corp.
C/O Penguin Group (USA) Inc.
Attention: Order Processing
405 Murray Hill Parkway
East Rutherford, NJ 07073-2316
Phone: 1-800-526-0275
Fax: 1-800-227-9604

DELILAH

SHELIA M. GOSS

ACKNOWLEDGMENTS

I thank God for showing me grace and mercy every day of my life. The best gift my parents, Lloyd (1947-1996) and Exie Goss, gave me was teaching me and my brothers, Lloyd F. (Jerry) and John, about Christ. For that I'll always be grateful.

I want to dedicate this book to Jasmine Hogan, my twelve-year-old cousin who has shown an unwavering faith at a young age, and my grandmother N.E. Hogan, who at eighty-eight is still on the battlefield.

Of course, my unofficial street team, Hattie Hogan Jones and Nicolette Hogan, get a special shout out, along with three cousins who buy all of my books: Demetrius Hogan, Mary Jean Foster and Dorothy Hodges. I want to thank my local book club, Cedar Hill Divine Women of Faith, for agreeing to choose *Delilah* as their first book of the month for 2011 (smile).

Although this is my tenth book, this is my first work of Christian fiction. Thank you, Joylynn Jossel, for making this book possible. I also want to thank my agent, Maxine Thompson, as well as Carl Weber and everyone else at Urban Christian.

I also want to thank the following for their prayers and encouragement: Kemmerly Beckham, Carla J. Curtis, Kandie Delley, Peggy Eldridge-Love, Linda Dominique Grosvenor, Deborah Hartman-Fox, Sheila L. Jackson, Shelia E. Lipsey, Michelle McGriff, Angelia Menchan, and Anthony Rivers.

Acknowledgments

I've had a great support system behind me on this literary journey, and I would like to thank the following people: Mrs. Til (Jokae's Book Store in Dallas); Abiola Abrams; Vincent Alexandria; Gwyneth Bolton; Tina Brooks McKinney; Jennifer Coissiere; Yasmin Coleman (APOOO Book Club); Ella Curry (EDC Creations); Essentially Women; Eleuthera Book Club; Brenda Evans; Sharon "Shaye" Gray; Bettye Griffin; Cynthia Harrison (one of my test readers); LaShaunda Hoffman (*Shades of Romance* magazine); Yolanda Johnson-Bryant; Live, Love, Laugh and Books; Lutishia Lovely; Rhonda McKnight; Darlene Mitchell (another one of my test readers); Michelle Monkou; Celeste O'Norfleet; Debra Owsley (Simply Said Accessories); Onika Pascal; Tee C. Royal (RAWS.I.S.T.A.Z.); and the list goes on and on.

Thanks, Cedric Ceballos, my favorite former NBA player, for being a man of your word.

If your name wasn't mentioned, it's not that I forgot about you; I just ran out of room. Thank you _____ (fill in your name). I appreciate you all.

Shelia M. Goss

Chapter 1

"Dee, either you do what I asked you to do or else I'll let your church family know all about your prostitution days," William Trusts said, from the other end of the phone.

Delilah opened her mouth to speak but nothing came out at first. She was caught off guard by this revelation. She assumed her past was like a bad dream, long forgotten. "How did you . . . How did you know about that?" she stuttered.

"Why do you think I chose you to handle this important task? Money seems to rule your world, baby. Now do me a favor; hurry up and get what I want. Your life just might depend on it."

The phone remained up to Delilah's ear until the automated recording came on. "If you'd like to make a call, please hang up or call your operator." William Trusts had hung up on her.

Delilah refused to go back to the life she led before she got her latest job as a project coordinator at Trusts Enterprise. She would do whatever she had to do to remain on top, and if that included deceiving people who had come to trust her—then so be it. She had done it once. She could do it again. Only thing was, she wasn't Dee anymore. She had chosen to go by her birth name,

Delilah S. Baker, when she started attending Peaceful Rest Missionary Baptist Church a few months ago.

She turned and stared at the man who had finally succumbed to her advances after numerous one-on-one counseling sessions. He was the man she hoped to marry one day, the man the members of Peaceful Rest Missionary Baptist Church called Reverend Samson Judges. His snoring was a welcomed sound after their night of passionate lovemaking.

Delilah couldn't believe her luck. She had seen him on television and when William Trusts, her boss, asked her to find out as much as she could about Samson, she knew it was a sign for her to attend his church. She had fallen in love with the local television evangelist as soon as she saw him walk across the stage live on TV.

He had swagger like the rapper Jay-Z and good looks that mimicked Denzel Washington's, except Samson's skin was lighter. With his naturally wavy jet-black hair, fair skin, and thick mustache, Samson was an immediate turn on. Despite their situation, Delilah didn't want to think the man she watched weekly had any flaws. She had met too many men who disappointed her time after time. In her mind, Samson was perfect.

William, on the other hand, believed that every man had a skeleton in his closet. He offered Delilah financial security if she took on the task of finding out Samson's Achilles' heel. Once she agreed to do so, she started attending Samson's church and had quickly become part of several of the ministries, most notably the singles' group and Pastor's Aide committee. She originally joined Peaceful Rest for the wrong reasons, but through her interactions with other church members and learning more about God and Christ because of Samson's teachings, she renewed her relationship with God.

God was the last thing on her mind right now, however, as Samson stirred beside her. She felt his leg brush against her. "Good morning," Delilah said.

Samson didn't respond right away. "I'm sorry about last night," he said with remorse.

"Why are you apologizing? Nothing happened that we both didn't want to happen," she assured him.

He sat up in bed, making sure the comforter covered his lower body. "I'm not a drinker, and I should have told you so when you insisted I drink the glass of wine."

"Like I told you, it had little alcohol in it," Delilah lied. She knew the sweet taste of the wine masked its potent effect. She would have to thank her friend, Keisha, for the bottle later.

He rubbed his temples. "I have a lot to repent for."

"The Good Book says it's okay to drink in moderation," Delilah said as she moved closer to him in the bed.

"The Lord frowns on fornication. And what we did last night, well, it just wasn't right." Samson pushed her away.

Delilah felt embarrassed. She slipped her naked body under the comforter. Samson reached to the side of the bed for his clothes. "I think I better get going."

"You can wash up in there." Delilah pointed toward the master bathroom connected to her bedroom.

He barely said thanks before she saw him walk in the bathroom and close the door.

Delilah frowned because it seemed her plan had backfired. She hoped he could look past last night. They had become so close, and she didn't want to think about going back to a life without him. She grabbed her pink satin robe from a nearby chair and put it on before sitting back on the bed. A few minutes later, Samson walked out of the bathroom fully dressed and looking refreshed.

"In light of what happened, I think we should keep our distance," Samson said.

"But . . . it was bound to happen. We have chemistry. We're meant to be together," Delilah responded.

Samson hung his head before looking back up. "Delilah, you're a sweet woman, and any man would be blessed to have you in his life. But you must be forgetting—I'm already spoken for. I'm getting married in two weeks, and this shouldn't have happened."

Just the thought of Samson's fiancée, Julia Rivers, put Delilah in a foul mood. "Whatever, Samson. I thought you were different. Now I see you're just like the rest of the men out there. You got what you want—now just leave." Delilah turned her back to him.

Samson walked up to where she sat. "Delilah, don't be like that. What we did was wrong. You know it, and I know it. Let's just end this as friends." He reached out with both hands to hold her hand.

Delilah became livid and pushed his hands away. "I have enough friends."

"I'm sorry. Let me know what I can do to make it better," Samson said.

Delilah gave him the silent treatment and wouldn't look him in the face. Samson stood and waited, but a minute later he said, "Just tell me what I can do to make it up to you, and I will. I'm so sorry I let it get to this. Will you forgive me?"

Delilah looked him directly in the eyes. "Ask God to forgive you, but as for me, I need you to leave *now*!"

Samson didn't delay leaving after she raised her voice. It wasn't long before she heard the front door close. Delilah ran to the bedroom window and watched Samson get in the black SUV the church had leased for him two months prior.

"Samson, you're going to be mine one way or another. You having a fiancée don't mean nothing to me," Delilah said out loud.

A smile swept across Delilah's face as she thought of how Julia would respond once she learned of Samson's indiscretion. Delilah removed the small camera she had hidden behind the clock. She hadn't planned on using the video; she planned on telling William the camera had malfunctioned. But now, Samson's actions left her with no choice.

Chapter 2

"Julia's been trying to reach you all night," Kelly Judges, Samson's mom, said to her son over the phone.

Samson could hardly get a word in. At times, he would hold the phone away from his ear. When he tried to say something, he was cut off again. He finally said to his mother, "I'll call her."

"You do that. I hope you weren't unavailable because of Delilah. I told you there's something about that woman I just don't like."

Samson wondered how his mom seemed to always know what was going on in his life. He assured her, "Mom, nothing is wrong. I'll call Julia and all will be well. Trust me."

"In God I trust only," she responded. "Just make sure you straighten it out. Your wedding is two weeks away. There's still a lot to do."

He listened to his mom go on and on about his upcoming nuptials. One would think she was the one getting married instead of him. "I've waited all my life to see my only child get married. Now whatever is going on with you, deal with it before you say the words 'I do,'" Kelly said.

"Yes, ma'am," he responded. At least she cut off her usually long lecture before she got to the part about how long she had prayed for a child and after twenty years of marriage, the Lord blessed her and his dad with a son. His mom informed him at an early age that she had given him to God the moment she found out she was pregnant.

Because of the constant reminder of his obligations, Samson, at thirty years old, did his best to stay on the straight and narrow. Even in his teen years, when some pastors' kids, or PKs as most people called them, were being rebellious, he did the opposite. He avoided trouble and didn't mind spending most of his time in church right under his dad's coattail as he learned more and more about God's Word.

As soon as Samson hung up the phone with his mom, he reminisced about the night before. It had been obvious to him from the moment he met Delilah that she was different. He was used to putting off women's advances, but there was something about Delilah and her model height that caused him to throw caution to the wind and give in to the desires she stirred up in him.

He knew he shouldn't be having the carnal thoughts that crept in his mind every time she came into view. Delilah changed her hairstyle like most women changed clothes. He never knew what to expect. One thing that didn't change was her curvaceous figure and sweet, alluring perfume. His father had warned him about what to expect as a pastor when it came to women. That was one reason why his father insisted he get married. He said a single man over a church would cause many to sin, and he was right about that. He had only been the pastor for a year, and although Peaceful Rest had seen an increase in membership, it was obvious many of the new female members were there only in hopes of snagging a husband, and not just any man—him as their golden prize.

The phone rang again. Elaine Benjamin, his secretary, would answer and let him know if he needed to pick up the call. He was lucky Elaine decided to stay and work for him when his father, Regis Judges, decided to retire at the age of seventy-six. He knew stepping into his father's shoes as pastor would be a challenge.

Elaine, five feet even with heels on, walked into Samson's office handing him a pink slip of paper. "William Trusts says he'll be waiting on your call," she said.

Samson took the paper and balled it up before aiming for the trash can as if he was shooting basketball. "I hope he's not holding his breath."

"Would it really hurt you to meet with him? At least one more time?" she asked as she stood in front of his mahogany wooden desk.

"It's only a waste of time. Unless the Lord places it on my heart to give up the land that Trusts wants, I will not, nor will Peaceful Rest, have anything to do with him," Samson said sternly. Samson and the church had agreed to use the land they had purchased on the south side of the neighborhood to build a community action center, something that in Samson's opinion would be more beneficial than a shopping center.

"It would be something good for the community. It'll bring jobs," Elaine added.

"I refuse to make a deal with the devil. And Trusts should be wearing a red suit instead of those black pinstriped ones he likes to wear," Samson said.

"Pray about it again. I have to finish up the programs

for Sunday, so I'll let you do what you do." Elaine turned around before walking out the door. "I forgot to tell you, Julia will be here any minute."

Before Samson could take in what Elaine had said, Julia stormed into the room almost running Elaine over. "I'll be out here if you need anything," Elaine said with a raised eyebrow before shutting his office door.

"Samson Judges, I've been calling you all night," Julia said, sounding agitated.

"I—" he stuttered.

Julia stood in her cream-colored designer suit with her hands on her hips. Her arched eyebrows were coming together due to the frown on her face. She used her freshly manicured nails to illustrate her frustrations as she talked.

"Don't even think about lying to me because I sat outside of your house until two in the morning and you, mister, didn't return home."

"What had happened was . . . someone called and needed prayer. It took longer than I had expected, so I just spent the night."

Julia walked closer and stood over Samson. "Who was the person? You could have prayed for them over the phone."

"You know I like to be sitting face-to-face with people when I can," Samson responded.

Julia folded her arms and tapped her feet. "I'm waiting. Who was this person in desperate need of prayer?"

Samson mumbled, "Delilah," but it sounded like he said, "David."

"Oh, now you act like you can barely talk," Julia said.

"It doesn't matter. It's done and over with. I'm here.

You're here," Samson said as he stood up and tried to wrap his arms around Julia.

Julia resisted at first. Samson touched her chin. "Come on. Let me see those dimples. Pleeeease," he cooed.

Julia pouted. "Samson, I don't know if I'll be able to deal with this as first lady—the midnight calls and not knowing when you'll be home. I just don't know."

Julia turned away from Samson and walked near the large bookshelf located on the opposite side of his office. Samson went and stood beside her. He reached for her hand. "Julia, you'll be a perfect first lady. You are my Proverbs thirty-one woman. Peaceful Rest will be blessed to have you as its first lady. Not to mention me."

Julia's frown turned to a smile. "I guess the wedding is stressing me out."

"It's going to be all right. In two weeks, we'll both look back on this time and laugh." Samson rubbed her hand and then pulled Julia in for a hug. He got a strange feeling that between now and their wedding, the drama was just beginning, and it'd be no laughing matter.

Chapter 3

Delilah sat in the church parking lot listening to her favorite morning show as she attempted to calm her nerves. She could slap Elaine for not putting her call through to Samson. She knew why her calls were being filtered when she pulled up on the lot and saw Julia's green Mercedes parked next to Samson's SUV. Delilah watched from a distance as Samson walked Julia to her car.

He's such a gentleman, Delilah thought as she watched him hold Julia's door open.

She waited until she was sure Julia was off the church grounds before zooming in to the parking spot Julia had just abandoned. Before Samson could re-enter the church, Delilah was on his heels. "Just the man I wanted to see," Delilah said as she touched his shoulder.

Startled, Samson jumped before turning around. "Whew, Delilah. You almost gave me a heart attack."

Pretending to be shy, Delilah apologized. "I hated the way you left this morning."

Samson interrupted her. "Let's stay outside. I don't want anyone to hear our conversation."

"But, Pastor, it's eighty degrees out here, and you know brown sugar melts," Delilah teased with her eyes.

"It is hot for April. Follow me to my office. I'll just tell Elaine to hold all of my calls."

Delilah smiled as she followed him to his office. She didn't bother to speak to Elaine as they passed by her. In the past, Elaine had made it obvious that she didn't like Delilah, and as far as Delilah was concerned the feelings were mutual.

As soon as Delilah closed and locked Samson's office door, she pounced on him. Samson didn't resist her as she stuck her tongue down his throat. He moaned, giving her the desired effect she wanted, and that's when she pulled away from him. She straightened her skirt and took a seat in one of the chairs across from his desk.

It took Samson a minute to recover from the French kiss. "Delilah, we can't keep doing this," he said as he took a seat behind his desk.

Delilah made sure the short skirt she wore eased up even more as she crossed her legs, giving Samson a view of what he would be missing if he didn't continue their liaison. "You still have time to call off your wedding," she said.

"Why would I do that?" Samson asked, looking puzzled.

Delilah leaned in closer, showing her cleavage. "You could have this every night if you would tell Ms. Prissy to take a hike."

"I love Julia," he responded.

Delilah laughed. "Yeah, right. If you loved her so much, there's no way you would have been in my bed."

"That was an accident. I had too much to drink."

Delilah enjoyed watching Samson squirm. He didn't think she would let him get off the hook that easily, did he? She was not a piece of old clothing he could just throw away. No, she was human. She was flesh, and she was in love with him.

"Is that the excuse you're going to give her when she finds out about us?" Delilah asked.

"There's no need for either one of us to say anything to Julia. It happened one time, and it won't happen again," Samson said in a low voice.

Delilah stood up and eased her skirt up over her hips. She walked around the desk and swirled Samson's chair around.

"What are you doing?" Samson asked, stuttering.

She sat her naked bottom on his lap. "Oh, you might be a man of God, but you know exactly what I'm doing. And if you don't, he sure does," Delilah said, pointing between his legs.

Samson panted, "The door. Anybody could walk in."

"The door is locked. The only way anyone will know what we're doing is if you make noise."

"We can't," Samson said unsuccessfully as Delilah unbuttoned her shirt.

Samson's resistance turned into participation as he played with Delilah's chest, and they both went at it as if they were at a buffet and hadn't eaten in months.

Less than thirty minutes later, Delilah viewed herself in the mirror and fixed her hair. She put on more lipstick so she wouldn't raise any suspicion with Elaine. "Now what was that you were saying about us?" Delilah asked as she turned around to face Samson.

Samson scared her when he fell down on his knees and started praying. "Father God, please forgive me. Lord, I'm weak. Temptation keeps knocking at my door, and I keep answering. Please remove the desires of my loins so that I can remain faithful to you, Lord. Lord, please forgive Delilah, as she is only a pawn of the enemy. Change her heart so she too can resist the temptations of evil. In Jesus' name I pray. Amen."

Delilah didn't know if she should be mad or throw in an amen herself. There was some truth in his prayer. She was being used by his enemy to get him to do something he didn't want to do. Now, the fact that he was a willing participant in sleeping with her not once, but now twice, didn't have anything to do with William Trusts or the devil. He slept with Delilah of his own accord. Delilah knew it, and Samson did too. Delilah wanted to tell him while he was down praying to ask God to forgive him for lying—lying about not wanting her the way she knew he did, or the way she wanted him.

"Pastor, I'm leaving you for now. This thing between us"—Delilah pointed her finger at him and then back at herself—"is just getting started."

Delilah left Samson staring at her as she walked out of his office. Elaine rolled her eyes at her when she walked by her desk. Delilah put more bounce in her step and slung her shoulder-length hair weave as she walked toward the bathroom.

While Delilah was washing her hands, Elaine entered the bathroom. "I know what you're doing, but it's not going to work," Elaine said with clenched teeth.

Delilah viewed herself and Elaine in the mirror. "I have no idea what you're talking about."

Elaine stepped closer. "Look. I can see through the games. Pastor can't, but I can. There are plenty of single men in this church. Go try to snag one of them."

"It sounds like someone is a little jealous," Delilah said. "What is it about me that you wish you had?"

Elaine didn't bother to respond. She left Delilah in the bathroom with a huge grin on her face. "I don't know who she thinks I am," she said to her reflection in the mirror. "I don't care if you're short or tall, big or small, I come from the Grove, and in the Grove we'll snatch anyone up who steps to us the wrong way."

Elaine had Delilah reminiscing about her earlier years when she had to fight just to survive the streets. That was an era in her life she was really trying to forget, but folks like Elaine and William just wouldn't let her.

Chapter 4

Samson did his best to concentrate on his upcoming nuptials, but thoughts of Delilah in his office a few days ago seemed to be on the forefront of his mind. He prided himself on walking in the Spirit of the Lord, but lately lust for Delilah had taken center stage. He stared out the window at the open space in his backyard. Thoughts of Delilah were soon replaced with thoughts of the family he would have with Julia—the woman he loved.

"Lord, why now? I've been able to control my carnal nature for years. Now that you've sent me the woman I've prayed for, why now?"

He walked away from the window and took a seat behind the desk in his study. He picked up the black leather Bible his father had given him the day he dropped Samson off on the campus of Grambling University his freshman year. He could recall the speech he'd given him also. "Son, I've tried to protect you as much as I could. You're going to be faced with many temptations. Don't try to fight them on your own. I'm giving you a new Bible to start a new stage of your life. Use it. Let God fight your battles."

During his time at Grambling, Samson was able to resist drugs and alcohol, but he wasn't prepared for the onset of girls who constantly hounded him. His innocence and Creole good looks, combined with his Southern charm, was an automatic attraction. He spent many nights going from one young woman to another. He barely passed his freshman year. He gave his parents the lame excuse of trying to adjust to being away from home for his lackluster grades.

The cell phone ringing brought him out of his thoughts. He hadn't bothered to look at the caller ID. The voice of the one person he had been trying to avoid for the last few days squealed from the other end. "Why aren't you returning any of my calls?" Delilah asked.

Samson leaned his head back in his chair and swiveled it around. "I've been busy."

"We need to talk."

"There's nothing else we need to talk about. What happened in my office the other day was a mistake."

Delilah seemed to purr her words. "We both know you wanted it as much as I did."

Samson couldn't argue with her. Delilah told the truth. He hated himself for succumbing to her, so his only recourse was to keep his distance—by any means necessary. "Let's pretend like none of this happened. We can go back to being just friends."

"Friends? You have got to be kidding." Delilah laughed.

Samson's doorbell rang. He held the phone, listening to Delilah go on and on. He was grateful for the interruption. He would thank whoever it was responsible for getting him off the phone. He opened the door, and to his surprise Delilah stood on his front porch. She closed her flip phone. "Surprise," she said, with an evil grin, moving past him into his house without waiting for an invitation to enter.

She turned and looked around. "You have a nice home, Samson. I've wondered why you never invited me over before."

Samson stood by the door, never taking his hand off the door knob. "Delilah, what are you doing here?"

She removed the dress jacket from her shoulders and threw it on the chair. "Like you don't know." She began to unbutton her shirt.

Samson rushed from the door and grabbed her jacket. "This has to stop."

Delilah swayed her body from side to side. "It doesn't have to." She continued to unbutton her blouse.

Samson's reflex automatically threw the jacket at Delilah, throwing her off guard. She bent down to get it, but while stooped she moved closer to Samson.

"What is going on here?" Julia asked, as she whisked through the opened door.

Samson, stunned and lost for words, couldn't talk. Julia asked again, "Samson?"

Delilah winked at Samson as she stood up. "I lost one of my contacts on the floor, so Samson, I mean Pastor Judges, stood still until I could locate it." Delilah plastered a fake smile on her face as she faced Julia. "And I did, so I'll be going." She turned around and with her back toward Julia winked at Samson again. "Pastor, thank you for the advice. I feel better now."

Delilah held her jacket in front of her, and Samson hoped and prayed she wasn't showing too much cleavage when she whisked past Julia. Julia slammed the door behind Delilah, missing her back by inches. "Good riddance."

"You could have tripped her," Samson said.

"Humph. Like I care." Julia moved closer to him. "When we get married, these home visits by your parishioners—that's going to stop."

Samson didn't know if he liked this side of Julia. "Dear, you can't dictate how I run my ministry."

She crossed her arms in front of her. "If you think for a minute that I'm fooled by the likes of Delilah and other women like her who come to Peaceful Rest, you have another thing coming."

"There's nothing going on between me and those women. I'm their pastor."

"Uh-huh." Julia never did uncross her arms.

Samson attempted to kiss her on the lips, but she turned her head so fast his lips landed on her cheek. She pulled away. "Samson, I'm going to give you the opportunity to change your mind if you want to. Are you sure you're ready to marry me?"

"Yes, I'm ready to marry you," Samson didn't hesitate to respond. "You're the woman I've prayed for. I love you, Julia."

She sulked. "It's hard to tell."

Samson rubbed her back. "We're both stressed, so just chill out, okay?"

Julia faced him. "I love you so much, Samson, but I'm not going to be like some of these first ladies in the city. I refuse to share you with anyone."

"You're not going to have to share me. I'm a one-woman man." Samson hoped God wouldn't strike him down. In his heart, he was a one-woman man. He just had to figure out a way to get Delilah out of his system. He would keep his distance from her—he had to.

He embraced Julia and blinked a few times when

he glanced at one of the living room windows and saw Delilah blowing him kisses. Before he could react, she walked away. He squeezed Julia without once taking his eyes off the window. He had to think of a way to deal with Delilah or risk losing Julia—and that's one thing he wasn't ready to do.

Chapter 5

Delilah laughed all the way to her car. She got a rise out of watching Samson squirm around Miss Goody Two Shoes. She couldn't wait to burst Julia's bubble when she walked away with her man and the status of first lady. Samson wanted to play games with her emotions; she would show him how to play. Delilah thought about the video of her and Samson together. She wouldn't give it to William, but she sure would use it to get what she wanted from Samson.

Two hours later, Delilah sat across from several other church members as they all discussed what the Pastor's Aide committee would be doing for their pastor's upcoming wedding.

Dorothy Neely, the president of the Pastor's Aide committee, said, "Julia says she doesn't need our help, but I feel we should be doing something. What do y'all think about helping out at the reception?"

Dorothy was the oldest member on the committee. She went to school with Samson's mother and never let the other committee members forget it.

As far as Delilah was concerned, there would be no wedding. She leaned back in her chair and waited to see what the other eleven members had to say.

With arms adorned in big, red bangle bracelets,

Michelle Thompson spoke first. "Ms. Dorothy, it is their wedding, so I think we should honor Julia's wishes." Some of the other members, including Delilah, nodded in agreement.

"Nonsense," Dorothy responded. "I say we take a vote. All in favor of not doing anything at the reception raise your hand."

Six hands went up. Dorothy smiled, but her smile soon faded when Delilah's hand went up, making the number seven and sealing the majority. Dorothy huffed. "Well, we can at least take up a special collection so we can get them a nice gift."

Delilah uncrossed her legs and leaned forward. "No disrespect, Ms. Dorothy. I don't know about y'all, but I'm on a budget." Delilah looked around the room. "I can't afford to buy them an individual gift and then donate money for another gift."

Michelle jumped into the conversation. "I say, let's chip in for one huge gift and then sign our names to the card."

"I've already gotten them something, so I'll pass," Delilah responded.

Lora Stampley, who was about the same age as Dorothy, said, "Dorothy, why don't we just all get individual gifts?"

Dorothy rolled her eyes and ignored her. She looked around the room and said, "All in agreement with one big gift instead of doing individual gifts raise your hand."

Several of the other women had bought their gifts already too. Those who hadn't raised their hands. Dorothy said, "You ladies can still sign your name to the card."

Lora whispered in Delilah's ear, "I can't stand her sometimes."

Delilah couldn't help but chuckle. She was glad to learn she wasn't the only one who had her fill of Dorothy. Delilah smiled as they continued to discuss other upcoming church events. The only reason she joined the Pastor's Aide committee was so that she could get closer to Samson. She used being part of the committee as an excuse to see him one-on-one in his office. She was sure Elaine could see past that, but Delilah didn't care. She watched the other women in the room, and besides Ms. Dorothy and Michelle, who was happily married to a prominent Shreveport attorney, she had a feeling most of the other women were on the committee for the same reason she was. They could step back because as soon as she got rid of Julia, Samson was all hers.

Delilah heard her name being called a few times before snapping back into reality. "Just ignore Dorothy," Lora said.

Too late. Dorothy had Delilah's full attention. "You ladies need to start setting an example for the young women of the church. How are we to tell them how to be modest if we're dressed any kind of way?"

Delilah rolled her eyes. "I dress for me, not everybody else," Delilah said.

"Don't think I'm singling you out," Dorothy said.

"It sure sounds like it. I don't see you saying anything to anyone else in the room."

All eyes were on Delilah. "Ms. Dorothy, why don't we table this discussion for another time?" Michelle asked as she pulled the top of her blouse closer together, covering her cleavage.

"That's the problem now. Nobody ever wants to talk about things." Dorothy pointed at one of the other women in the room who had on a very short skirt. "Dear, what you have on would be inappropriate for church. God is not pleased with you showing all of that." She moved her hands up and down from her waist to her lower body.

The other women remained quiet. Delilah refused to sit and be insulted because of her style of dress. "Just because you've let your body go doesn't mean the rest of us have to hide behind long, ugly dresses."

Dorothy put one of her hands on her hip. "I will not be insulted by the likes of you."

Delilah stood up but remained in front of her chair. "I was taught to respect my elders, but you have to give respect to get it. I think I better leave before we both say some things we'll regret later."

"Yes, you better because I might be old, but I haven't forgotten how to throw down."

Michelle jumped up and intervened. "Ms. Dorothy, this is so not like you." Michelle wrapped her arm around Dorothy's shoulders and glanced in Delilah's direction. "Delilah, I think you leaving now would be a great idea."

Delilah reached down and grabbed her purse. She had to pass Dorothy to get to the front door. "Let that be the last time you disrespect me. Elder or not, I have no problem kicking your behind." Delilah heard the women murmuring as she strutted out the door.

Chapter 6

Samson said a silent prayer before leaving his office to head to the sanctuary. "Samson, we need to talk," his mom said before he could reach the entryway to the sanctuary.

He turned around to face her. "Mom, is it life-threatening?" he asked, noticing the worried look on her face.

"No, but—" she said.

"Then it can wait until after church. Love you." He kissed her on the cheek.

The soloist's voice rang out the words, "So I'll just say thank you, Lord . . . I won't complain," while the other ministers in the pulpit stood up and greeted Samson as he made his way to the center seat. There was not an empty seat in the church as people of all ages began to feel the Holy Spirit. As the song ended, Samson made his way to the podium. The music continued to play as Samson sang the words, "So I'll just say thank you, Lord . . . I won't complain."

He paused and said, "You know, sometimes you just have to say, 'Thank you, Lord.' When your husband won't act right, say, 'Thank you, Lord.'" Shouts were heard throughout the sanctuary. "When your wife won't act right, say, 'Thank you, Lord.' When the kids won't act right," the people in the congregation shouted along with him, "Thank you, Lord.'

"Don't let that fire stop burning; we're just getting started. Ushers, I'll let you take over from here," Samson said as he backed away from the podium and took his seat.

Assistant Pastor Michael Monroe whispered in his ear, "We took up $5,000 in Sunday School this morning."

Samson wasn't concerned about the money. He knew that as long as he preached the Word, the people would come, and he trusted that God would take care of all of the church's needs. Money was the last thing on his mind as he mentally prepared for his sermon. The choir sang an A and B selection, getting the members spiritually ready to receive the Word. The pianist sang the hymn "Amazing Grace."

Samson, with his mind on delivering God's Word to His people, eased his way to the podium. "Turn your Bibles to the fourth chapter of James. Let's read verses one through three together. I'm going to use the New Living Translation."

The congregation stood and read along with him. "What is causing the quarrels and fights among you? Don't they come from the evil desires at war within you? You want what you don't have, so you scheme and kill to get it. You are jealous of what others have, but you can't get it, so you fight and wage war to take it away from them. Yet you don't have what you want because you don't ask God for it. And even when you ask, you don't get it because your motives are all wrong—you want only what will give you pleasure."

Samson asked, "Do you sometimes wonder why it seems God isn't answering your prayers?"

"Yes," could be heard throughout the congregation.

"Well, ask yourselves, Where is God in my prayers? How does He fit in? Are we asking for things just to satisfy our earthly needs, or is what we're asking for going to help uplift or build the Kingdom of God? Don't go getting quiet on me now."

Samson read more scriptures out of that chapter and said, "Thank God for His mercy because He knows what we're going to pray for before we utter a word."

Forty-five minutes later, Samson stepped out of the pulpit, and with his cordless microphone, walked back and forth in front of the first pews for the altar call. "God gave His only begotten Son so that none of us will perish. Accept Christ as your Lord and Savior. Don't wait until next Sunday because today is all you have. Come now and be saved."

Several people—men and women—accepted the invitation and walked down to the altar. Souls were saved, and the saints rejoiced. Samson and his associate ministers fellowshipped with the members after service. Samson smiled as he thought about the souls that had been saved. The smile on his face turned to a frown when Delilah, dressed in a hot pink suit, bypassed some of the other ministers to get to him.

"Pastor Judges, I really enjoyed your sermon today," she said, extending her hand.

Samson knew if he didn't shake her hand, it would draw attention. "Sister Delilah, I'm just God's vessel." He plastered on a fake smile and shook her hand. Delilah gripped his hand, and he had to pull it several times before she released it.

Before walking away, Delilah moved closer and whispered, "We need to talk."

"We have nothing else to talk about," he said.

"I think we do," she insisted.

Samson watched Delilah walk away. He felt someone tugging on his sleeve then turned around. "Julia, dear. I was wondering if you were here." He gave her a hug.

"I was running late, so I sat in the back." Not once did Julia stop looking in the direction Delilah had walked. "I see your fan club is in full effect."

Samson chuckled. "Now, Julia, don't even start."

She held out her hand, showcasing her three carat diamond engagement ring. "Some of these women forget who is wearing your ring."

Before Samson could respond, other members walked up to him. Julia stood in the background until he greeted the rest of his church members. "See, that didn't take too long, now did it?" Samson asked as he led them to his office.

Samson was startled to see his mom in his office when he opened the door. Standing next to her was Dorothy. "There you are. Baby, we need to talk about one of your members," Kelly turned and said.

Before Samson could respond, Dorothy blurted out, "That Delilah girl. She had the nerve to threaten me at the last Pastor's Aide meeting. Something needs to be done about her."

Samson removed his black robe and hung it up as he listened to Dorothy recount the events of their meeting. Samson took a few deep breaths in an attempt to remain calm as he thought about the best way to handle the situation.

Julia stood in the corner with her arms crossed. She said, "I never did like that woman."

"Ms. Dorothy, I'm sure Delilah didn't go off on you for no reason," Samson said.

Kelly was appalled at her son's comment. "I can't believe you're taking up for that woman. Dorothy is like an aunt to you, and here you are siding with Delilah."

"Mama, I'm not taking sides. As pastor, I have to look at things objectively," Samson explained.

"This is Dorothy we're talking about, a woman you've known your entire life."

"Forget it, Kelly. I can handle Ms. Jezebel." The sweat was popping off Dorothy's forehead as she talked.

"Ladies, there's no need to do any name-calling. I'll talk to Delilah and see if she can apologize."

Julia said, "No, you're not going to do anything. I'll talk to Delilah. If I'm going to be first lady, it'll be my duty to talk to the women of the church when issues arise."

"She's right," Kelly said. "She might as well start now."

Samson had to think quickly. He didn't want Julia anywhere near Delilah. "You're busy with last-minute wedding details. I'm not trying to put more responsibilities on you."

Julia walked up to Samson and gave him a tight hug. "Dear, I'll take on this responsibility with great pleasure."

Before Samson could protest, Julia was out the door. The satisfied look on the faces of his mom and Dorothy made him wonder if he was worrying for nothing. He prayed Delilah wouldn't tell Julia about their indiscretions.

Chapter 7

Delilah's house was located in the Eden Garden neighborhood, not too far from the church. Delilah hadn't been home long enough to change clothes when her doorbell rang. She looked out the peephole and chuckled. Delilah opened the door. "Well hello there," she said.

"No need for pleasantries," Julia responded.

Delilah started to say, "In that case, we can hold this conversation on the porch," but instead she said, "Come in and have a seat."

She wanted Julia to see that she too was living large. No, she didn't have the big house, but her home was filled with nice furniture, and Black art covered the walls. Each room was color coordinated to fit a certain theme. "Would you like something to drink?" she asked as she took a seat across from Julia.

"No. I doubt if I'll be here that long."

"Whatever." Delilah turned and looked Julia directly in the eyes. "So why are you here?" Delilah watched Julia squirm in her seat. *Not too cocky now are you?*

"Ms. Dorothy told Pastor Judges about your altercation."

"First of all, if you're going to come to me with some mess, get your story straight."

"All I know is what she told Pastor Judges."

"Did Samson send you over here?"

"As the future first lady, it will be my job to diffuse situations like this, so I wanted to squash this before it got out of hand."

"There's nothing to squash. We had a meeting. She said a few things I didn't like, and I said a few things she didn't like. End of story."

"Well, Ms. Dorothy said you attacked her."

Delilah didn't allow Julia to finish. "Ms. Dorothy is a bitter old woman who y'all let get away with talking to folks crazy. I respect my elders, but when she questioned how I dressed, that was it for me."

Julia cleared her throat after looking Delilah up and down. "You have to admit, you do dress provocatively."

Delilah stood up. She pressed her hands down on her knee-length skirt. "Am I to be ashamed of the body that God blessed me with? Unlike you, I don't have a problem flaunting my body."

"You can choose to wear something else."

Delilah laughed. "Julia, if I wore a sack, your man, the good reverend, would still notice the body hidden underneath it, so stop hating."

Julia turned beet red. "You have no shame do you?"

"I haven't done anything."

"God is not the author of confusion."

Delilah placed her hand on her hip. "Are you calling me a devil?"

"I'm just saying you could have handled that situation with Ms. Dorothy better."

"Maybe so, but I didn't grow up at Peaceful Rest and will not let her or you disrespect me."

Julia stood up."I should have known coming over here wouldn't do any good."

"Then why did you come?" Delilah asked.

"Let's drop it. It's probably best that you resign from the Pastor's Aide committee," Julia said before walking toward the door.

"Ohhh. Now I see what this is about. You don't care about Ms. Dorothy; you're just concerned about Samson." Delilah, with a pout on her lips, said, "Until Samson kicks me off the committee, regardless of what you or Ms. Dorothy want, I will remain on the Pastor's Aide committee. Now if there's nothing else, I have things to do."

Julia turned around when she got to the door. "Dee— Isn't that what your friends call you?—Samson and I are getting married next weekend, so if I were you, I would give it up, honey. The best woman has won."

Delilah gritted her teeth. "You're the she-devil. Get out of my house now."

"Gladly," Julia said.

Delilah slammed the door behind her. The wall shook. Delilah rushed to locate her cordless phone and dialed Samson's number. "Samson, I need to see you tonight," she shouted.

"I have plans," he responded.

"I suggest you break them or your future bride will find out all about us?"

"Delilah, I'm tired of you threatening me with this. Julia's meeting me for dinner. Afterward, I'm telling her myself. Are you happy now?"

That was not the response she expected to get from Samson. Delilah hung the phone up. She had to think and think fast. Thoughts raced in Delilah's head as she imagined how Julia would respond once she found out about her and Samson. Delilah was confident there would be no wedding. Samson wouldn't have to worry because Delilah planned on being there to console him.

"Samson, yes, tell her. That means you'll be mine sooner than later," Delilah smiled.

Chapter 8

The palms of Samson's hands were drenching with sweat. He grabbed another napkin off the dining room table to wipe them. He listened to his mother and Julia go over last-minute wedding details while they ate dinner. He couldn't wait to get Julia alone so he could find out what happened at Delilah's. He dreaded telling her about his indiscretion, but Delilah had left him no choice.

"Son, I can't tell you enough how proud I am of you and this beautiful woman here," Regis said between bites.

"Thanks, Dad." Samson hoped Julia would forgive him because between her parents and his, they had spent a lot of money on their upcoming wedding.

"Julia told me about her visit with Delilah," Kelly said.

Samson saw the looks exchanged between Kelly and his dad.

"We'll talk about it later," Julia said to her fiancé.

"Dear, the first thing you need to learn is to never, ever sugarcoat things when you talk to your husband," Kelly advised. "He'll appreciate your honesty." Kelly looked in Regis' direction. "Won't he, dear?"

Regis dropped his head. "And son, you'll learn to never disagree with your wife."

Samson and Julia looked at each other and laughed. "This will be us in thirty years," Samson said.

Kelly didn't seem to find it amusing. Her nose twitched. "Well, Samson you already know how I feel about Delilah."

"Everybody at this table knows how you feel," Samson responded.

Kelly ignored Samson and continued to give Julia advice. Their conversation transferred from the dining room table to the den. Samson was relieved when Regis finally took over the conversation.

"These two probably want to spend a little time together before it gets too late," Regis said.

Kelly smiled. "Oh, I was young once. Julia, why didn't you stop me? I would have let you two go a long time ago."

Julia looked at Samson. Samson shrugged his shoulders before Julia spoke. "Mrs. Kelly, I always enjoy our conversations."

Samson's parents walked them to the door. Kelly reached out to hug Julia goodbye. "Remember what I said." Kelly then hugged Samson and whispered in his ear when he bent his head down, "Take care of your mess."

Samson and Julia exited the house, and less than an hour later, Samson and Julia were sitting on her couch watching a romantic comedy on DVD. Samson couldn't enjoy the movie or Julia's company because he dreaded telling her about him and Delilah. He visualized Julia's reaction to the news in his head several times. He was positive her response would mimic the woman's reaction in the movie they were watching. It was enough to change his mind. He would have to figure out another way to deal with Delilah. He couldn't dare risk losing Julia by telling her about his lack of restraint.

Samson yawned. "I don't know about you, but I'm getting sleepy, so I better go."

"You could spend the night," Julia said in a low and sultry voice.

"I don't think that's a good idea." Samson moved and Julia stood up.

"Why? We're getting married next week, so why not?"

"We decided to wait until after we're married, so waiting one more week won't hurt."

"I'm a woman, and I have needs." Julia waved her hands back and forth in the air. "This no sex before marriage was your idea. I've been waiting two years to have sex with you. We're about to get married, so come on. Let's just do it." Samson could hear the frustration in her voice.

"I have needs too, but baby, we've come this far. We can wait." Julia had no idea how hard it was for him to resist making love to her. He had never seen her so aggressive with him before.

"I bet you if it was Delilah offering her body to you, you wouldn't turn it down?"

"This has nothing to do with her and everything to do with us."

"Prove it." Julia started kissing him and unbuttoning her blouse.

Samson pushed her off him, almost tripping on her coffee table. "Hold up. I'd better be going before things get out of hand."

"You don't have to go," Julia said as she licked her lips.

"I don't want to go, but if I don't, we both might do something we'll regret tomorrow." The sweat popped off Samson's forehead.

"You're right. I don't know what came over me. Let me walk you out." Julia buttoned up her blouse.

"Baby, in one week, we can sleep in each other's arms every night," Samson said.

"I know. I let my lust take over for a minute."

Samson smiled. "It happens."

"Call me when you make it home."

Samson kissed her goodnight and exited her house. He let out a sigh as he slid into the driver's seat of his SUV. BeBe and CeCe Winans' latest gospel CD blasted through the speakers. Julia had no idea how much he wanted her, but he would not break his vow to God by sleeping with her and desecrating their relationship. He could wait until Saturday night.

His conscience seemed to speak out loud. *You would rather mess around with Delilah instead.*

Samson turned the music up louder in a failed attempt to drown out his own thoughts. He sped home and immediately called Julia when he pulled up in his driveway. "I miss you already," he told her.

"You could have stayed."

"And have you hate me in the morning? I don't think so." Samson turned the ignition off and exited his vehicle

"Tonight will be the only night I can sleep. There's so much more on our wedding to-do list."

"I'm confident you have it all covered."

Samson blinked twice. He couldn't believe Delilah stood on the opposite side of his tinted windows. "Samson, are you in there?" Delilah yelled. She placed her face on his tinted windows when he didn't immediately respond.

"Julia, I'll talk to you tomorrow. Good night." He didn't wait for her to respond. He prayed Julia didn't hear Delilah yelling from the outside of his SUV. He removed his keys from the ignition and opened the door.

"Delilah, you need to go home." Samson tried not to brush up against her when he exited his SUV. Delilah reached out for him. He hit her hands every time she tried to touch him.

"Come on, Samson. I know you're hurting. I waited for you to come to me, but when you didn't come, I decided to come to you."

Samson looked around, hoping none of his neighbors were looking. He grabbed Delilah by the arm. "Come on. Let's take this inside."

Delilah giggled. "That's what I'm talking about."

Samson struggled with getting the key in the lock with one hand, while never losing his grip on Delilah's arm with his other. Once he entered his house and they were behind closed doors, he released Delilah's arm. "Delilah, we need to talk."

"We can save the talking for later," Delilah said. She slid her hand up and down his chest.

Samson's body hadn't fully recovered from being around Julia. Delilah's touch only increased the sexual urges. He shouted, "Get thee behind me, Satan."

Delilah stopped. "This is the second time today someone's accused me of being the devil, and I'm not going to stand for it."

"Good. Now maybe you'll stop. Sit so we can talk."

This time Delilah obeyed Samson. She waited for him

to sit down first and then she took a seat across from him. She crossed her legs, deliberately exposing her thighs. Samson did his best to keep eye contact but found himself peeking at her legs during the course of the conversation. "This thing between us has to stop."

"Samson, if I could stop what I feel for you, believe me, I would."

"Delilah, you're a pretty woman, and there's not a man alive who wouldn't want you, but I'm taken. End of story."

Delilah walked over to his stereo. She found a radio station, and as the latest R&B songs blasted from the speakers, she began dancing seductively. "If you can resist me after what I'm about to do, then I'll walk away and never bother you again."

"Good," Samson said.

The Commodores' song "Brick House" played next as Delilah swayed her body from side to side. Samson squirmed in his seat. He should have gotten up and walked out of the room, but watching Delilah dance had him hypnotized.

There was something about Delilah that seemed to have a hold on him. She had a vulnerable side that she didn't like to expose. He wanted to heal her. Samson knew pushing her away would hurt her, but giving in to her demands could jeopardize not just his life, but Julia's.

The hold Delilah had on him was hypnotic, and as much as he knew she was bad for him, he couldn't seem to get enough of her. He had been able to resist temptation for years, but since the moment he met Delilah, she became his Achilles' heel.

Delilah made her way over to where Samson was sitting and straddled him. Defeated, Samson gave in to his carnal desires once again. The next morning, Delilah rolled over and whispered in Samson's ear, "Ready for another round?"

Chapter 9

Delilah pouted and complained, but Samson wouldn't budge. "You can still call off the wedding," Delilah said.

"That's never going to happen, so you might as well let me go."

She did something she said she would never do in front of a man. She cried. Samson reached out to her. She pushed his arm away. "Don't touch me."

"Delilah, fine. It's almost eight o'clock, and I have things to do."

"I can see myself out."

"You can't stay here. When I leave, you leave."

"So you're kicking me out?" Delilah yelled.

"Calm down. Nobody's kicking you out."

Wiping her eyes, Delilah got out of the bed and put on her clothes. Samson avoided looking at her. Delilah should have felt some type of shame, but she didn't. She never made Samson do anything he didn't want to do.

"I'm going only because I have something to do myself," Delilah said.

"Be careful," Samson said as he walked her to the door.

She was disappointed he didn't at least give her a hug. She dialed her best friend's number as soon as she was seated behind the wheel of her car."Keisha, let's meet for lunch. My treat."

At one that afternoon, Delilah met Keisha at a local eatery. The crowd had thinned since the lunch rush hour passed. "Girl, I love that hair color on you," Delilah said as she sat across from Keisha.

"Platinum blond. You should try it." Keisha ran her fingers through the end of her hair.

Delilah loved changing her hairstyle, and having a best friend who was a hair stylist worked in her favor, but she would leave the platinum blond to Keisha.

"I ordered your favorites," Keisha said.

"Good, because I haven't eaten anything since yesterday."

Delilah listened as Keisha gossiped about the patrons at her salon, but the news didn't compare to what Delilah had going on in her life. The waiter brought over their food. Delilah explained her dilemma. "Samson wanted it as much as I did, so I don't know why he keeps tripping with me."

"You're going to burn in hell for messing with that preacher," Keisha said. She dipped her French fries in ketchup.

"Did you not hear a word I said? He wants me too, but he doesn't want to disappoint his parents."

"Delilah, I don't know what planet you're on, but the preacher is just using you. He's getting sex from you, but he's still marrying his virtuous woman. Move on. Save yourself from heartache, but most importantly, save your soul."

Delilah's cell phone rang. "That's probably him now." Delilah retrieved her phone from her purse with a huge grin on her face. "Hello."

"Are you making any progress?" William asked.

Delilah rolled her eyes. "Just give me some time."

"Time is money. I need that land to build my shopping center, so I need to see some results. He still won't take my calls."

"I'm working on it. I have a trump card I haven't played yet. He'll do whatever I want when I play it."

"Well, what are you waiting on? Give me the results I want or you'll be jobless."

William disconnected the call without waiting on Delilah's response. "Are you okay?" Keisha asked.

"Yeah," Delilah responded, as she slipped her cell phone back in her purse. "Just my boss getting on my nerves."

"You need to find you another job."

"Where else am I going to work and make twenty dollars an hour in this city? Plus, I'm getting a bonus for this special assignment," Delilah said. Delilah, feeling distress, had shared with Keisha details of her special assignment.

"You can find something. I can get you a job on the riverboat with me. Girl, with my tips, I easily pull in a thousand dollars every week."

"I know nothing about a crap table or blackjack."

"You don't have to. There's a training class you go through."

"Well, if this doesn't work out, I'll think about it."

"You have options," Keisha said.

"If Samson marries that woman, I don't know what I'll do."

Keisha stopped eating. "Do I need to slap some sense into you? You're delusional if you think he's going to drop Ms. Prim and Proper for an ex-hooker."

"I was an exotic dancer. Big difference." Delilah looked around the room to make sure no one was listening. "Besides, you don't have to tell the world my business."

"I just want you to see how ridiculous all this looks. You slept with him. The sex was good. Now move on."

"You just don't understand. I'm a better person because of Samson."

"I've seen him on TV and yes, he's sexy, but he's not the only man in Shreveport."

To Delilah, he might as well have been because Samson was the only man she wanted, and she'd stop at nothing to get him.

Chapter 10

"Samson, you haven't heard a word I said," Julia said. She might as well have been talking to herself because Samson's mind was on Delilah and the countless number of text messages she had sent him since Monday morning.

He had avoided her all week, but he was sure his luck would be changing soon since it was now Wednesday night and Delilah rarely missed Wednesday night Bible Study. He looked at his beautiful bride-to-be. His insides fluttered as he thought about how much he loved her. He recalled the first time he realized he was in love with Julia.

They had known each other since childhood because both of their fathers were prominent men of the cloth; however, it wasn't until after they both graduated from college and they ran into each other at a church conference that his feelings changed from admiration to love. That was more than two years ago. Julia was soon to be his queen, and he couldn't let anyone stand in the way of making it happen. Delilah had to be dealt with, but there was no one he could trust, or was there?

"I don't know where your head is tonight, but I hope you get it together before you go in there trying to teach your congregation," Julia said.

"Michael's teaching tonight."

"Good, because you are not yourself."

Samson took Julia's hand in his. "Come on, let's go before we're late."

"Aww, how sweet," Delilah said when she ran into them in the hallway.

"Just keep moving," Samson told Julia.

"Is something going on I should know about?" Julia looked back and forth between Samson and Delilah.

Samson was caught off guard with her question. "No," he lied.

"That's all I needed to know."

Samson sighed as they walked into the sanctuary and took their seats on the front pew.

He could feel someone watching him, and when he turned around, Delilah's smiling face was staring back at him. He jerked his body back around and did his best to concentrate on Michael's discussion on the eighteenth chapter of Matthew.

"Pastor Judges, would you like to add anything to what I said about leading others to sin," Michael said, staring at him from the podium.

"Uh, no. Minister Monroe, you've done an excellent job explaining." Samson wiped his sweaty hands on his pants leg. He heard Delilah snicker. He glanced at Julia from the corner of his eyes. His attempt to reach for her hand resulted in her crossing her arms. The rest of the time, Samson blocked out everything else and looked directly at Michael.

"I didn't mean to put you on the spot earlier," Michael said later in the pastor's study.

"Man, I'm just nervous about Saturday."

"I'm surprised you're here tonight. I was a nervous wreck when I was about to get married."

"Julia and I are going to be gone all next week, so we wanted to be here."

"Well, if there's anything you want me to do, let me know."

"My mom and Julia have it all covered. All I need to do is show up."

Michael looked over Samson's shoulder. "Looks like you got company," Michael said as Delilah walked into his office.

"I hope I'm not interrupting anything. Pastor, I wanted to ask you something." Delilah batted her eyes.

"Pastor, I'll catch you later," Michael said.

"No, don't go. There's something else I wanted to discuss with you," Samson said.

Michael didn't read in between the lines that Samson didn't want to be left alone with Delilah. "Call me on my cell when you finish." He smiled in Delilah's direction. "Delilah, nice seeing you."

Delilah licked her lips. "Same here. Tell that wife of yours she's a lucky woman."

"I'll be sure to tell her that."

Once Michael was gone, Delilah closed the door.

"What are you doing?" Samson rushed to the door to open it.

Delilah jumped in front of it. They were now face-to-face. He could smell the cherry blossom lip gloss on her lips. "Your fiancée is in the restroom. Why haven't you returned my calls?"

"I'm beginning to sound like a broken record—because I'm busy. I am getting married in a few days."

"I know. That's all anybody is talking about."

Samson moved and left Delilah standing with her back to the door. "I hate to rush you, but I need to go."

"Okay, but I wanted to drop off something with you." Delilah reached into her purse and pulled out a disk. She handed it to him but wouldn't let go of the case. "If I were you, I would watch this in private."

Samson needed Delilah gone before Julia came to his office, but he was curious to know what was on the disk. He looked at both sides of the disk, but there was no writing. Before he could ask Delilah any questions, the doorknob turned and Julia walked in. "What's going on here?" she asked.

Samson thought to himself that a closed door meant nothing because it seemed as if people still just burst into his office without knocking. He snapped out of his thoughts at the sound of Delilah's voice.

Delilah smiled. "Nothing. I just dropped off something to the pastor. You two make such a cute couple."

Julia responded, "Well, now that you've dropped it off, you can be going."

Delilah turned to face Samson. "Remember what I said." She winked at him, turned, and twisted out of the room.

"I know it's wrong, but I can't stand that woman," Julia said.

Samson threw the disk Delilah had given him in his briefcase. "Come on, I'll walk you out."

Samson and Julia were in separate vehicles, so instead of leaving one at the church, they each decided to drive. He followed Julia home to spend a little time with her before heading home.

It wasn't until later that night, while lying in his bed, that he remembered the disk Delilah had given him earlier. He retrieved it from his briefcase and placed it in the DVD player. For some reason the disk didn't immediately start playing like it normally would, so he played around with the remote. The screen remained fuzzy, but when he turned the sound up, he realized that what he was watching was no ordinary video. Within seconds, the visuals became clear and he saw his naked bottom staring at him on the screen.

There was no misunderstanding what was going on. The video showed him and Delilah in the heat of passion. He watched the video, wishing he could turn back the hands of time. He had been celibate for years, and Delilah had him breaking vows to his fiancée and, more importantly, to God. He could try to lie his way out of it, but the proof of his sin was not only a vision in his head, it was recorded for anyone to see.

Chapter 11

Delilah slept with the phone by her ear. She expected Samson to call her as soon as he saw the video. Morning crept up on her. She glanced at her phone and didn't have one missed call. "I wonder if he even watched it."

Delilah knew her obsession with Samson was on the borderline of being considered psychotic, but she loved him and wanted him like she had never wanted any other man before in her life.

She dialed Samson's phone number. Her phone beeped. Trusts Enterprise's number flashed on the caller ID screen. She disconnected the call with Samson and clicked over. "Delilah speaking," she answered.

"Any news?" William asked.

"I'm working on it," she responded.

"Don't disappoint me," he said before hanging up.

"I can't believe I made a deal with the devil." Delilah slammed down the phone.

After the conversation with William, Delilah took a long shower. Her phone rang while she dressed. A smile crept across her face when she saw Samson's number displayed on the caller ID. "I knew you would call," she answered.

"I'm coming over now," was all Samson said.

"I'll be waiting."

Delilah changed her clothes several times. She wanted to look sexy for Samson, but then again, she wanted to play hard-to-get. The problem with Samson was, in her opinion, that she had been too accessible to him. She would be less forward from this point on.

She reached for the room fragrance and sprayed it in the air. The fruity aroma spread throughout the house. She did a clean sweep of her living room to make sure everything was presentable.

Before Samson could ring the door bell, Delilah greeted him at the door. "Come in."

Samson didn't say a word. He walked directly to the living room and sat down. Delilah left him there and returned with a twelve ounce can of his favorite soda.

"You can keep that," he said.

"Suit yourself." Delilah popped the cap off a can of Sprite and took a sip before sitting down next to him.

Samson moved farther away from her. She didn't move again. He reached into his jacket pocket and waved the disk she had given him in her face. "You had no right taping us."

The forceful tone of his voice concerned Delilah. She had never seen Samson this angry.

"I can't see you every night, so I needed some reminder of our time together."

"Where's the hidden camera?" Samson stood up and started picking up the figurines around the room. "Is it in here? Is it under here?"

"There's no camera, Samson."

"I forgot, the video shows us in your bedroom." Samson placed the figurine back on the table and looked directly in Delilah's eyes. "Lately, people have said some bad things about you, and I've taken up for you. But now . . ."

Delilah stood up and walked in front of him. "Now what? Can I help it that I fell in love with you? How do you think I feel knowing that I'll never be good enough for you? That you only want to use me?" Tears formed at the corners of her eyes.

Samson turned away from her. "It's not like that. I can't have this video get out. This could affect my ministry." He turned around and looked Delilah in the face."Do you really love me?"

Delilah whimpered. "Yes, I love you more than I've loved any other man."

"Then destroy the video and promise me no one else will see it."

"I can't make that type of promise," she responded.

Samson reached for her hand and held it. "Please. I'm begging you. Get rid of it. I'll do anything."

Delilah had Samson exactly where she wanted him. Julia was history. She imagined replacing Julia in Saturday's wedding. Where would she get her dress on such a short notice? Delilah squeezed his hand. "You can call off your wedding and tell Julia you and I are getting married instead."

"Delilah, you know I can't do that." Samson released Delilah's hand.

"Well, you did say anything," she pouted.

"Anything but that. You know I love Julia."

Delilah thought about William and Trusts Enterprise. She could now fulfill her obligation to William, and get him off her back and collect the rest of the money he promised her. "You can sell the property to Trusts Enterprise. That would make me happy."

Samson released Delilah's hand. "Why are you concerned with Trusts Enterprise?"

"I work for them. My boss told me they were interested in the church property. I need the commission, so if I make the sale, I get the bonus."

"Sorry to disappoint you again, Delilah, but I refuse to sell out. Selling the property to Trusts Enterprise is not an option."

"Please. Do it for me." Delilah batted her eyes a few times.

"Never in a million years."

Delilah picked up the disk from the sofa. "Then what am I to do with this?" She waved the disk in the air.

Samson took the disk and broke it in two. "That's destroyed. Now promise me you'll destroy the video so I won't have to worry about this showing up again."

Delilah moved closer to him. "Promise me you'll always be a part of my life."

Samson cleared his throat. "I can promise you that I'll be there as your pastor, but nothing more."

"That's not what I was talking about and you know it."

"You'll find someone else who is available and will make you forget all about me. Watch." Samson pulled her into his arms.

One minute Delilah was angry with Samson, but with this kind gesture, it melted the anger away. "No one could ever replace you," she whispered. She rested her head on his chest.

"So do we have a deal? Will you destroy the video?"

"Yes," Delilah said. She crossed her fingers to cancel out the lie. She had no intentions of getting rid of the video. Not yet, anyway.

Chapter 12

Samson hoped he could trust Delilah. He destroyed the disk, but he wondered if she had the recording saved on her camera. If word ever got out about his affair with her, Julia would cancel the wedding, and his parents would be disappointed. He had to do whatever he needed to keep the thing between them private. He loved Julia, and he was still going through with the wedding.

The attraction he had for Delilah was a distraction, but he couldn't allow it to overshadow his good judgment. Allowing himself a few minutes of pleasure shouldn't hurt anything. He worked hard in the ministry, and sometimes the stress from being everyone's confidant became a little too much for him to bear. Even with all the prayer and meditation, he needed an outlet.

Samson knew Delilah wanted him the moment he met her. He encouraged her to open up to him, and when the opportunity presented itself, their counseling sessions overlapped into something more. He could be an imperfect Samson around Delilah. She didn't expect anything from him—that was one of the things that attracted him to her.

He never expected their secret relationship to get out of hand. For him, it was only an affair, but Delilah allowed her feelings to cross the line. Now he had to figure out a way to pacify her enough so she wouldn't destroy the relationships he had built up around him.

Samson attempted to justify his actions as he quoted, out loud, a scripture from the third chapter of Romans. "For all have sinned and come short of the glory of God."

Samson's phone ringing brought him back to the present. "Son, I need to see you," Regis said from the other end of Samson's cell phone.

"I'm driving now, so where do you want me to meet you?" Samson asked.

"Your mother's gone, so just swing by the house."

Samson ended the call with his father. His dad normally asked him how he was doing, but today he didn't waste any time. He wondered if there was something wrong with his health. Samson turned his vehicle around and headed to his parents' house.

Fifteen minutes later, Samson used his house key and entered his parents' home. He called out for his dad but got no answer. He located his dad in the den, sitting in a brown leather recliner and engulfed in a movie.

Regis's body jumped a little when Samson appeared next to him. "Son, you startled me."

"I called out your name." Samson took a seat in one of the other brown recliners in the room.

"You know when I'm watching something I tend to tune things out around me. Years from being with your mother." Regis laughed and so did Samson.

"I can come back another time."

"Nonsense. I called you over, remember?" Regis located the television remote and muted it.

Samson decided to get straight to the point. "Is everything okay with you? With Mom?"

"Couldn't be better," Regis responded. "I called you over here to talk about you."

Samson, puzzled, said, "I'm doing fine."

Regis positioned his body so he would be looking directly in Samson's face. "Some people have been telling me some things, and frankly I don't like what they are saying."

Samson fidgeted in his chair. "Like what?"

"Now, I have never been one to judge because the Bible says, 'Judge not that ye be not judged.' But from what I can see, Delilah Baker is nothing but bad news."

"Dad, you know you can't believe everything people tell you."

Regis laughed. "Son, I might be old, but I'm not dead. Women like Delilah have been trying to bring down the men of God for generations."

It was Samson's turn to laugh. "Come on now. It's not even that serious. She comes to me for advice. That's it. Nothing more, nothing less."

"If you think I believe that, then you, my son, have a bigger problem than I thought. Do you think you're the only man who's been tempted?" Samson didn't answer. Regis said, "Answer me."

"Dad, maybe we should talk later."

Regis ignored him and said, "Do you think it was easy for me to resist temptation when I was a pastor of Peaceful Rest? No, it wasn't."

Samson had always known his father to be faithful to his mother. He never heard any rumors of him stepping out on her. Now he wondered if that was the case.

Regis said, "We've been blessed to have some good genes. And women around here love men with good hair because in their minds we would make good-looking babies."

"I'm not trying to have any kids right now, but when I do, it'll be with Julia."

"Good intentions can lead to lifelong despair if God is not involved."

Samson stuck out his chest. "Dad, I got this. Everything is under control."

"From where I sit, things are about to get out of control. Anytime people are murmuring about something and it gets back to me, there's an issue."

"Who is saying these things?" Samson asked.

"It doesn't matter. What matters is that you be careful. Every day, you have to put on the full armor of God in order to resist temptation that surrounds us."

Samson thought about what his dad said. "I don't drink. I don't smoke. I don't chase women like some of the preachers I know. I'm a pretty stand-up guy."

"But you're not perfect. Even I, who've been in the ministry since I was twenty-five years old, have fallen short. Don't ever think you're above reproach. Every man has an Achilles' heel, and Satan knows it."

"Dad, I've never known you to step out on Mom. So are you telling me you cheated?"

"I cheated, but not the way you think."

Samson shook his head from side to side. "I don't understand."

"My addiction was alcohol. Being a minister can be stressful, so instead of taking my burdens to the Lord like I preached to my congregation, I turned to the bottle. My love for alcohol almost destroyed my marriage and my ministry. But thank God for His grace and mercy. See, that's why I can sit here and tell you, son, that without putting on the full armor of God every day, you can't fight this battle by yourself."

Samson listened. If his dad could get over drinking alcohol, he surely could resist Delilah. But did he really want to? That's the question that plagued his mind.

Chapter 13

Delilah felt guilty about lying to Samson. The original video of them together was saved on her flash drive. She wouldn't destroy it, but Delilah had no plans to give William a copy. She couldn't pinpoint the moment her assignment for William turned into a quest for her to get the man of her dreams. If only Julia weren't in the way.

Julia appeared to have it all—the looks, the education, and most importantly, her past was different from Delilah's. Julia grew up in a two-parent household and had all the luxuries her parents could afford. Delilah couldn't compete with her on that level, so she used the one thing she knew she had: her looks. Julia, although pretty, couldn't hold a candle next to Delilah's natural beauty.

Delilah knew it was wrong for her to go after Samson, but until he said I do, she would continue to pursue him. Delilah felt like she knew exactly what Samson needed, and that's why he was drawn to her. She could give Samson the desires of his heart. Samson could be himself around her. He didn't have to put on any pretenses. In her ideal world, Samson would allow her to be in control, and Delilah would take care of all of his needs.

Delilah lay across her bed and recalled how Samson's

demeanor changed when he approached her about the disk. She saw a side of him she didn't know existed. It was a dark side, a place she never would have thought existed in a man like Samson. She tried to think of something else, but Samson filled her mind.

She fumbled in her nightstand drawer and retrieved her Bible. One of the church programs fell out. Samson's handsome face stared back at her. She placed the program to the side and flipped the pages of the Bible open to the book of Judges. She read, in her opinion, one of the greatest love stories ever told—the story of Samson and Delilah.

Delilah didn't recall falling asleep, but before she knew it she and Samson were being transported in time. In her dream, Samson married her instead of Julia. Many men tried to get Delilah to leave Samson, but Samson would fight them off. Each time, their love grew stronger and stronger. Their lives were perfect until William appeared and jolted Delilah awake.

Startled out of her dream, Delilah decided to give Keisha a call. Her friend answered on the third ring. "Guess what? Samson's going to be all mine," Delilah spat off.

"Say what?"

Delilah could tell she caught Keisha off guard. "I threatened to show Julia the disk of him and me together, but get this—he wants to be self-righteous and tell her himself."

Keisha blurted: "Girl, have you lost your mind? Blackmail? Really, Delilah?"

"I'm not going to show Julia the video. I just wanted Samson to see how serious I am about us. He needs to break things off with her so we can move on with our lives together."

Keisha attempted to be the voice of reason. "Girl, stop it before you get yourself into something you can't get out of. You're a beautiful woman. Find an available man and leave your pastor alone."

"But I love him. I think he loves me too; he's just afraid of what people will think."

"Do you blame him? You're throwing yourself at him like you're desperate. Stop the madness now."

Delilah wasn't getting the response she wanted from Keisha. She wished her friend were more supportive of her quest to get Samson. She had to convince Keisha she was right in pursuing Samson. "Just think about it. Julia will leave him once she finds out about me. His parents I'm not too worried about. They'll eventually learn to love me. The church, well, the members all love him, so they'll forgive him."

"I will be praying an extra-long prayer for you because, girl, you have gotten out of control."

Delilah laughed. "Keisha, stop tripping. I'm serious. It's just a matter of time before Samson's all mine."

"You must be dreaming because if you believe he's going to cancel his wedding to be with you, Delilah, you have another thing coming," Keisha said.

"I can give him what Julia can't." Delilah refused to give up hope.

Keisha laughed on the other end of the phone. "Julia's not giving it up to him; you are. Why should she when you're her substitute?"

Ouch. That hurt. "Here I thought you were my friend." Delilah couldn't believe Keisha had said something so hurtful to her.

"I am your friend. That's why you can count on me to tell you the truth, whether you agree with me or not."

Delilah hated to admit it, but Keisha never bit her tongue when it came to telling her anything. Sometimes she could be a little too harsh. Keisha's blunt honesty, however, was one of the reasons Delilah cherished their friendship. Keisha was the sister she never had.

Delilah asked, "What do you think I should do with the video?"

"Erase it and act like it never existed. You're lucky Samson didn't go upside your head."

"He would never do something like that."

"You never know what a man is capable of doing until his back is up against the wall."

Keisha had a point. She recalled the way Samson's eyes darkened when he approached her about the disk. She wouldn't admit it to Keisha, but it did scare her for a minute.

"I'm not giving it to William, so you don't have to worry about that."

"Destroy it. Give William back his money and look for another job."

"I can't," Delilah whined.

"You can, but you won't."

"Have you read Samson and Delilah's story? It's one of the greatest love stories ever told. Samson and I are destined to be together. This isn't just fate, it's biblical, Keisha."

"Delilah, I would be remiss if I didn't share this with you. I hate to tell you, but the story of Samson and Delilah in the Bible is more of a tragedy than a love story. Do you want to destroy the man you claim to love?"

Here she goes again on one of her tirades, Delilah thought. "No, of course not."

"Then do as I suggested. Forget William and Samson and move on."

"William I can forget, but Samson, never. I love him too much to give him up that easily."

"But the love isn't reciprocated. You deserve so much better."

"Keisha, you just don't understand. You don't know Samson like I know him. My love for him won't allow me to give him up."

"I hope you don't live to regret this quest of yours. Samson is a man of God, and your trying to destroy him will only bring bad things on you."

"I'm the one standing in the gap for him. If I didn't agree to help William, he would have found someone else, and you can guarantee that person wouldn't be making things easy for Samson." Delilah said those things more to herself than Keisha, as she attempted to justify working for William.

"Your allegiance should lie with God, but it sounds like you've aligned yourself with the devil."

Delilah couldn't disagree because there were many days when she thought William was a pawn of Satan. "I love God, and I love Samson. Unless Samson does something to change my mind, I will protect him from William's wrath."

"From what I've heard about William, he's no one to play with. Be honest with him and get out while you can. Men like William will destroy anybody who stands in the way of them getting what they want. I love you, and I don't want anything to happen to you," Keisha said.

"Are you sniffling over there?" Delilah asked.

"No, I'm all right."

To Delilah, it sounded like Keisha was crying. Maybe her friend was right. Maybe she should get out from under William while she still could. She hadn't spent the money he had given her yet, so all she had to do was return it. Delilah knew it wouldn't be that easy, so she pushed thoughts of returning William's money to the back of her mind.

"Keisha, I'm a grown woman. I know how to take care of myself. Trust me. Things will work themselves out. William will get his land, and I will get what I want—Samson."

Chapter 14

Samson felt bad about how things played out with Delilah. She claimed to love him, and his male ego ate it up, but he knew it was wrong. He had no business sleeping with Delilah. He knew God was not pleased with his behavior. Samson headed straight to church after he left his parents' house. Elaine's car was the only one in the parking lot, and he assumed she was in her office.

He kneeled down before the altar. "Father God, please hear your servant's prayer. I have been obedient to you in so many areas of my life, but lately I've succumbed to the desires of the flesh. I know you're not pleased with my actions, and the video was a wake-up call. Lord, forgive me for the sins I've committed against you and against the woman that you've blessed me with.

"Delilah has a good heart, but her affections are directed in the wrong place. I pray that she gets peace of mind and that she realizes her worth. Only you can change her mind and heart. With you all things are possible.

"Lord, please remove the yoke from around my neck. Free me from my carnal desires. Forgive me, Father, and guide my steps so that I won't be a hindrance to anyone trying to serve you."

Samson finished praying and stood up. He turned around and came face-to-face with William Trusts. "What are you doing here?"

"If the man of God won't come to you, you have to go to the man of God, right?" William, wearing a red pin-striped suit and matching hat, sat down on the closest pew, his cane in hand.

Samson remained standing. "Let me get my bottle of holy oil. Better yet, let me get the whole box."

William leaned on his cane as his sinister laugh filled the sanctuary. "You got jokes I see."

"If you're here about the land, forget it."

William tapped his cane on the floor. "No, we have another matter to settle. I understand you've been getting a little cozy with one of my employees."

"I don't entertain rumors."

"Must be some truth to it because you never asked me which employee." William leaned back on the pew.

"William, you have one minute before I forget I'm a pastor and kick your butt out of my church."

Getting straight to the point, William said, "What would your fiancée think about you messing around with Delilah Baker?"

"I have no idea what you're talking about, so you can get out of here with your threats."

William stood up. "Oh, I'm going, but know this: I'll give you until the end of the month to sell me the property. If not, I'm taking it."

William picked up his cane and tipped out of the sanctuary. Samson fell back down on his knees to repent of the sinful thoughts that filled his mind about William. After praying, he got up and headed to his office. Elaine was on the phone when he entered the office. "Hold on, that's the pastor now." She looked up at him. "Julia's on the phone for you."

"I'll pick it up at my desk," Samson said as he rushed to his desk. "Hi, beautiful," he greeted Julia after picking up the phone.

"I stopped by this morning, but I guess I missed you," she said.

"I had some last-minute errands to run," Samson responded.

"Are you nervous about Saturday?" she asked.

"Is fat meat greasy?"

They both laughed. After going over wedding details, they got off the phone. Samson called Elaine on the intercom. "When Deacon Thompson gets here, I would like for you to hold all my calls unless it's my parents or Julia, please."

"Will do," she responded.

Samson turned on his computer and checked his e-mails. Sometimes some of the members would send prayer requests via e-mail, and he didn't want to miss any. He made a mental note of the prayer requests and kneeled down at his desk and prayed for his church members. He had just gotten off his knees when someone knocked at the door.

"Come in," Samson yelled.

Deacon Calvin Thompson entered, standing more than six feet tall and wearing a custom-made suit. They greeted each other with a brotherly hug.

"So what can I do for you, Pastor?" Calvin asked.

"Calvin, you're probably one of my best friends." Calvin was not only one of Samson's best friends, he also was the church's attorney.

"You've helped me out of plenty of messes," he said.

"This time it looks like I need you to get me out of a mess."

Calvin leaned forward in his chair. "Is William Trusts badgering you again? If so, I'll get my people on it."

"William is persistent. He's not going to give up until he gets the church property."

"As the church attorney, I've checked into it, and he has no legal claim unless the church decides to sell it to him."

"That's good to know. I've prayed and prayed about it. I don't think we should give up the land. I think Peaceful Rest will grow, and we'll need that land to build a new sanctuary twice as big as the one we have here."

"Some people think we should sell it, but I trust your judgment."

"I appreciate that, man."

"Let me deal with Trusts," Calvin said.

"I wish that were all there was to it. I don't even know how to say this." Samson walked to the window and stared outside. "Have you ever had to get yourself out of a compromising position?"

Calvin laughed. "You're talking to a lawyer. If there's a will, there's a way."

Samson turned around and sat back down behind his desk. "I can trust you, right?"

"I wouldn't be the best man in your wedding if you couldn't," Calvin responded.

Samson leaned his head back and let out a few deep breaths. "I have a situation. I thought I could handle it, but it's not going away."

"Samson, whatever you need me to do, I got it covered." Calvin sat up straight in his chair.

"What I tell you must not be repeated. I mean it. Don't even tell your wife."

"I'll treat it as attorney-client privilege."

Samson sighed with relief. "It's Delilah Baker." Samson went on to tell Calvin about his encounters with Delilah. He felt a weight lift off his shoulders when he confessed.

"Women like Delilah are plentiful. She won't go through with her threats. If she were going to tell Julia anything, she would have done it a long time ago."

"I need you to make sure she doesn't get anywhere near Julia before the wedding." Samson was relieved that Calvin didn't seem to judge him.

"Consider it already done."

Calvin exited Samson's office, leaving Samson alone with his thoughts. He had no idea of Calvin's plans, but he hoped whatever they were, they would convince Delilah to back off with her threats.

Samson leaned back in his chair. What was he thinking? Calvin was no match for Delilah. Sending someone over to clean up his mess would set her off.

Samson dialed Calvin's number. "Don't confront Delilah. Just have my back if something goes down."

"Are you sure?"

"Positive," Samson responded as he twirled his chair around to face the window. Samson hung up the phone and dropped his head as he prayed for another solution.

Chapter 15

William was the last person Delilah wanted to see. She wondered if she should ignore his knock and pretend she wasn't home. William shouted from the other side of the door. "I know you're in there, so you might as well open the door." He beat on the door again.

Knowing if she didn't answer he would come back, Delilah decided it was best to deal with him now and get it over with, so she opened the door. "William, good to see you." Delilah moved to the side and allowed him to enter.

"Your preacher man is a hard one to crack," he said. His six foot two inch frame towered over her as they walked to her living room.

"Told you it isn't as easy as you think it should be."

William picked up a few of her figurines. "I don't want you to do anything else until after the wedding. Once he's married, he'll have more to lose if he's caught in an affair with you."

Delilah wasn't too sure she liked William's plan. Threatening Samson with the video didn't give her the results she wanted. When Samson left her house earlier, she had a long talk with Keisha. Keisha reasoned with her, and although Delilah didn't completely agree with her, Keisha had a point. Delilah had to let him go—let him go and see for himself that marrying Julia would be a mistake.

"So are you down? If so, I'll throw in another $25,000. Half now and the other half with the other money I owe you," William said.

"I really like Samson. I don't want to see him hurt."

William touched her chin and tilted her face so she would be facing him. "If he cared about you, and I mean really cared about you, he would not be leaving your bed to go marry some other woman. Your allegiance is to the wrong man."

Before she could blink, William's lips were on top of hers. She pushed him away. "Stop. What's gotten into you? I can't believe you kissed me." Delilah wiped her lips with the back of her hand.

"Sweet Dee. You'll be calling me when the good Rev. is no longer taking care of your womanly needs."

Delilah rolled her eyes. "I would rather be celibate than sleep with you."

"Be careful what you say now. I am your boss." William's signature laugh sounded throughout the room.

"Boss or no boss, I will not sleep with you."

"Good. Because I want you to stop playing around and sleep with Samson." William removed a stack of money from his jacket pocket. "Here's the down payment."

"I'm not a whore." Delilah didn't take the money.

"Well, according to my sources, you used to drop it like it's hot every night at The X Spot."

"I'm a changed woman. You know that."

William placed the money in her hand. "I know that I've invested a lot of money in this shopping center project, and you, my dear, are going to close it for me. I'll be in touch."

Delilah remained in the same spot until she heard the front door close. "I hate you William," she yelled as she removed the money from the paper wrapper and counted it.

She promised Keisha she would let things be, but William's offer to pay her more money drew her back in. William could be so persuasive when he wanted to be. She would not let William win this round. She loved Samson, and she would not allow him to destroy her one and only love—even if it meant forfeiting any other money.

She dialed William's number. He answered on the first ring. "You can come back and get your money. I'm not doing it."

"Oh, you will do it or else the good Rev. will get a package on his wedding night with your personal resume—you know the one where you opened up shop for the highest bidder."

"You wouldn't dare." Delilah bit her bottom lip.

"Trust me, I would," William said. "So do we have a deal?"

She blinked her eyes a few times and shook her head. "I'll think about it."

"I'll take that as an affirmative." He laughed. "Good day. I have more pressing business to take care of."

Delilah paced the floor. She could tell Samson William's plans. Would that make him trust her more? Would he still go through with the wedding? Probably. So who was she fooling? She gathered up the mail that had accumulated on her desk in the den and started going through it.

"What do we have here?" she asked out loud. She removed the gold seal from the opening of the envelope. "I should have opened up my mail sooner," she said after reading the enclosed invitation.

Delilah placed the envelope in her purse and went to her closet to find something to wear. She tried on several outfits until she found the perfect one. It was a shimmering red form-fitting, knee-length dress accenting all of her curves. She applied a minimum amount of makeup but lined her lips with ruby red lipstick. She puckered up and looked in the mirror. "Ladies, don't start the party without me."

Delilah stopped by Mall St. Vincent and picked up a last-minute gift for the bride-to-be. She paid extra to have the set of lingerie gift wrapped. She now stood outside on the porch of Michelle's brick home. Rushing because she was running late, Delilah almost broke her heel on the sidewalk leading up to the house. She rang the doorbell for a second time.

A young woman whom Delilah didn't remember seeing before answered. "Are you here for Sister Julia's bridal party?" the young woman asked.

"I sure am," Delilah responded.

"I can help you with your gift." The girl attempted to take the gift from Delilah's hand.

Delilah held on tight to her package. "I got it."

The girl looked at Delilah strangely but said, "Everybody is in the den."

"Lead the way."

Delilah could hear plenty of laughter as she followed the girl. She admired the decor and felt she and Michelle had similar taste. Once they entered, the young woman announced, "We have another guest."

Every eye in the room was focused on Delilah and the girl. The room fell silent.

"What is she doing here?" Dorothy asked out loud.

Delilah walked over to where Julia sat and handed her the gift she had been carrying. "This is for you." Delilah turned in Dorothy's direction. "And to answer your question, Ms. Dorothy, I'm part of the Pastor's Aide committee, and this is a Pastor's Aide-sponsored event, so I'm here." Delilah twitched her head and smiled before turning around to find an available seat.

Julia said to Dorothy, "It's okay." She looked up in Delilah's face. "Delilah, thank you for the gift."

"You're welcome." Delilah took a seat and crossed her legs. "Is this a party or what? Why all the frowned up faces?"

Elaine said, "She's right. One monkey don't stop the show."

Delilah uncrossed her legs and then crossed them in the other direction. Not once did her smile crack. "Flip Wilson said it could, but that's a conversation for another day."

Kelly intervened, "It's game time."

Delilah said under her breath, "Yes, let the games begin."

Chapter 16

Samson was enjoying the bachelor party some of the men insisted on throwing him until Calvin said, "Michelle just called me. Delilah's at the bridal party."

"I better get over there," Samson said, placing his can of soda on the table.

"Nonsense. Michelle's going to play interference. If anything jumps off, she'll call me."

As much as Samson tried to forget about what was happening at Calvin and Michelle's place, he couldn't. Delilah hadn't called him once since he'd left her place earlier that day, and that scared him. He slipped away from the men and walked out on the patio. He dialed a number.

"Delilah, I hadn't heard from you, so I just wanted to make sure things were cool between us." Samson knew it was a bad idea to call Delilah, but he didn't hang up.

He could hear women laughing in the background. "You miss me already?"

"Are we cool?"

"Do you want to talk to her?"

"No. Are you crazy?"

"Not certifiable." The noise level decreased on Delilah's end. "I'm surprised to hear from you."

"Just checking on you."

"I'm fine, and your wife-to-be is fine too. After the games, we'll be opening up gifts."

"What are you doing there, Delilah?"

"Are you jealous? Would you rather I be at your party instead? You know I can leave here and come where you are. All I need is the location."

"I would feel better if you left. You don't even like Julia."

"No, I don't, but I love you. So if she's going to be a part of your life, I'll have to adjust."

"Man, what are you doing out here? The fellows are looking for you," Michael said, interrupting the words Samson was about to speak.

Samson didn't hear him coming, but turned to face him as soon as he realized he wasn't alone. Samson held up his hand. "I'll be there in a minute."

"I'm sorry. I didn't realize you were on the phone." Michael turned away and went back into the house.

Samson turned his attention back to the phone conversation with Delilah. Slightly above a whisper, he said, "Leave before any drama starts, okay?"

"You should be getting back to your party, and I'm about to get back to mine." Delilah hung up on him.

Samson re-entered the house and whispered in Calvin's ear. "Man, we need to go crash the bridal party. Delilah refuses to leave. I don't trust her around Julia."

"Calm down. Forget Delilah for a minute and enjoy your night. Are you my partner or what? Because I'm ready to show them who the dominoes kings are."

Samson decided to take his friend's advice and relax and enjoy his party. "I'm counting every time I lay a bone down," Samson said.

"That's what I'm talking about. Let's do this." Calvin followed Samson to the den, where the other men were waiting.

Samson sat across from Calvin, and after a few hands played, Calvin slammed a domino on the table. "Thirty."

When it was Samson's turn, he counted, "Twenty-five."

Michael and his partner barely counted. When it was Calvin's turn again, he shouted, "Y'all really don't want none of this." He counted again. He and Samson stood up and high-fived each other.

Michael pretended he didn't care that he and his partner were losing. "I just haven't been getting any good hands."

"Oh, you was talking noise when Samson wasn't here," Calvin said as he placed his dominoes on the table.

When Samson's turn came around, he turned and looked at Michael. "Just because I feel sorry for you, I'll let you get ten in." Samson, with a wide smile across his face, placed his domino on the table.

Michael counted and a few minutes later Calvin yelled, "Domino."

Samson did a little dance move in his chair. "Who's the man?"

"Y'all want a chance to redeem yourselves?" Calvin beat on his chest.

"They can't handle the dynamic duo," Samson said.

Michael pulled out a deck of cards from his pocket. "Spades is my game. Anybody down?"

Samson looked at Calvin. "Might as well beat them at spades too."

"Let's do this," Calvin said.

During the course of the game, several of the men brought up Delilah's name. Samson's guilt ate at him. He did his best to refrain from commenting.

Michael said, "Samson, no disrespect, but if I were a single man, I don't think I could resist her."

"I'm not single; I'm getting married Saturday." Samson switched from friend mode to pastor mode. "And if you were single, I would have to counsel you against committing fornication."

One of the deacons said, "I guess he told you.'"

The men laughed. The chatter among them went back and forth. Many would be surprised at the openness between Samson and some of the men in his congregation. Although he was their pastor now, he grew up with some of the men, so they were used to being open with him on their views. He didn't always agree with them, and he had no problem letting them know it, either.

Samson ended up having a good time at his bachelor party. Delilah didn't cross his mind again until he was getting ready to leave. Samson approached Calvin and said, "Man, I want to thank you for everything."

"That's why I'm the best man," Calvin said.

"Seriously, I was about to run over to your house until you stopped me."

"Michelle hasn't called me, so I'm sure everything is fine."

"Julia hasn't called me either."

"I'm headed home. Tomorrow's another long day. We have the rehearsal dinner. I plan on sleeping late, so don't call me before ten."

"I'll be tied up in court all day, so I'll talk to you tomorrow at rehearsal."

"Thank you, Lord, for allowing this night to end drama-free," Samson said out loud, although in the back of his mind he knew at any moment Delilah could say to Julia or his mom something that would change his night. He tried not to think of anything negative as he drove straight home.

Chapter 17

Delilah's face seemed frozen with the fake smile she wore the entire night. As much as she hated to admit it, Julia could have made a good friend under different circumstances. But life handed them different roles to play, and unknowingly, Julia was her enemy. She's the one who had Samson's heart, and she was the one he would vow to love until death.

Julia read a card that Kelly had given her from Samson. The women were *oohing* and *ahhing* at the sweet words written on it. Tears formed in the corners of Delilah's eyes at the thought of losing Samson forever.

"It is touching isn't it," Elaine said sarcastically to Delilah.

Lord, I'm trying to be good, but if this heifer says one more word to me, I'm going to snatch that low-grade yaki hair off her head. Delilah tried to ignore Elaine and continued to watch Julia open her presents.

Julia held Delilah's gift in her hands. "Who's this from?" she asked as she removed the pretty pink ribbon from the pink Victoria's Secret box.

Michelle read the card. "It's from Delilah."

Delilah smiled. Julia removed the pink tissue paper and held up the black and red laced lingerie. A few women said, "Sexy. I like it."

"Women should pick out their own lingerie," Dorothy said, not once taking her eyes off Delilah.

"Ms. Dorothy, this is a bridal party," Michelle said. "I know when Calvin and I got married, I got some of the cutest lingerie, stuff I wouldn't dare buy for myself but was glad I got."

"Me too. Michael never knows what I'll be wearing when he comes home at night," Michael's wife said.

"I don't know a man who can resist a woman who wears something like that," Delilah said.

"Listen to her, honey, 'cause you know she has a lot of experience with men," Kelly said.

If Kelly wasn't Samson's mother, Delilah would have walked up to her and slapped the taste out of her mouth, but she kept quiet. The rest of the gift-opening occurred without any snide remarks. Julia stood up afterward and said, "I want to thank you all for coming and for the wonderful gifts. I'm overjoyed right now."

Some of the women went to Julia and hugged her. Delilah remained seated. The doorbell rang. "That must be Calvin. He must have forgotten his key," Michelle said. She left the area to go answer the door. "Who are you?" Delilah heard Michelle ask.

A male voice responded, "I'm here for Julia Rivers."

"Who is it?" Dorothy asked.

Delilah wished Dorothy would mind her own business. She sat down and watched everyone's reaction when a man walked in wearing a pair of tight jeans, a cowboy hat, and no shirt.

"One time for the rodeo," someone shouted as the male dancer started putting on a show.

"Who's responsible for this?" Dorothy asked

Michelle responded, "I don't know, but I need to thank them because brother man got it going on."

"Ladies, this is inappropriate behavior for Christian women. We should not be partaking in this foolishness," Kelly said.

The dancer took that opportunity to shake his body in front of Kelly as some of the women stuffed his shorts with dollar bills. Delilah rolled over with laughter when Kelly almost fainted.

The male dancer collected money as Dorothy and Kelly looked on with disgust. Julia seemed reserved, but she slipped the dancer a few dollars when she didn't think Kelly was watching her. Delilah even participated in the fun. She should have, since she was paying for the dancer to be there.

"Ladies, looks like I came in just in time," Calvin said from the living room entryway. Michael stood beside him.

The male dancer took that as his cue to leave. He grabbed the money and his clothes. Michelle said to her husband, "Baby, we're wrapping things up now."

"I see," Calvin said, with a raised eyebrow.

Delilah grabbed her purse and followed the dancer outside so she could pay him the money she promised.

"I'll walk you out," Michael said to Delilah.

"Sure, but your wife might get jealous." Delilah twisted out of the room.

The male dancer waited near Delilah's car. "Good job. Here's your money. Thanks for the entertainment." She handed him an envelope.

He moved closer to her. "The party don't have to stop. We can take it to your place."

She pushed him away. "I don't think so. I'm a Christian woman, and I don't do dancers."

He retreated. "Your loss, baby. I got another show to do anyway. I'm out of here."

Delilah threw up two fingers. "Peace."

"It figures she would be trying to get with that dancer," Delilah heard one of the women from Julia's party say to another.

She turned around to face them. "Y'all better be glad I'm saved because the old me would have commenced to throw down." Delilah didn't wait for a response. She hit the car alarm button and slid into her driver's seat.

When driving away, she eased her car as close as she could to the women. They both jumped. Delilah laughed and sped away.

Chapter 18

Tensions were flying high the entire day. Samson found himself putting out one fire after another. If it wasn't one of his church members calling and needing prayer, it was his mother or Julia calling with last-minute wedding changes. Elaine had taken off early to go get her hair done, so he was left answering the phone.

"Thought you could use some relaxation," Delilah said as she entered his office carrying a white Styrofoam plate. "I come bearing food."

Samson hadn't eaten all day. "You didn't have to bring me anything."

"I figured all the women in your life would be busy getting ready for your big day." She opened up the plate. It was filled with baked chicken, macaroni and cheese, greens, and corn bread.

Samson couldn't resist the food. Delilah sat and watched him as he devoured the food. "This was right on time," he said as he ate the last bite of greens.

"I aim to please."

"Thank you for behaving yourself at the bridal shower last night."

"Samson, I love you. I would not do anything to deliberately hurt you." Delilah's eyes twinkled.

"We can be friends. I won't be able to talk to you like

I talk to you now, but when we see each other, we can be cordial."

"I am on your Pastor's Aide committee, so we'll still have a lot to discuss."

"I've been meaning to talk to you about that. Maybe you should resign from the committee."

Delilah looked worried. "Please don't kick me off the committee. You'll never find another member more committed to your cause than me," Delilah pleaded.

"That's not what I was going to say. I just think you should let Ms. Dorothy or Michelle handle reporting stuff to me from now on."

Delilah twisted around in her seat. "You're afraid to be alone with me, aren't you?"

Samson didn't respond. "Delilah, you know our history."

She leaned forward. "I promise to behave as long as you do." She winked.

"I dropped by to bring you lunch, but it seems someone else beat me to it," Julia said, entering the room. She placed the brown paper bag on the nearest table in Samson's office.

"Hello to you too, Julia," Delilah said.

"Why is it every time I turn around, I find her here?" Julia looked directly at Samson.

Samson stuttered, "What had happened was, I was working. Delilah decided to drop me off something to eat. That's it."

He stood up and hugged Julia. Her arms remained to her side. Delilah leaned back in her chair with a smug look on her face.

"Jules—I can call you Jules, can't I?—there's no need

for you to be jealous. You're the best woman, remember?" Delilah assured her.

"I don't like the sight of this one bit," Julia said, obviously frustrated from the tone of her voice.

"Delilah's been having a hard time lately. She needed some advice," Samson lied. He looked at Delilah and with his eyes tried to tell her to help back him up.

Julia placed her arm around his waist. "When we get married, this spiritual counseling needs to cease."

Samson knew Julia didn't care for Delilah, but he was not too fond of the jealous streak his fiancée possessed. His church had more women members than men, and on any given day some would need counseling. He wondered if Julia would have the same possessive spirit with those women. Besides, he only agreed to counsel Delilah so he could keep tabs on her. He felt as long as Delilah got to spend a little time with him, she would be satisfied and wouldn't resort to ruining his world by revealing their affair. He would not allow Julia to interfere with his plans.

"Julia, this isn't open for discussion." Samson then addressed Delilah. "Delilah, thanks for the lunch. I hope I solved your problem. If you don't mind, I need to speak with my fiancée alone."

Delilah eased out of her chair at a slow pace. "The next time I see you two, you'll be walking down the aisle."

"You're coming to the wedding?" Julia asked.

"Of course. I wouldn't miss seeing my two favorite people tie the knot. Tootles," Delilah said as she sashayed out the room.

"I have to pray every night for God to forgive me for

the evil thoughts that run through my mind concerning that woman," Julia said.

"Baby, you have to get past this. There will be plenty of women who need my spiritual guidance." Samson moved and sat down behind his desk.

Julia sat on the corner of his desk. "She just rubs me the wrong way. I used to not have a problem with her, but this crush she has on you seems to be more than just a crush."

"She can't help it. I am kind of cute, don't you think?" Samson hoped his joking would ease the tension between them. "Forget Delilah, baby. In less than twenty-four hours, you are going to be Mrs. Judges, and I can't wait."

"You still have time to back out, and I won't be mad at you," Julia said. Her eyes didn't reflect the words that came out of her mouth.

"God has sent me a treasure in you. Julia Rivers, the day I marry you will be the happiest day of my life." Samson took her hand in his and kissed the back of it.

"It's hard to tell when every time I turn around, Delilah is up in your face and you seem oblivious to what she wants. Then again, maybe you enjoy the attention." Julia jerked her hand away.

"Julia, don't be like that." Samson didn't attempt to reach for her hand. "Delilah has issues, but you don't have to worry about me and her."

"I don't trust her." Julia stood and folded her arms.

Samson walked up to her and looked her directly in the eyes. "Forget Delilah. The question is, Do you trust me?"

Julia tilted her head. "Should I?"

"Of course," Samson responded.

"Yes, Samson, I trust you, okay?"

Without saying a word, Samson wrapped his arms around Julia. She was unable to see the look of relief on Samson's face.

Chapter 19

Delilah dragged herself out of bed Saturday morning. As much as she pretended to be okay with Samson's upcoming nuptials, she wasn't. If only she had met him before he got engaged to Julia, both of their lives could be different.

Keisha would never understand her fascination with Samson. His TV ministry is what saved her life. She wanted what he talked about on the screen week after week. One day she retrieved her grandmother's Bible from her attic. After wiping off the dust, she started reading chapter after chapter. No matter how long it took, she was determined to read it from beginning to end.

Her mind marveled at how many times God forgave people in the Bible for doing stupid things. Her personal turning point came one Sunday morning when Samson preached about Rahab. Delilah turned her Bible to the scriptures and read Rahab's story. She forgot all about her original reason for attending Peaceful Rest Missionary Baptist Church and walked down in front of the altar and joined the church that Sunday.

She'd never forget the day she decided to give her life to Christ, nor would she forget the man responsible for it. Samson was part of her destiny but, unfortunately, not entirely the way she wanted him to be.

Delilah peeked at the clock. The wedding would be in three hours. She needed at least an hour to get ready. She wouldn't be the one getting married, but she could guarantee she would look just as good as the bride, if not better. Over an hour later, Delilah stood in front of the full-length mirror and admired her knee-length, white satin dress trimmed in lace and pearls. Delilah loved her appearance. She placed the matching hat on and adjusted it so the ringlets from her hair wouldn't fall in her face.

She located the new pair of shoes she bought from DFW and put them on. The crystal five-inch heels made her legs look even slimmer. She grabbed her designer clutch and set out for Peaceful Rest Missionary Baptist Church.

Delilah wanted to be early, but it appeared others had the same idea. She circled the parking lot several times to find an available parking place. She admired her face in the rearview mirror and reapplied her lipstick. Satisfied with her looks, she made her way to the church entranceway.

"Hello, Sister Delilah," one of the ushers said as he handed her a wedding program.

"Good afternoon," she responded.

She took the wedding program and followed the sound of the music coming from the main sanctuary. She stopped short of the doors to sign the guest book. With the program tucked under her arm, she went inside. The pews were embellished with an array of pink and white flowers. Delilah asked, "Which side should friends of the groom sit on?"

The male usher responded, "The right."

"Thanks. I'll be sitting on the right." Delilah smiled and walked around him.

She saw some of the women from Pastor's Aide sitting on the bride's side of the church. She waved and found a seat near the front. "Ma'am, we're going to have to ask you to move to this next pew. This pew is for immediate family only."

Delilah pretended not to be embarrassed. "I have to go to the restroom anyway," she said.

Instead of going in the direction of the restroom, Delilah headed toward the pastor's study. The usher directing her to change seats was all the nudge she needed to seek out Samson. She wanted to see if she could talk him out of marrying Julia.

"Oh, no you don't," Calvin said as he jumped in front of her, causing them to collide.

"Last time I checked we were free to walk the halls."

"Samson told me all about you. This is his day, and you, Ms. Delilah, will not spoil it. So turn around." He used his hands and turned her around in the opposite direction of Samson's office.

"But I need to talk to him. It's important."

"He doesn't have time to talk to you right now. Whatever problem you have, call the office."

"Who made you his gatekeeper?"

"I did, when I took on the role of best man. And as his best man, I feel you're up to no good. He doesn't need this type of drama on his wedding day."

"This is not right. I should be able to talk to my pastor."

"You can, just not today," Calvin responded.

No matter how much Delilah protested, Calvin had a response. By now, she was back near the door. He held it open for her. "See you after the wedding," he smiled.

She re-entered the sanctuary and located a seat near the aisle. She retrieved her cell phone and sent a few text messages back and forth with Keisha as she waited for the ceremony to begin. She held out hope that Samson had changed his mind since it was thirty minutes past the time the wedding was supposed to start.

Samson seemed to glide into the sanctuary when he entered with Calvin and Reverend Regis Judges, Samson's dad. Delilah watched his every step. When her eyes met Samson's, Delilah saw her dream of them being together dissipate into thin air.

Chapter 20

Guilt swept through Samson's being when he laid eyes on Delilah. Seeing her there reminded him of his broken vows to God. Her beauty had blinded him on many occasions. He refused to let his mind wander.

Calvin nudged him in the side. "Man, you all right? You look like you've seen a ghost."

"Just nervous." His mind should have been on Julia only, but 'here he was minutes away from saying I do, and he couldn't break eye contact with Delilah.

Delilah's smile glowed. She mouthed the words, "I love you."

Calvin looked in Delilah's direction. "Man, just ignore her. She'll have to get through me to ruin this day."

"I hope she behaves." The increased sound of the music playing broke the trance.

"Samson, are you ready?" Samson's dad asked.

Julia originally wanted her father, Reverend Rivers, a noted minister in the community, to preside over the wedding, but he wanted to walk her down the aisle instead. Samson's dad was more than happy to take on the role of marrying his only child. Regis called out his name again.

"I'm just ready for this part to be over with."

"It's about to start, so if you're having any second thoughts, now's the time," Regis said.

"I love Julia, and I'm ready to make her my wife." Samson confessed those words to his father, but his eyes were looking in Delilah's direction.

The organist played "How Great Thou Art," and the ushers signaled for everyone to take their seats. The time was at hand.

"You do have the ring?" Samson asked Calvin.

Calvin patted his chest. "It's right here. I got you. No need to be nervous."

Samson chuckled. The tension from his body eased as the wedding party entered the sanctuary. His heart skipped a beat as the traditional wedding march rang throughout the sanctuary. Everyone in the church stood up. Samson would remember for the rest of his life the moment Julia and her dad entered the sanctuary.

Julia glided down the aisle like an angel dressed in a strapless white satin dress adorned with pearls and diamond studs. Her long train followed behind her. Samson's smile widened the closer she got to him. He heard both his mother and Julia's mother sniffling.

"Who gives this woman to be married?" Regis asked.

Julia's father responded, "I do." He placed Julia's hand in Samson's.

Samson and Julia turned and faced Regis. Regis stated the occasion and followed up with a prayer. One of the associate pastors of Peaceful Rest Missionary Baptist Church stood at the podium and read the second chapter of Genesis verses eighteen through twenty-four. ". . . Therefore shall a man leave his father and his mother, and shall cleave unto his wife: and they shall be one flesh."

Samson knew the passage from memory. After a scripture from the New Testament was read, all eyes were on the couple. Regis said, "The couple has written their own vows."

Samson pulled out the slip of paper he had written his vows on. He glanced at it then looked into Julia's eyes. "I don't think I'll be needing this." He placed the paper back in his pocket. "Julia, you're my best friend, my heart, the love of my life. I have been shown the favor of God by having you take my hand in holy matrimony. I promise to love you like God loves the church. I promise to honor you and treat you like the royalty that you are. My heart overflows with joy as I stand here before you, and our family and friends. I vow to love you, cherish you, be faithful to you, and support you. You have my heart, and I commit to you on this day that nothing will ever tear us apart."

Julia wiped a few tears from her face and said her vows. "Samson, my love, God answered my prayers when He sent you my way. I promise to be the supportive wife to you and your ministry. With everything in my being, I promise to make our home a safe haven for us and any children we may bear. I promise to honor you and love you unconditionally. You're my heart, my best friend, and the love of my life. I commit to you in front of family and friends my loyalty and eternal love."

Regis said, "If anyone feels this couple should not be united in holy matrimony, speak now or forever hold your peace."

Someone cleared her throat. Samson and Julia turned around in the direction of the noise. Delilah looked away. Regis proceeded with the ceremony. Calvin handed Samson the rings. Regis recited some of the traditional vows as they exchanged rings. "By the power vested in me, I now pronounce you husband and wife. Ladies and gentlemen, I present Mr. and Mrs. Samson and Julia Judges. You may now kiss the bride."

The crowd cheered as Samson lifted Julia's veil and kissed her. Samson noticed the smiles on people's faces as he held Julia's hands and marched down the aisle. Everyone was smiling, except for Delilah.

Chapter 21

Delilah's heart broke into several pieces as she watched Samson and Julia exchange their vows. They looked so happy when they walked past her down the aisle. She waited for the crowd to dissipate before leaving the church.

She called Keisha while on the way to the reception. "Why are you putting yourself through the torture?" Keisha asked.

"It wouldn't look right if I wasn't there," Delilah responded.

"From what you tell me, nobody would care if you were there or not, so just go home or come by here. I'll order us some pizza, and we can have a girls' night out."

Delilah wanted to see this through. If she could come to grips with Samson and Julia's relationship, maybe—just maybe—her heart would let go of the love she felt for Samson. "I'm almost there, so thanks, but no thanks."

She ended her call with Keisha and searched for a parking place. The hotel where the reception was being held had valet parking, and she opted to use it when she couldn't locate a close parking place.

The wedding party hadn't arrived, so Delilah took the opportunity to take a bathroom break. She ran into

Ms. Dorothy coming out of one of the stalls. "You're looking pretty today, Ms. Dorothy."

Dorothy looked Delilah up and down. "Thanks." She washed her hands and left the bathroom without saying another word to Delilah.

"I hope someone tells her there's tissue stuck to the bottom of her shoe." Delilah chuckled.

Delilah relieved her bladder. She heard familiar voices so decided to remain in her stall until after they left.

"Can you believe that heifer? She had the nerve to sit on the groom's side," one of the women said.

"Julia better watch out because Delilah's nothing but a Jezebel, and I wouldn't trust her around my husband," another said.

"I told Calvin that if I ever caught him talking to her, he would have some explaining to do." Delilah recognized Michelle's voice.

Calvin thought he was all that and then some, so as far as Delilah was concerned, Michelle didn't have to worry about her or any other sensible woman wanting her man.

"You have to admit, though, the heifer knows how to dress," the other woman said. *She got one more time to call me a heifer,* Delilah thought to herself.

"Not better than me, but she does all right," Michelle said.

Delilah waited until they exited the bathroom before leaving the stall. She washed her hands and got in line to greet the wedding party during the reception procession.

"Congratulations," Delilah said as she shook Julia's hand.

"Thank you," Julia was forced to say. They both knew she wasn't sincere.

Julia ignored the next person in line as she watched Delilah shake Samson's hand. She rolled her eyes at Delilah. Delilah left the line but felt like she was being watched. Delilah filled her plate with appetizers and found an empty seat as close to the wedding party's tables as she could.

She attempted to ignore the conversations going on around her. "Is this seat taken?" an Idris Elba look-alike asked.

"No," Delilah responded, barely looking at him as he took a seat next to her.

After dinner was served, Delilah watched the happy couple get on the dance floor for the first dance. Luther Vandross' "Here and Now" rang in her ear. Other couples began filling up the dance floor.

"Would you like to dance?" the guy next to Delilah asked.

She thought about declining, but after hearing Samson and Julia laugh on the floor, she changed her mind. "Sure."

The song was replaced with another slow tune. This gave Delilah time to size up the man who had been sitting beside her. He wasn't bad-looking at all. She noticed how some of the women reacted when they passed by their tables to reach the dance floor. Delilah pulled him closer when she caught Samson looking in her direction. They danced a couple of songs then exited the dance floor.

"So what's your name?"she asked after returning to their table.

"Luther," the gentleman replied.

"I'm Delilah."

"I know," he responded.

"Who told you that?" Delilah was curious.

"My brother-in-law was more than happy to after I inquired about the prettiest woman in the room."

Delilah blushed, but curious about his brother-in-law's identity, she asked, "Who is your brother-in-law?"

"He's your church's attorney."

It didn't immediately register with her. "Oh, Calvin. I didn't know. In fact, you two look more like brothers than brother-in-laws. "

"But I'm the better looking one."

They laughed then Delilah said, "I don't know. Calvin is handsome."

"And married. Me, I'm single and available."

"Oh, really now?" Delilah leaned closer to him.

"Very much so. I understand you are too."

Delilah pulled back. "I'm single, but my heart belongs to another man."

"One way to get over one man is to start dating another one."

"That's what people say."

"Let's make it happen." Luther pulled out his Blackberry. "How can I reach you after tonight."

"I like a confident man, and because of that I will give you my number." She recited her number to him.

"Do you want mine?"

"I'll get it when you call me."

"I'll be sure to do just that."

Delilah peeped Calvin's game. He thought sending his brother-in-law over would distract her from the glowing couple. She enjoyed the diversion, but Samson was still on her radar, and no matter how good-looking Luther was, he could never replace Samson in her heart.

Chapter 22

Samson couldn't recall ever feeling this happy about any other woman. Only two other days of his life rivaled this one—the day he confessed Christ at the age of eight and the day his father ordained him as a minister.

"Mrs. Judges, I think we should be making our exit soon, don't you think?" Samson said to Julia.

Julia read between the lines. She tapped Michelle on the shoulder. "Michelle, it's time to throw the bouquet."

Michelle went to the deejay table and grabbed the microphone. "All the single ladies come to the front."

The crowd dissipated only to be replaced with women, young and old. "Come on, Ms. Dorothy," someone yelled out. "You're single. Get on up there."

"Child, I'm too old for a man," Dorothy replied.

Delilah said, "She got that right."

Samson watched Delilah as she made her way into the middle of the crowd of women. To everyone's surprise, the bouquet landed right at Delilah's feet. She picked it up and held it in the air to showcase her victory. The disappointed single women left the dance floor. Delilah walked toward Julia, who bore a frown on her face.

"Smile or you'll mess up your pretty wedding album," Delilah advised as she stood next to her holding the bouquet. She leaned close to Julia as if they were best buddies.

Samson moved out of the way as the photographer snapped their pictures. He heard Delilah say to Michelle, who was standing nearby, "Your brother's kind of cute. I think I might take him up on his offer and go out with him on a date."

She didn't waste any time moving on, Samson thought to himself, feeling a tinge of jealousy as he stood on the sidelines, still within earshot.

When Delilah walked away Michelle said, "She'll find out soon enough, Luther's nothing but a player. Ms. Delilah has met her match."

Julia stared at Samson. He knew she was trying to see how he would respond to Michelle's comment, but he didn't. Instead, he took Julia's hands in his. "Can I have this last dance?"

Samson pulled Julia close to him as they danced. There were other people on the dance floor, but Samson's heart and mind were on his wife only. Julia laid her head on his chest, and they rocked back and forth. The song ended, but they were still dancing.

"Baby, it's time we made our escape," Samson said.

"Give me a few, and I'll meet you out front," Julia said.

Samson said good-byes to the groomsmen and his parents.

"Don't worry about things here. Enjoy your new bride," Calvin told Samson.

"Oh, I definitely plan on doing that. It's been a long time coming." Samson said thank you and good-bye to guests as he left out of the reception area.

"Hold up. You're telling everybody good-bye but me." Delilah rushed up to him.

Samson looked around to see if he could locate Julia. He and Delilah were the only ones in the hallway. "Good-bye, Delilah."

"Aww, come on now. You can do better than that. Can a sister get a hug like the other women?"

"I don't think so."

Delilah pouted. "All I'm asking for is a hug."

Samson ignored his reservations and hugged her. Delilah held on tight. "Think of me when you're making love to your wife tonight."

Samson pushed her away and Delilah giggled. "Good-bye, Samson."

He was glad no one saw the exchange. His body wasn't supposed to react the way it had, not toward Delilah anyway. Disappointed in himself, Samson said a silent prayer. He was still trying to gather his senses when Julia approached him.

"Let me get that." Samson reached down and took the small suitcase Julia was now carrying.

A long, white stretch limousine with the words "Just Married" on the windows filled several parking spots in front of the hotel. The driver held their door open as they headed in the direction of the limousine. Samson helped Julia in, and they waved at people standing outside of their limousine as it pulled away.

"You just don't know how long I've been wanting to do this," Julia said.

"What?" Samson asked.

Julia removed her shoes. "They've been hurting me all day."

Samson laughed. "I don't know why women like to torture themselves."

"We do it all for you men," Julia said as she leaned closer and they shared a kiss.

Samson picked up a bottle of champagne on the bar and poured them each a glass. "To Mrs. Judges." Samson held up his flute.

"I like how that sounds." They tapped their glasses together.

"Where are you taking me?" Julia asked.

"It's a surprise."

"I might not have the right outfits packed."

"Your mother has packed for you." Samson couldn't stop smiling. He couldn't wait to surprise his bride. She had always wanted to go to the Bahamas, and thanks to the good deal he got with his travel agent, he was about to make it happen for her.

She kissed him. "As your wife, I demand you tell me."

"We're going to Dallas. I thought we would take a limousine drive there instead of flying since it's so close, and from there you'll just have to wait and see."

"Great. I can do some shopping."

"We'll only be there for one day, dear."

"I don't need but a few hours."

Julia didn't drink or smoke, but she had one vice, and that was shopping. Samson had dated Julia so long this didn't come as a surprise. They kissed and cuddled during the three-hour drive to Dallas.

Samson checked them into their honeymoon suite at the Adam's Mark hotel in downtown Dallas. Julia screamed with joy when he picked her up and carried her over the threshold. "Oh, this is beautiful," Julia said, admiring the suite.

"You can put the bags over there," Samson said to the

bellhop. After putting Julia down, he retrieved a ten dollar bill out of his wallet and handed it to him. Samson made sure the door was secure after the bellhop left.

Samson smiled at the excitement Julia displayed as she marveled at how beautiful their hotel suite was. "Let's continue to explore." Samson hoped the hotel had done what he had asked. When he opened the bedroom door, rose petals met them at the doorway and led directly to the huge king-sized bed. Chocolate-covered strawberries and a chilled bottle of champagne sat next to the bed. "Where's my bag? I want to freshen up," Julia said.

Samson fetched one of her bags and asked, "Is this it?"

Julia opened the bag and looked inside. "Yes this is it. I won't take long." Julia left to go to the bathroom to freshen up.

Samson removed his tuxedo and went to the other bathroom in their hotel suite. Shortly thereafter, he lay across the bed anticipating Julia's return. "I'm waiting," he shouted.

"Close your eyes," she replied a few seconds later.

Samson closed his eyes. He could sense Julia's presence. Samson inhaled her fragrance. He felt her touch him, and his eyes immediately opened. "Oooh. There are no words to describe how good you're looking, baby," Samson complimented.

"Good. Because talking is the last thing I want to do."

They kissed and caressed each other's bodies. He removed the sheer white lingerie from her body. Samson could tell Julia was ready for him. This was the moment they both had been waiting for, but his body wouldn't respond. Of all the nights, nothing. His body had no problems reacting to Delilah's presence. Was his body trying to tell him something he didn't want to believe? Was Delilah right? Should he have chosen her and not Julia? All those questions and more ran through Samson's mind as he tried to ease the situation by cuddling with Julia.

Although Julia's back was toward him in the bed, he heard the soft sounds of her crying. Her whimpering tugged at his heart. He squeezed her tight until they both fell asleep.

Chapter 23

"I'm going to be celibate," Delilah said over dinner the following week at Keisha's place.

Keisha burst out laughing. "Please. I would love to see that day."

"I'm serious. If I can't have Samson, I would rather be celibate." It had been a week since Samson's wedding. Delilah imagined him and his new bride having the time of their lives on their Bahamian honeymoon. She happened to overhear Elaine and Michelle talking about where they were going last night after Bible Study.

"So what's up with the guy you met at the reception?" Keisha asked.

"He's been calling, but I don't have time for games."

"Girl, you're going to have me choking. You're a natural comedian tonight."

Keisha poured them both some more soda.

"This lasagna is good," Delilah said.

"Don't be trying to butter me up. You know I'm going to tell you the truth whether you like it or not."

"A best friend would be supportive." Delilah played around with the food on her plate.

"Let's see. We're not having anything special going on at my church tomorrow, so I'll go to church with you tomorrow so I can give you moral support on the couple's first Sunday back as husband and wife."

Delilah hadn't thought about them returning tomorrow. Yes, she would need to be around at least one friendly person. "Good. Now make sure you wear something cute. You'll be representing me."

"Hold up, sister. You got it twisted. I always look good."

Delilah disagreed. Keisha was her friend, but she seemed to dress more flashy than stylish. She would keep her comments to herself though. One wrong word from her could set Keisha off on a tangent, and from her experience, it could be days before they spoke again. She needed Keisha to be there for her.

Delilah went home and picked out an outfit for the next day. She fell asleep as soon as her head hit the pillow but tossed and turned the entire night with nightmare after nightmare. She remembered none of them the next morning as she wiped the sleep from her eyes.

"I feel like I just got hit by a freight train," Delilah said as she popped a couple of ibuprofen into her mouth. She washed the pills down with water.

It took her longer than usual to get dressed due to the tension that filled her head. She called Keisha to let her know she was running late. An hour later, she and Keisha were sitting on a pew in the middle of the church where she could get a good view of everyone entering and leaving the sanctuary.

"Girl, I might have to move because I can't see nothing with that big old birds' nest on that woman's head," Keisha said. She shifted in her seat in an attempt to get a better view.

"That's Ms. Dorothy. She's the head of Pastor's Aide. She hates my guts," Delilah informed Keisha.

"Interesting."

Delilah went on to identify several other people, mainly women, in the congregation who didn't like her for whatever reason. "Girl, I don't even see why you want to come to this church if nobody likes you," Keisha said.

"Because I'm not here for the people. I'm here to get the Word, and Samson brings it like no other pastor I know."

"That's because you haven't branched out and been to other churches."

"I visit other churches all the time," Delilah said.

"Only when Samson's not preaching."

Music began to fill the sanctuary. One of the ushers tapped Delilah on the shoulder. "Excuse me," she said. "I'll need for you ladies to hold it down. Church is about to start."

Keisha mimicked the usher. Instead of getting upset, Delilah laughed. "So where's the happy couple?" Keisha asked.

"That's what I want to know."

After one of the associate pastors said a prayer, everybody stood up as the choir marched in singing, "Shake . . . shake . . . shake. Shake the devil off. In the name of Jesus, shake the devil off."

Delilah turned to face the front of the church as the choir made their way into the choir stand. Delilah tapped Keisha on the arm. "There they are."

Julia, wearing a knee-length, peach-colored suit, walked in front of Samson. Both had smiles on their faces. Julia walked and stood near the front pew. Samson greeted the other ministers as he made his way into the pulpit. He lowered his hand to indicate everyone could be seated.

Delilah's mind should have been on worshipping God; instead, her heart filled with envy the moment she saw how happy Julia appeared. The choir rocked the sanctuary. Everyone, including Keisha, seemed to be filled with the Holy Ghost. Delilah and a few children remained in their seats as the choir sang, "Where the spirit of the Lord is there is liberty."

Delilah felt like a captive and could not relate to the lyrics of the song at the time. Delilah's headache subsided, but she wasn't enjoying the service. Keisha, on the other hand, seemed to be having a good time.

"Girl, Peaceful Rest's choir is off the hook. I need to see about getting y'all for our next musical," Keisha said.

"Oh, okay." Delilah halfway listened.

Forty minutes later, Samson made his way to the podium. "My lovely bride and I would like to thank each and every one of you for the gifts, cards and well wishes. We wanted to also thank Calvin and Michelle and everyone who worked with them to move Julia's stuff to my house while we were gone. We just got back late last night and, yes, we did miss our church family." Samson looked in Julia's direction. "Honey, did you want to say anything?"

Delilah couldn't hear Julia's response over the noise from the congregation, but it must have been no since Julia remained seated. "I know some of you came to hear me preach, but I decided to let Associate Minister Michael Monroe bring today's message since technically I'm still on my honeymoon." A few laughs were heard throughout the congregation. Samson continued to say, "Well, after the choir gives us an A and B selection, the next voice you hear will be Minister Monroe."

After the choir sang a couple of selections, Minister Monroe stood behind the podium and sang "Precious Lord" along with the congregation. A few minutes later, he began reciting a couple of verses from the sixth chapter of Matthew, taken from the New King James Version. "Take heed that you do not do your charitable deeds before men, to be seen by them. Otherwise you have no reward from your Father in heaven. . . . But when you do a charitable deed, do not let your left hand know what your right hand is doing, that your charitable deed may be in secret; and your Father who sees in secret will Himself reward you openly."

"Amen," several people around Delilah said.

"Today, I'll be talking about charity." He stopped talking and looked at one of the ushers. "Ushers, you can be seated."

He faced the congregation. "Some of us are doing stuff for the wrong reasons. We want our sisters and brothers to pat us on the back for things we should be doing for our fellow man anyway." He paced back and forth in front of the podium. "Some of us only do stuff for people who can do something for us."

"Preach," someone yelled.

"When was the last time you did something for someone and didn't expect anything in return?" he asked.

Thirty minutes later, as the sermon ended, Keisha said, "Minister Monroe was good, but I'll have to come back so I can hear your pastor."

"Yes, Minister Monroe is good, but he's no Samson."

They got out of their seats. Delilah started to head to the front of the church instead of going toward the front door. Keisha grabbed Delilah's arm. "Where are you going?"

"I'm going to stand in line to greet the happy couple like everybody else."

"Ugh. Come on. Let's go," Keisha said. She kept her hold on Delilah's arm.

Delilah attempted to pull away, but Keisha had a strong grip. "You win," Delilah said.

She followed Keisha toward the door. Delilah turned around and caught Samson looking in her direction. She waved, but he didn't wave back. Maybe there was no more hope after all.

Chapter 24

Samson sighed when Delilah left instead of standing in the receiving line like some of the other patrons. He pretended not to see her wave at him. He smiled at his wife who was going to make a good first lady. They attempted to thank everyone personally as they made their way through the line.

Calvin and Michelle walked up to the couple. "I guess we'll be seeing a Samson Junior running around here in about nine months," Calvin said.

Julia's smile vanished. Michelle said, "Calvin, you need to shut up sometimes."

Samson attempted to diffuse the situation. "Man, give us some time to ourselves. We have plenty of time for kids. Right, baby?" He placed his arm around Julia and pulled her to him.

"Right," she responded. Her smile seemed forced.

Samson and Julia retreated to his office. He removed his robe. "That went well, don't you think?" he asked as he hung up his robe.

"I guess." Julia walked to the window. People could be seen talking and getting into their cars.

Samson walked up behind her. "Service was good. Michael's doing an outstanding job. I won't be surprised if someone doesn't call him to pastor his own church soon."

"Why didn't you wave back at her?" Julia asked.

Samson pretended not to know the identity of "her." "Baby, I'm not sure I know what you're talking about."

"You didn't see Delilah when she waved at you?"

"No," he lied.

Julia rolled her eyes and turned away. "I thought after we married, I wouldn't have to worry about her. Man, was I wrong."

"You're the only one fixated on her. I told you there wasn't and never will be anything going on between Delilah and me."

Julia turned and faced Samson. "That's what your mouth says, but your body says something totally different."

A knock on the door interrupted their conversation. "Come in," Samson yelled.

"There goes my favorite couple," Kelly said as she entered. She hugged the newlyweds.

"Ms. Kelly," Julia stated.

"It's Mom now," Kelly corrected her. "Will I be seeing y'all for dinner?"

"Mom, I think we'll pass on dinner today. Samson and I want more alone time."

"Oh, I get it." Kelly winked her right eye. "Julia, call me so we can catch up later this week."

"I took a short leave of absence from my job, so we'll talk later," Julia responded. As soon as Kelly was out of the door, Julia said, "Samson, I'm supposed to be this happy, glowing bride, but look at me."

"Baby, we can get through this. Tonight. Watch."

Julia laughed. "I heard that for an entire week. I waited two years." She held up two fingers. "Two years to marry the man of my dreams, and he couldn't get it up. Do you know how that makes me feel?"

Samson started to reach for her but stopped when she wrapped her arms around herself. "I'm sorry. I prayed and . . ." his words trailed off.

"And what, Samson? You prayed to God that you would be able to perform for your wife? This is embarrassing."

"Nobody has to know but us."

Julia rolled her eyes. "Come on. Let's go. I don't want to talk to anyone else."

Samson followed Julia out of his office. Julia plastered on a fake smile while they greeted a few people who were hanging around the church as they made it to their car. Her smile left her face as soon as they were seated behind the tinted windows of Samson's SUV. Julia looked out the window the entire trip home. Samson, left with his own thoughts, felt bad. They had been married a week and one day, but due to his impotence, they had not consummated their marriage.

The silence between them remained after they got home. Samson spoke first and asked, "What do you want for dinner?"

"Whatever you want. I'm going to take a nap. Just wake me up when you get back from wherever you decide to go."

Samson tried to be understanding about Julia's frustrations, but she didn't have to be so cold toward him. He changed into a pair of jeans and a button-down starched shirt. He thumbed through the flyers from different dining spots he had in his kitchen drawer. He decided to drive to the other side of town and get some barbeque from Uncle Buck's.

"Isn't that your pastor?" he heard someone say from behind him as he stood in line at Uncle Buck's and placed his order.

"Hey, Pastor," Delilah said.

Samson bit his bottom lip. He turned around and greeted Delilah and the woman with vibrant red hair.

Delilah said, "This is my best friend Keisha."

"I've heard so much about you," Keisha took the liberty of saying.

"All good I hope," he responded.

Keisha looked at Delilah and smiled. "Where's your bride?" Delilah asked.

Samson had no business talking to Delilah, but he answered, "At home taking a nap." The line was getting longer behind them. "Ladies, I'll let you place your orders. Looks like we're holding up the line."

Samson took a seat in the back corner as he waited on his food. He pulled out his cell phone and started playing a game. "I'm surprised she let you out of her sights," Delilah said as she slipped in the chair at his table. Keisha sat at another table.

"We're married, not in bondage."

"Mmhmm. So how was the Bahamas? Or did you stay in the room the whole week and not get a chance to take in the sights?" Delilah's perfume filled his nostrils to the point of being overpowering.

"My relationship is not up for discussion," Samson said.

"Sort of testy. You would think that after a week of consummating your marriage, you wouldn't be so tense." Delilah seemed to be teasing him.

"Pastor Judges, your order is ready," the cashier yelled over the noise.

Samson slid out from his chair. His leg grazed against Delilah's thigh as he tried to get by her. "See you."

He grabbed his food and sped home. Julia was still sleeping when he arrived. He woke her up and, although she still was a little reserved with him, they talked as they ate dinner. Afterward, they cuddled and watched a couple of movies.

Later that night, back in the bedroom, Samson disappointed Julia again. Frustrated, Julia turned her back to Samson. When he reached for her, she moved closer to the edge of her side of the bed. Samson couldn't believe how things were turning out. He closed his eyes and thoughts of seeing Delilah earlier that day filled his head. He felt his body begin to respond to the thoughts. He screamed internally, *Noooo*. Was his body was trying to tell him something again?

Chapter 25

Delilah squeezed her pillow. The dreams of Samson soon turned to nightmares as she fought the evil witch of the south—Julia. In her dreams, Julia got to walk away with the grand prize. Delilah held a consolation prize: a box that made an annoying buzzing noise. The sound of the phone ringing jolted Delilah out of her sleep. "I'm coming," Delilah yelled, as she reached over to answer the phone. "Hello," she said, barely above a whisper.

"Rise and shine, sweetheart," William said.

She stretched and sat up in bed. "What time is it?"

"It's time for phase two. Now get your butt out of bed and start earning the money I paid you."

Delilah's eyes adjusted to the daylight. She glanced at the clock. "William, it's just seven in the morning. There's nothing I can do this early."

"I saw your boy on TV, so I know he's back from his honeymoon. I'm giving you two weeks to get something on him that I can use."

Delilah attempted to go back to sleep after hanging up with William, but sleep evaded her. She tossed the comforter to the side and started her morning ritual. She put her coffee on, showered, and then ate her breakfast while reading the *Shreveport Times*. Out of habit, she checked the obituaries. She never knew her father, but her mother had given her his name. She checked the paper every day to see if his name was listed.

A part of her blamed her deadbeat dad for the life she'd led. If he hadn't abandoned her mother when she was born, they might not have been forced to live in the projects. Her mom worked for a wealthy white family and cleaned their house for lackluster pay. Her mom literally worked herself to death. The day the police stopped by the apartment with a social worker to tell Delilah the news is the day something inside her died. At that point, the ten-year-old girl felt like she had no reason to live. Placed in foster care, Delilah got moved from house to house due to her bad-girl ways.

No one heard the cries when some of her foster parents took advantage of her physically and abused her mentally. The last time she tried to seek help from an adult, her foster parent beat her into silence. When she turned sixteen, she ran away and lived on the streets. An elderly woman with bluish gray hair found her stealing food from her garage. Ms. Shadows took Delilah in, fed her, and clothed her. She was thrilled when Ms. Shadows worked it out with the state and became her foster parent. For a year, Delilah felt happy. Ms. Shadows didn't have much, but the little she had she freely shared with Delilah. Ms. Shadows dressed her up and took her to church weekly, and rarely would she find the woman without her Bible.

She lost hope again the day she walked home from school and found Ms. Shadows permanently asleep in her rocking chair. The paramedics had to pry Delilah away from the woman's body as she hugged her tight, refusing to let go. *"Don't leave me too, Ms. Shadows,"* Delilah had said.

No one cared about the skinny teenager with thick wavy hair. She was now seventeen—too old for the system and not old enough to be the head of household on her own case file. With no one to support her and a need to survive, Delilah got a fake ID and started dancing at an area strip club when she overheard some women brag about how much money they made.

At first she didn't make much money, but when Mercedes, one of the highest paid strippers in the club, took her under her wings, it didn't take Delilah long to learn the tricks of the trade. She made enough money to rent out Ms. Shadows' house from her surviving relatives, and she lived there until Ms. Shadows' nephews decided to sell the house.

As she got older, Delilah realized she wouldn't be able to make money with her body for the rest of her life, so, like Mercedes, she enrolled at one of the local colleges. That's when she ran into Keisha. Keisha remembered her from her old neighborhood, and their friendship rekindled.

She had to credit Keisha for getting her away from the nightlife because she didn't have the courage to leave it on her own. Keisha not only encouraged her, she helped Delilah get a regular job. The pay was far less than what she was accustomed to making, but the benefits outweighed the pay. She no longer had to deal with men who fawned over her like she was a piece of meat.

Delilah would never admit to Keisha that with stripping she offered other services on the side. Those services were the ones that William had found out about. How, she didn't know. She never mentioned any of it when she applied for a job at Trusts Enterprise. Making twenty dollars an hour at a regular job was a dream come true for her; little did she know that it would come with a price.

The water in the shower turned lukewarm, bringing Delilah back to the present. Through most of her twenties, Delilah lived the fast life filled with men, money, and booze. Whenever Delilah felt she'd turned her life around for the better, something evil lurked and attempted to draw her back in. Her life always seemed to spiral out of control. This time, though, she had come too far to lose it all. She had lost Samson. Could she afford to lose her soul as well?

Chapter 26

Samson and Julia's honeymoon ended before it ever got started. Only two days back from their trip to the Bahamas and Julia was giving him the cold shoulder. Disappointed in how his married life had started, Samson headed to the altar as soon as he got to church Monday morning.

"Father God, I come to you with a humble heart." Samson prayed for the sick and shut-in. He ended his prayer on a personal note. "I know my actions before I got married were not pleasing to you. I don't want my wife to pay for the sin I committed. Please restore me physically so that I can please my wife in every way possible."

Samson ended his prayer and slowly made his way toward his office.

Elaine, sitting at her desk, greeted him when he entered. "Pastor Judges, William Trusts called."

William was the last person Samson wanted to talk with. "If he calls again, don't take a message."

Samson sat in front of his computer and got caught up with his e-mails. Many of them were congratulatory messages from other ministers and people he knew who were unable to come to the wedding.

Elaine stepped in his office. "I have a doctor's appointment at one o'clock, so I probably won't be back today. Is there something you want me to do before I leave?"

"Just leave the door open. I'll see you tomorrow."

"Trusts called again, so you might want to look at the caller ID before answering the phones."

"I'll let the calls go to voice mail, and you can check them tomorrow."

"I'm out," Elaine said before closing the door behind her.

"What in the world?" Samson said as he clicked on an e-mail in his inbox. A video of Delilah swinging around a pole played. At the bottom of the e-mail, the note read, "Can your wife do this?"

The e-mailer with the name of "Deedancer" sent him an instant message. "I see you got my e-mail."

"Delilah, anybody could have checked my mail."

Delilah responded: "But they didn't. Do you miss me yet?"

Samson typed, "Unless it's church-related, I suggest you don't e-mail me."

"You never did answer my question."

Samson hated to admit it, but he did miss Delilah. He missed how her back arched when they made love. He was tempted to watch the video she sent again.

"How have you been?" he asked, hoping to change the subject.

"As well as can be expected after losing the man I love," she responded.

Samson hated that he had to hurt Delilah, but he didn't love her. He was now married, and she would have to move on. "Other than that, how have you been?"

"Do you really want to know?" she asked.

"I sincerely want you to be okay, Delilah."

"Well, I've been having nightmares lately. I've tried to forget my past, but the dreams won't let me."

"Set up an appointment, and I'll have one of the associate pastors talk with you about it."

"Can you do it?"

"Now, Delilah, you know our track record."

"I promise I won't try anything."

Samson wasn't worried about Delilah. He was more concerned about how his wife would react if she found out he was counseling Delilah, especially in light of the problems they were having in the bedroom. "Delilah, I won't be able to do it."

"Please," she wrote, adding a few frowning faces for effect.

Samson felt torn between his pastoral duties and his responsibility as a husband. He had prayed about Delilah and felt he was strong. He would not allow the devil to win. "I have an opening this evening at four, but I have to be out of here by five," he typed.

"I'll be there."

"Hi, hubbie," Julia said. She entered his office holding two brown bags.

"What a surprise." Samson remained sitting as he determined Julia's mood. Julia shortened the distance between them.

Julia removed two plastic containers from the bag and placed one in front of him. "I know I haven't been the nicest person to live with, so this is a peace offering."

Samson turned the monitor off. "My favorites."

"I know how you love my mama's macaroni and greens, so I bribed her into cooking it for you."

"I'll have to call my mother-in-law to thank her."

"She put you some peach cobbler in there too."

"I married the wrong Rivers."

"Watch it now," Julia said.

For the first time in days, they were actually laughing again.

"I left my phone in the car. Can I use your computer to check my e-mail?" Julia asked.

"Uh, well I was in the middle of doing something. Can it wait?" he asked.

"It'll only take a minute."

Samson had to think fast. He felt around on the floor for the plug. Julia moved the mouse around. The screen remained blank. Samson's heart rate increased. His foot hit the button on the power plug at the same time Julia hit the power button on the monitor.

"What's wrong with your computer?" she asked.

"It has a mind of its own sometimes." Samson used his foot to turn the power back on. The computer beeped. "See. It's working now."

"I'll check them later. I told your mom I would meet her."

"You sure? Because it's not going to take long to log back on."

"I'm sure. I'll see you tonight at home," Julia said. She kissed him and left his office.

Samson didn't exhale until Julia had left his office. He logged back on to his account. Delilah had logged off. He sent her an e-mail canceling their four o'clock session. He didn't know what he was thinking making plans to see Delilah without anyone else being in the office. The two of them alone equaled trouble.

Chapter 27

Delilah sprayed her body down with her favorite designer fragrance. Instead of wearing a skirt, she changed into a pair of hip-hugging jeans and a satin low-cut blouse. Satisfied Samson would be salivating before she left him, Delilah drove to the church.

Delilah was thrilled when she noticed Elaine's car was not there. She zoomed into the parking spot next to Samson's SUV. She applied some more ruby red lipstick, puckered her lips, and blew a kiss at herself in the rearview mirror. "Are you ready for me, Samson?"

She exited the car and walked briskly up the walkway to the church. She jiggled the knob on the church front door. "He should keep this door locked," Delilah's voice echoed as she entered the church. She headed straight to Samson's office.

He seemed to be in deep thought as she stood in the doorway and watched him for a few minutes. "Knock, knock," she said.

"You came."

"Yes, four o'clock, remember?" She pointed to the clock on the wall.

"I sent you an e-mail to cancel."

"But I didn't get it," Delilah lied. She got it, read it, and hit the delete button without responding.

Samson stood up. "Well, you're here now."

Delilah reached for the door and closed it.

"It's just us here, so you can leave it open."

Delilah did as she was told and re-opened the door. "Thank you for taking time to see me today, Samson."

"Like I told you before, I'm here for you in a pastoral capacity if you need me."

Delilah sat down in the chair across from his desk. She fanned herself. "It's so hot. I don't know how I'll be able to get through the summer."

"Would you like something to drink?" Samson asked.

"Water would be fine."

Samson retrieved a bottle of water out of the mini-refrigerator in his office and handed it to Delilah. She took several sips before placing the bottle on the desk in front of her.

He took a seat and picked up a pen and began writing something on a yellow steno pad. "I'm not sure I'm comfortable with you taking notes of our session," Delilah said.

"You don't have to worry about anyone else seeing this. As you talk, the notes will help me better counsel you."

Samson seemed to be in control of things. His reactions were totally opposite of what Delilah expected. She wanted him to sweat. She wanted to feel the heat that normally materialized whenever they were in the same room. Right now, she was feeling nothing. Maybe he really was happy with his new wife.

Melancholy sat in her spirit. She had lost so much. Tears formed in the corner of her eyes. Samson passed her a tissue. "It's okay. Get it out."

She dabbed her eyes with the tissue. "It all started when my mom died. I've never told anyone this, but my foster parents weren't the nicest of people. In fact, some were downright cruel to me. People think I'm self-ish, but I'm really not. I've had to fight for everything I've gotten. Life hasn't always treated me right."

"Sister Delilah, you appear to be doing well for your-self now, so you have to stop holding on to those ill-gotten feelings. Let the past bury itself."

"I wish it were that easy. Everything could be go-ing great, but when something life-changing happens, those old thoughts return." Delilah revealed a part of her-self to Samson that no one else got to see. "Your wed-ding made me remember some things."

He placed his pen down." I know you were disappoint-ed about my marriage, but you knew beforehand I was getting married."

"I'm in no way blaming you for this last episode, Pastor. I was just hoping you could help me exorcise these de-mons once and for all." Delilah thought she deserved a Best Actress award for faking sincerity.

"The first thing we need to do, and I should have done this before you started talking, is pray."

Samson didn't see the smile that replaced Delilah's frown, due to his head being bowed. Delilah added, "Yes, Lord," in various places as Samson prayed.

"God, we know with You all things are possible. Your daughter needs some supernatural healing, Father, heal-ing of the mind. Heal her so that she can find peace—peace that only you, Lord, can give her."

Delilah followed his prayer with an "amen."

Samson ignored the ringing office phone. Seconds

later, his cell phone rang. After checking the caller ID he said to Delilah, "That's my wife. Hold on for a minute."

Delilah crossed and uncrossed her legs as she waited for him to end his call. Samson's demeanor seemed to change. His forehead tensed up. He swiveled his chair around. Delilah could tell something was wrong.

Samson turned the chair back around and faced her. "Sorry about that."

"Everything okay?" she asked. She really was concerned. He had just gotten married, so there shouldn't be any problems at home. She leaned forward, revealing some cleavage.

Samson's eyes were glued to her chest. He cleared his throat. "This isn't about me, Delilah. It's your time."

"If there's something you need to take care of, we can do this another time."

He looked away. "Maybe you're right. But before you go, I want to give you scriptures to read when you get home." He scribbled on his steno pad and handed a sheet of paper to Delilah.

Delilah reviewed it."Matthew fifth chapter and the sixth chapter of Luke."

"I want you to think about forgiving the people in your past who have wronged you. Reading those scriptures should help. Read them daily and meditate on them."

"Can I come back tomorrow around the same time?" Delilah asked.

He glanced through the calendar on his desk. "I don't see anything scheduled, so four tomorrow is fine."

"Great." Delilah extended her hand to shake his.

"Be careful," Samson said as he shook Delilah's hand.

"I will." She bent over to retrieve the paper she let slide onto the floor. "See you tomorrow," she said before leaving the room.

Chapter 28

Samson remained seated. He didn't want Delilah to see the effect she had on him. If Julia ever found out, she would be devastated. The last thing Samson wanted to do was commit adultery in his heart. Once his office door was closed, he picked up his Bible, and the pages automatically flipped open to Proverbs chapter six, verse twenty-five: *"Lust not after her beauty in thine heart; neither let her take thee with her eyelids."*

He knew in his heart this was a sign from God. "Lord, I love my wife. I want to build a life with my wife."

Samson continued to read more scriptures. As he read, his sermon for the following week came to him. He jotted down some notes. Time had crept by. The phone ringing jolted him out of his deep thoughts of meditation.

"What time are you coming home?" Julia asked from the other end of his cell phone.

"Baby, I'm sorry. I started reading and praying. Time just got away from me."

He couldn't tell if Julia was upset from her tone. "I'm almost through cooking. It should be ready by the time you get here."

"Give me at least thirty minutes. I'm almost through working on my sermon." They ended their call, and

Samson typed up some more notes on his computer before logging off. He locked up his office and the church and jumped in his SUV.

Traffic stood still on I-49. He called Julia to alert her. This time there was no mistaking what mood she was in.

"Is this something I should expect every night?" she snapped.

"Julia, you know better than that. I got lost in time, that's all."

"I'll have to warm the food up when you get here."

Samson didn't want to argue. He said good-bye and discontinued the call. He listened to a gospel CD as he weaved in and out of traffic. When he finally made it home, Julia greeted him at the door with a hug and kiss. "Sorry about earlier," she apologized. "I've had time to cool off, and I don't want to argue."

"All's forgiven," Samson responded.

"Go get washed up, and I'll bring the food to the table."

Being married to Julia was definitely different from dating her. Her demeanor had changed. He tried to understand her frustrations, but what she didn't take into consideration was that not being able to consummate their relationship also affected him. He pulled the printout he had about Viagra out of his briefcase. He laughed out loud. He was only thirty years old and never thought he would need a pill to help him perform. If his friends only knew. He threw the printout back in his briefcase.

The aroma of the food filled the air when he entered the dining room. Julia filled his plate with food and waited for him to take her hand in his to say grace. The conversation over dinner reminded him of a bad date. Julia's recounting the conversations she had with his mother earlier that day bored him. Maybe when Julia went back to work as plant manager she would have something more exciting to talk about.

"The food was good," Samson said.

"Thanks," Julia responded.

Samson went to his study while Julia cleared the dinner table and went to wash dishes. He retrieved his medical insurance information. He wrote down the information he needed so he could make a doctor's appointment the following day.

He leaned back in his chair and placed his legs on top of the desk. He owed his father a call. He picked up the phone and dialed his father's number. Regis answered on the third ring.

"Kelly tells me she feels something isn't right with you and Julia. Y'all having problems already son," Regis had asked after their greeting.

Samson closed his eyes. "We're okay. Trying to get adjusted. I forgot to thank you for helping to move her stuff in while we were gone." Samson hoped it would steer the conversation in another direction.

"That's what family's for. Now back to you and Julia. You know I do have a little experience under my belt when it comes to women." Regis chuckled.

Samson recalled hearing Regis and some of his friends brag about their younger days. Regis claimed to have calmed down when he met and married Samson's mother. Samson trembled. It sickened him to even think about his parents being intimate. He wouldn't dare talk to his father about the real problem within his and Julia's relationship. "We'll be all right, but thanks for your concern."

"Kelly wants to speak with you."

"Tell her I'll call her back," Samson said.

"Too late. She's on the phone," Regis responded.

His mother couldn't see him, but he automatically removed his feet from the desk and sat up. "Hi, Mom."

"You need to take care of your wife soon, son," Kelly stated.

"Excuse me?" Samson said in a high-pitched voice.

"Don't take that tone with me. You're not too old for me to knock you down a peg or two."

"What did Julia tell you?"

"Julia didn't tell me anything. I overheard her talking on the phone to one of her friends when she was at our house. You know there's medicine for your problem."

Samson, infuriated, held back his temper. "Look, Mom. I've heard enough. I've got to go."

"Remember what I said. Get you some medicine."

"I'm not trying to be disrespectful, but this is an issue between me and my wife."

"Well, if you want to keep your wife happy, you better get you some help."

"Good night, Mama." Samson slammed the phone down on the desk.

Steam seeped through Samson's pours. He paced the floor a few times. "One, two, three . . ." he counted out loud. He did his best to calm down as he went in search of Julia.

Samson stood in the doorway and watched Julia for a few minutes. Julia, oblivious to Samson's mood, moved her head up and down as she listened to the music coming from her headphones.

Samson walked up to her and snatched them from her ears.

"Hey, what's your problem?" Julia asked.

"I can't believe you," Samson yelled.

Julia, used to seeing a calm and mellow Samson, blinked a few times. "I have no idea what you're talking about."

"Lying will only get you in deeper." Samson stood with folded arms. "Why were you discussing our bedroom issue with your friend and at my mom's of all places?"

"So what if your mom heard me talking to Cookie. She's a woman. She's got needs too."

"I didn't know I married a sex fiend."

"I didn't know I married a hypocrite either."

The evening went nothing like Samson had planned. For now they were at a standstill. He's a preacher. He shouldn't be having these types of problems. Two people were in love, but sex stood in the way of them being happy.

While in bed that night, Julia wouldn't allow him to touch her. She moved her body close to the edge of her side of the bed. Samson, frustrated, lay on his back and closed his eyes. He went to sleep wondering if marrying Julia was a good idea.

Chapter 29

Delilah eased her car into the tight parking space in front of Keisha's hair salon and went inside. Every chair in the salon seemed to be filled. "What's up, Ms. Thing?" the receptionist said when Delilah entered.

"Is Keisha available? I need something done with this mess." Delilah ran her hands through her hair.

"I'll check." The receptionist yelled on the intercom. "Keisha, Ms. Thing is here." She looked at Delilah. "Just kidding." She spoke back into the intercom. "I mean Ms. Delilah."

Delilah was in a jovial mood, so she ignored the receptionist. The phone at the desk rang. The receptionist looked up at Delilah. "She said come on back."

Delilah spoke as she passed the stylists and went toward the back of the salon where she found Keisha styling someone's hair.

"You might as well have a seat and relax. You're my last client today so don't trip if we're here all night," Keisha told her.

Delilah hated coming in the evening for that very reason. She liked to be at the beauty shop for only two hours max, but because she and Keisha were friends and she did her hair pro bono, she came whenever Keisha could fit her into her busy schedule.

Delilah picked up a recent issue of a fashion magazine. She marveled at how dowdy some of the clothes looked for such extravagant prices. She was no fashion guru, but she did have a sense of style, and some of the things critics claimed were the in thing for the season shouldn't be seen anywhere in public, in her opinion.

Keisha dished out advice to some of her patrons. One woman was dealing with a cheating husband. Marsha, one of Keisha's regular customers who was now on her third husband, said, "Now ladies, don't get into a frenzy with what I'm about to say because you know I'm usually like, if he cheats, he'll cheat again so leave him. But, Cassandra, in your case, your husband has done everything you've asked of him, so why not give him another chance?"

Cassandra responded, "Because I'm just tired. He claimed he cheated one time, but I don't believe him. I've resorted to doing sneaky stuff like checking his phone records and car mileage. I even cracked the code to his voice mail, and I call his phone all day just to check it."

"How did you get his password?" Keisha asked as she curled Cassandra's hair with the curling iron.

"Put it like this: Most men like to keep their passwords simple. He used one of our kids' birthdays."

"Wow. So did you discover anything?"

"No, but that doesn't mean anything. All I know is I can't keep living like this. Divorcing him would give me peace of mind."

"Stay with him and cheat on him if that'll make you feel better," one of the other beauticians said.

"Two wrongs don't make it right," Keisha said. "Peace of mind is priceless, and if you have to leave him to get it, do you, sister."

"I know that's right," several of the women near them said.

An elderly woman interjected her opinion. "Back in my day, we didn't divorce our men. If he wanted to act up, let him. He has to answer to God for everything that he's doing."

"But, Mrs. Pearl, why should she stay with him just because? Adultery is grounds for divorce," Keisha said.

"Young lady, I think I know more about relationships, seeing how I'm seventy-two years old," Mrs. Pearl snapped.

Keisha stopped curling Cassandra's hair. "Yes, ma'am. I was just saying."

Delilah listened but didn't interject her thoughts. From the discussions going on in the beauty shop, whether young or old, she wasn't the only woman dealing with her share of drama.

Two hours later, Delilah sat in Keisha's chair. "I'm glad you let me clip your ends," Keisha said.

It was late, and the beauty shop had cleared out. There were only a few other stylists and clients remaining in the shop. Delilah removed the picture of the model with the hair style she wanted from her purse and handed it to Keisha. "I want it just like this."

Keisha viewed the picture. "I can do that." She turned on the crimp iron and waited for it to warm up. "So have you thought about what I said?"

Delilah looked around. No one appeared to be paying attention to their conversation. "I have a confession to make. I think he and his wife are having problems."

"Delilah, you know you like to exaggerate, and why would he confide in you about his relationship with his wife anyway?"

"He didn't actually verbalize it. I can just tell."

"We need to find you another man so you can stop bugging about Samson."

Delilah gave Keisha an "I'm innocent" look. "What?" she asked. "Don't nobody up in here know him, so what if I said his name."

"Just in case, let's keep his name out of it."

"See, now you know you must not be doing something right if you have to keep it all hush-hush."

"Don't trip just because I don't like my business all out in the streets," Delilah snapped.

"Testy." Keisha held up the crimp iron. "One piece of advice—never piss off your mailman or the lady who is about to do your hair."

Delilah looked up and saw Keisha's facial expression in the mirror. Keisha burst out laughing. Delilah said, "Girl, I was about to hop out the chair. You weren't going to touch me with that attitude."

Keisha swiveled the chair around. "You know I was just playing with you. But seriously though, if you want to get your mail, don't piss your mailman off."

They both laughed. Keisha had just applied the holding spray when Delilah's phone rang. One of Yolanda Adams' songs played as the ring tone. Delilah picked up the call right before it went to voice mail.

"It's about time you answered your phone. I've left several messages," Luther, the guy she met at Samson and Julia's wedding reception, said.

"Apparently, I haven't felt like talking," Delilah responded.

Keisha stood to the side with her hands on her hip.

"Look, I'm getting my hair done. I'll call you back later." Delilah hit the end button on her phone and placed it back in her purse.

"Who was that?" Keisha asked as soon as Delilah got off the phone.

"Nobody important. Just a bugaboo."

Keisha fixed a few stray strands on Delilah's head. "Anyway, back to you-know-who. If that man ever found out you were setting him up, do you think he would have anything to do with you?"

"I can handle my man," Delilah said, deluding herself. Delilah hoped Samson never found out her original mission for befriending him. She didn't want to give him a reason to cut all ties with her. She was not prepared to live without Samson in her life, even if his only role was as her pastor.

Chapter 30

Regis waved his hand in the air to get Samson's attention. Samson walked past several tables in the country club restaurant before reaching his dad's table. "Glad you could make it, son," Regis said as Samson took a seat.

"I only came here today because you bribed me with breakfast." Samson smiled.

"I learned that trick from your mama. Fill a man up and he's liable to be open to hear whatever you have to say is her way of thinking."

Samson eyed the food on the buffet. "Dad, I promise to listen to whatever you have to say after I fill my empty stomach."

Fifteen minutes later, Samson and Regis were each enjoying a full plate of breakfast. A waiter placed a pitcher of orange juice on their table. Regis said, "Your mother shared with me last night some personal things about you and Julia."

Samson held his hand up. "I don't want to talk about it."

"Look, I'm not here to ridicule you. I'm here to help."

Samson couldn't believe Julia's lack of secrecy had him discussing with his dad what should have been private between the two of them. He had never been so embarrassed. "Let's pretend like you never brought it up," Samson said as he took a bite out of his toast.

"Son, I don't have to tell you that I was surprised when your mother told me."

Samson didn't have a problem having sex. He just had a problem having it with Julia. The guilt of sleeping with Delilah before they were married marred their relationship. Samson wanted to confess to someone. Maybe releasing some of the burden would help improve things between him and Julia.

"Dad, before Julia and I married, I slept with someone. There I said it." Samson held his head down.

"Are you still sleeping with the woman?"

"No, I'm not. I swear on two stacks of Bibles." Regis had Samson feeling like a teenage boy being chastised by his father.

"Now, son, you can lie to me. You can lie to your mom and your wife. But you can't lie to God."

"I've been tempted, but no. I'm no longer sleeping with the woman."

"I don't have to tell you how important your wedding vows are, do I? You vowed before God to honor, cherish, and be faithful to her."

Samson felt at this point he had nothing to lose. Since his dad wanted to be blunt about things, Samson asked him a question that had been lingering in his mind. "Have you ever cheated on Mom?"

Regis placed his fork down. "My relationship with your mom has nothing to do with your situation, so don't go trying to change the subject."

"Julia and I will be fine. She needs to keep everybody out of our business, but otherwise we'll be all right."

"I saw how Delilah was looking at you at church Sunday. Don't let that woman mess up everything you've tried to build."

Samson wouldn't disagree with him. Delilah was a handful, but manageable. As long as he counseled her, he could keep her under control. She was beginning to open up to him more and more, and that would help him determine his next move. Samson's mission for the church and his wife would not be destroyed; he would protect it at all costs.

"Marriage is sacred. Please don't allow anyone, and specifically Delilah, to destroy it," Regis said.

Samson was disappointed that his father didn't have faith in him. But on another note, Samson insisted on getting an answer to his original question. "Dad, I know it's really none of my business, but I need to know if you ever stepped out on Mom."

"The answer to your question is no. Was I tempted? Many times. More than I can count."

"How did you get past the temptation?" Samson asked.

"Prayer, meditation, and not allowing myself to be alone with a woman I knew would cause me to sin."

"But there are times, as pastor, that you have to counsel people. You can't always be in control of every situation."

"Son, you're always in control of your actions." Regis refilled his orange juice.

"So did Mom ever know of these women?"

Regis laughed. "Now you know I can never get anything past that woman. She knew a woman's intention before I did. One way we stopped some of the madness was if a woman needed counseling, Kelly would be the one they spoke with or one of the other ministers' wives."

"I can see that happening with Julia later, but right now I think it's too early on in our marriage for her to be taking on that role," Samson said. The truth was, until things were right in their household, it was best that Samson and Julia kept their work lives separately.

"The Lord has led me to share this with you." Regis had a solemn look on his face. "Samson, you have been obedient most of the days of your life. You've come too far to allow the world to seep into your life and destroy all that has been built."

"Dad, it's not even that serious. The problem with Julia and me, it's temporary. It'll get handled."

Regis ignored him and continued to say, "You may feel that you're untouchable because of the special relationship you have with the Lord, but be warned. The enemy knows your weakness and will feed it. Stay focused on God's agenda. Don't succumb to the ways of the world."

Samson stayed in a solemn mood the rest of the time with his dad. He wasn't upset with him, but Samson felt like his father was judging him. His dad was one of God's messengers, so was it possible he was relaying a message from God? If so, Samson had decisions to make, decisions that could affect his walk with the Lord.

Chapter 31

Delilah sat in her car and contemplated whether to stay or leave the restaurant parking lot. She should have never agreed to meet Luther for lunch when he called earlier. He caught her at a vulnerable moment. She wasn't getting the attention she desired from Samson, so she agreed to meet Luther to give her ego a much-needed boost.

Delilah glanced at the clock on the dashboard. If Luther was already inside the restaurant, he could wait a few more minutes; Delilah was in no rush. She called Keisha but got no answer, so she left a voice message. "Keisha, please call me back. I need your advice about something."

She threw her cell phone in her purse and exited the car. Her long, curly hair bounced when she walked. She walked inside feeling confident. Men and women took notice as she strode past tables as if she owned the world.

"Glad you made it," Luther said. He stood up and pulled out her chair.

A gentleman, Delilah noted. She didn't expect that. "You've been blowing up my phone since the reception, so the least I could do was bless you with my presence."

Luther laughed. "You're more beautiful today than you were the day we met."

"Compliments might get you somewhere," Delilah said.

They chatted over lunch. "So what is a woman like you doing single?" Luther asked.

"I keep running into men like you." Delilah took a sip of her drink.

"So my brother-in-law tells me you have the hots for your pastor."

Delilah almost spit out her drink. "Calvin needs to mind his own business."

"Well, do you? You wouldn't be the first to be enticed with the man of God."

"In case you forgot, my pastor is now a married man."

"Maybe you need to remind yourself of that fact more than me." Luther winked his eye and continued to eat.

Delilah enjoyed the meal, but Luther was a little too cocky for her. He thought he had her pegged, but he was wrong. Yes, she was attracted to Samson, but her feelings ran deeper than anything physical. Men like Luther wouldn't understand.

He spent the rest of the lunch talking about himself, himself, and his favorite subject, himself. Delilah originally planned on spending more time with Luther, but after lunch, he could lose her number for all she cared.

"Look, lunch was good, but I have a few appointments this evening, so I'm out of here." Delilah picked up her purse.

"What about your half of lunch?" Luther asked.

Delilah looked down at her plate that still had half of her meal on it. "I'm full. If you want it, you can have it."

"No, baby. I'm talking about the bill. You ordered about fifteen dollars worth of stuff."

"Uh, you got me confused with some of those other women. Delilah doesn't pay for anything when she goes out with a man. So call one of your other chicks. Do whatever you have to do, but the meal is on you, boo." Delilah pushed her chair away from the table and left.

"You can't leave me with the bill," Luther yelled.

"I just did," Delilah said, as she walked away.

Luther could be heard shouting out obscenities. Delilah increased her pace as she walked to her car. She slid down into her seat as Luther walked past. Once he was out of clear view, she cut out of the parking lot.

Delilah was pulling out on Youree Drive when she received a phone call from Keisha. Delilah immediately recounted what occurred at lunch.

"Girl, you and these men," Keisha said.

"It's not like you have any better luck."

"But we're not talking about me right now. We're talking about you." Keisha laughed.

Delilah laughed as well. "It was funny. You should have seen the expression on his face. Pretty boy got stuck with the check." Delilah's phone beeped. She glanced at the screen. "Girl, that's him now. He must be crazy if he thinks I'm taking his calls after the stunt he just pulled."

"You need to answer it because I'm curious to know what he has to say for himself."

"Hold on." Delilah clicked over. "Hello."

"You know you wrong," Luther said.

"Baby boy, I don't know what kind of women you're used to dating, but I'm old school. When a man invites a woman out, he pays. End of story."

"I had to use some of my rent money to pay for that meal. You owe me eighteen dollars and fifty-seven cents."

"Did Calvin put you up to this? Tell him the joke stopped being funny a long time ago."

"Calvin? What's he got to do with this? I'm talking about you. You owe me some money."

"Get it from your brother-in-law; he's the big-shot lawyer. Now please forget my number and don't call me no more." Delilah clicked back over to her other line. "Girl, that fool got issues. What got me is he had it down to the penny."

Delilah soon ended her call with Keisha. She thought about Samson. Her attempt to forget him and move on didn't work. Luther was not the man to help her get over Samson. She walked into Trusts Enterprise.

"Look who graced us with her presence," the main receptionist said.

"Hi, Ms. Piggee," Delilah said with a smile on her face. She laughed inside because the receptionist lived up to her name literally. She was the company's busybody, yet people always told her their business. A couple of times Delilah even found herself confessing some things of her own to the fifty-something-year-old woman.

"Mr. Trusts got you working a special assignment, I hear. So what have you been up to?"

Delilah looked at her watch. It was after two. "It's coming along, but I've run into a few obstacles."

"Well, he's not here, if you came to see him. He's out of the office meeting with some contractors about plans for the new shopping center."

"Oh, that's fine. I came to get something out of my desk," Delilah lied. She really did want to see William. Her purse held a cashier's check for all the money he had given her. After going home the night before and praying, she realized bringing Samson down would not benefit her any. He was too nice of a man and didn't deserve it. Besides, Delilah wanted to make a last-ditch effort to get back in God's good graces. William would have to get his property another way. She would not be a pawn in his game.

Delilah left Trusts Enterprise and made it to her four o'clock appointment with Samson just in the nick of time.

"What are you doing here?" Elaine asked Delilah.

Delilah looked at her watch. "I have an appointment with Pastor Judges."

Elaine thumbed through her planner. "I don't see it here."

"Well, you need to check with him because I'm not going anywhere until I see the pastor." Delilah sat down in the chair and crossed her legs.

"Look, your shenanigans might work with men, but they don't have any effect on me."

Delilah shifted in her seat. "Elaine, you don't like me, and I don't like you, and that's fine because I'm not here to see you. So unless you're telling me Samson's ready to see me, I suggest you don't say anything else to me." Delilah emphasized the word "me" each time she said it.

Elaine stood up behind her desk. "Let me get the pastor so you can get out of my space."

Delilah was tired of the catfighting between her and Elaine. "Yes, please do. You're a secretary, so do your job."

Elaine blurted out, "Lord Jesus, please stop me from saying something to this heathen in my office."

Delilah was steaming inside. It took every ounce of patience for her not to get up and snatch the two-week-old weave out of Elaine's head. She counted to ten inside of her hand and patted her shoe on the floor while twitching in her seat. She was on a mission to get back not only in God's good graces, but in Samson's as well. She would not get distracted by the likes of Elaine.

Chapter 32

"Man, let me go," Samson said to Calvin, who was on the other end of the phone. "I hear some commotion going on outside my office."

Elaine burst through the door. "Delilah says she has an appointment with you, but I know the heifer is lying."

"Now, Elaine, that's not a nice thing to say."

"You need to come out here and tell her to leave because I'm tired of looking at her face."

"Send her on in," Samson said.

Elaine looked at him and shifted her head. "But she doesn't have an appointment."

"She does. I just forgot to tell you when I saw you this morning."

"I've told you to let me make your appointments. That's how you get double booked."

"No one else is scheduled for four, right?" Samson looked up at Elaine from his desk.

"No, but still, why am I here if you're going to make your own appointments?"

Elaine was making a big deal out of nothing. All of the women in Samson's life were tripping with him. He needed a vacation from everyone, including his wife. Julia was giving him the cold shoulder, and when he'd called her earlier she barely had ten words to say to him. Samson tuned Elaine out. When he saw her mouth stop moving, he said, "You're the best and I don't know what I would do without you." Although he was saying it to appease her, he really did mean it. She was a great assistant.

"As long as you don't forget it, we're cool. I'll send her in."

Less than a minute later, Delilah walked into Samson's office. "You need to get better help."

"Don't start," Samson said.

Delilah shut the door and took a seat. Samson hit the intercom button on his phone. "Elaine, hold all my calls unless it's an emergency."

Samson watched Delilah primp in her handheld mirror. To him, she looked flawless. Delilah placed the mirror in her purse. "I read those scriptures you gave me."

"Good. What message did you take away from reading them?"

She crossed and re-crossed her legs. Samson shifted in his seat. Every time she moved, her thin skirt would creep up a little more exposing her thighs. "In order for me to move forward, I need to forgive the people who did me wrong."

"Do you think you can do that?"

"I'm trying."

"Delilah, you have to do more than try. You have to make a conscious effort to forgive those people."

Delilah folded her arms and rocked from side to side as she opened up and told Samson about what happened at some of the foster homes. "I was a helpless little girl, and they took advantage of me. No one came to my rescue. No one."

Tears flowed down Delilah's face. Samson retrieved several tissues from the box on his desk and handed them to her. His heart tugged as he listened to Delilah recount her childhood trauma. It angered him inside to know that her innocence was stolen from her by people who were supposed to protect her. He got up from his seat and walked to where she sat and patted her on the back.

"Let it out. Crying is good for the soul. God's going to wipe those tears away."

"I'm sorry. I didn't mean to get so emotional." Delilah sniffled.

"No, I'm the one who's sorry. I hate that you had to endure all of this by yourself."

Delilah placed one of her hands on top of his. She squeezed it. She stood up, and they were now face-to-face. Samson could not get over the sadness in Delilah's eyes. He was drawn to her. The magnetic pull forced their lips to lock. The moan seeping through Delilah's mouth brought Samson back to the moment. He pushed her away. "I'm so sorry."

"We just got caught up in the moment," Delilah said.

"You don't deserve this. I'm under stress and then hearing your story. Lord, help me," Samson cried out. He walked to the window and turned his back toward Delilah.

She followed him over to the window and wrapped her arms around his waist. He could feel her chest on his back. This time he didn't push her away. He had to find a way to let Delilah down easily. With everything she had gone through, he didn't want to cause her any more pain. He gently moved away. He took Delilah's hand in his.

"Delilah, you're a beautiful young lady," he said. "You deserve the best. Unfortunately, I'm a married man, so any plans you had for me—for us—get over them."

Delilah took his hand and placed it on her chest. "My heart beats only for you."

He jerked his hand away. "These feelings you have for me, redirect them. You're part of the singles' ministry, right?"

"Yes," Delilah responded.

"I want you to become more active in it. You'll meet available godly men."

And get out of my hair, Samson thought.

Elaine called him on the intercom. "Your wife's on the phone."

"I need to take this call. I'll be right back." Samson needed to take a breather. He left Delilah in his office and went out in the lobby to talk with Julia.

Elaine must have told Julia about Delilah being in his office because she had a foul mood that evening. Being married caused him many restless nights. On days like today, he wished he had remained single.

Chapter 33

Delilah hated feeling vulnerable. She touched her lips, the same lips Samson had kissed. He initiated the kiss, and she would treasure those few seconds they seemed to be in sync with each other.

She should have been the one to leave his office so he could have a private conversation with his wife, but he rushed out of there so fast, she knew the kiss must have gotten to him too.

The door remained closed. Delilah wasn't trying to snoop but her eyes glanced at the paper on Samson's desk and the word Viagra caught her attention. *Should I? Shouldn't I?* She glanced back at the door to see if Samson was returning. Since he wasn't, she leaned down and picked up the paper. It had detailed information about the drug Viagra. "Wow. He needs medicine to get it up for his wife." Delilah felt bad for Julia because he didn't seem to have a problem with her.

Delilah's cell phone rang, and she scrambled to locate it. The missed call was from William. She called him back. "Do you have anything for me?"

"I'm at his office now," she whispered. Her eyes remained glued to the door. She couldn't chance Samson walking in and overhearing their conversation.

"I met with my investors earlier today, and they are

eager to move forward with this project. His property is the only thing standing in the way of me finalizing my plans."

"I stopped by the office to give you a cashier's check. I don't think I can go through with it."

"Either you do, or I will make sure everybody at your church gets personal copies of that video showcasing your talents on the stage and off."

Delilah couldn't have that. Although some of the women at church didn't like her, there was no way she would be able to face any of them if they found out about her past. They wouldn't understand that she had changed. Samson's wife would more than likely be the ringleader. She was no longer the woman William kept throwing in her face. She was Delilah—a queen who happened to fall in love with the wrong king.

"Your choice. Which is it?" William asked again.

Delilah gritted her teeth. "I'll go through with it."

"I knew I could count on you. I'll be in touch."

Delilah held the phone. She recalled something she heard Ms. Shadows say once; "Never make a deal with the devil because you'll always end up on the losing end."

All these years later, her words rang true to life. She could see the writing on the wall. She needed to update her resume because her time as a project coordinator at Trusts Enterprise would be ending.

Samson had been gone for several minutes. She wondered if he was ever coming back. She noticed for the first time a small white bag. She rushed to open it before Samson returned. She held the medicine bottle up and read it. "It's true. He's taking Viagra. Oh my goodness."

"What are you doing?" Samson asked.

Busted. She held the medicine bottle behind her back as she turned around and leaned on his desk. "Nothing."

Samson walked around her. She scrambled to put the medicine back in the bag. "Were you looking in my bag?"

"No. It fell, and I picked it up."

"A bag doesn't mysteriously fall on the floor." Samson sounded perturbed.

"Well it did. I was looking for a blank sheet of paper. If your desk wasn't such a mess, it wouldn't have fallen."

"Julia's expecting me, so we'll have to cut our session short."

"Didn't you tell her you were counseling someone?"

"What my wife and I talk about is none of your business, Delilah?"

"Excuse me. You don't have to snap my head off."

Samson sighed. "I'm sorry. I just have a lot going on. If you want, you can come in Thursday. Stop in with Elaine so she can put it on the calendar."

Delilah could tell something was really bothering Samson. She wanted to help him relieve some of the stress. He was a man of God, and it seemed his wife or somebody was causing him unnecessary stress. Since she was part of Pastor's Aide, it was her duty to make sure her pastor was taken care of.

She was not going to leave him in the state he was in." Samson, why don't you meet me at my place. I'm sure it's hard to talk around here with Ms. Nosy Body outside and the phones ringing off the hook."

"Thanks for the offer, but it's not a good idea."

Delilah walked up to Samson and hugged him tight. His body tensed. She looked into his eyes and said, "Julia's a lucky woman."

"I'm a lucky man."

She removed her arms from around him. "That you are. Not too many men get to hug me like that." Delilah winked and left Samson standing in the middle of the room.

"Did you get some spiritual healing?" Elaine asked Delilah as she exited Samson's office.

Delilah smiled. "I sure did, and I feel greeaaat."

Chapter 34

Delilah had no idea how close Samson had been to taking her up on her offer. It took him almost fifteen minutes to calm Julia down. Elaine would need some talking to because the argument he had with Julia could have been avoided if Elaine hadn't told her about Delilah being at his office.

He knew it wasn't Elaine's fault that he and Julia were having problems, but she sure added fuel to the already scorching fire. Samson had to think of something soon or he and Julia were not going to make it. He knew his parents would be disappointed, but when he married Julia a little over two weeks ago, he didn't expect it to be like this.

The only person he trusted talking with was Calvin, but he couldn't bring himself to tell him about the personal issue that stood between him and his wife. He couldn't chance Calvin telling Michelle. Michelle would tell God knows who. His mom knew, and that was embarrassing enough.

He grabbed his prescription and headed home. He smelled the aroma of food when he entered the house. "Julia, I'm home," he yelled.

"I'm in the kitchen," she replied.

He slipped a pill in his pocket and threw the prescription in his briefcase. He headed to the kitchen. When he bent down to kiss his wife, Julia turned her head, so his lips landed on her cheek instead of her lips.

"What's for dinner?" he asked.

"A roast and baked potatoes." She picked up an oven mitt and opened the stove. The steam from the roast filled the area around the stove.

"Smells good."

"Samson, there's something I want to discuss with you over dinner."

"Sure," he said as he left to get washed up. He wished she would have just come out and said what she wanted instead of making him wait. That was his biggest pet peeve with women. He made it a point when counseling others to let women know that men preferred one of two things: either come out and tell the man what you want, or don't say anything and only talk when you're ready to discuss the issue. Otherwise, it's a moot point as far as the average man is concerned.

Silverware hitting the plates was the only noise heard in the dining room. Samson didn't know what to say to Julia, so he waited for her to initiate the conversation. He bit into the last bite of food on his plate. "I want to quit my job," Julia blurted out.

Samson remained quiet. Julia repeated herself. He'd heard her the first time. "Why?" he finally asked.

"So I can have more time for your ministry. I was thinking there are some things that I can do. There's an available office at the church, and we can drive in together each day."

Samson felt there was more behind her wanting to quit her job. "Baby, I don't think it's a good idea."

"Well, I've prayed about it, and God said I should quit and give Him more of my time."

"So why are you just now telling me this?"

"Because we haven't been talking."

Samson sneered. "It's not because I haven't tried. It would have taken you only a few minutes to discuss this with me."

"Get over it. I'm discussing it with you now."

"So when is your last day?"

"That's just it. I haven't quit yet. I'm just thinking about it."

"Julia, I'm going to pray about it. When I get an answer, I'll let you know."

Julia seemed to calm down. "That's all I want you to do, honey. See, with us being together more, that may help us in other areas."

She gathered up their empty plates and took them to the kitchen. Samson, full and confused about how to handle Julia's request, hung his head and prayed. The carnal man wanted her to continue to work. With everything so fickle, the more money they had coming into the household, the better. His salary from Peaceful Rest was enough to take care of both of them, but he was by no means one of the wealthiest preachers in the area.

People assumed with his TV ministry, he would be. What they didn't realize was that it took money to broadcast every week, and if sponsors were low, the church had to pay the difference. There had been several times he forfeited his salary so that the Word could be preached to the masses.

Julia came and wrapped her arms around his neck and kissed him on the head. "I love you. I really do. I'm sorry I've been such a you-know-what lately."

"I'm sorry too. I've been taking out my frustrations on you."

"Well, that's in the past. Let's promise we'll both do better, okay?"

"Deal," Samson said. By now, he had Julia sitting in his lap. They kissed. Still no reaction and more disappointment for Samson.

"Why don't you go upstairs and change into something sexy," he suggested.

Julia smiled. "You don't have to tell me twice. I'll be waiting." Julia kissed him and twisted out of the room.

When Julia was out of eyesight, Samson retrieved the pill from the bottle he had hidden in his pocket. Before he could take it, his cell phone rang. "Delilah, I'm at home now. Whatever it is can wait until tomorrow?"

Delilah wailed from the other end of the phone. "I don't know what I'll do, Samson. All the memories just came flooding back."

"Let's pray." Samson prayed, hoping Julia wouldn't walk in at this time.

Delilah responded from the other end. "Thanks for the prayer, but I need to see you."

"I can't," Samson insisted.

"If you don't come, I don't know what I'll do," Delilah cried from the other end of the phone.

Samson didn't want Delilah to do something crazy. Knowing he would probably live to regret it, he responded, "Okay. I'll be there. Don't do anything irrational."

"Julia," he called. Samson knew Julia was not going to be happy if he didn't come to the bedroom and deliver.

"Come here, big boy," Julia said, as she slipped from under the covers wearing sheer, pink-laced lingerie.

Samson moved closer. "Baby, that was a church member. They are having suicidal thoughts. I have to go stop them from doing anything crazy."

Julia plopped down on the bed. "Are we ever going to do it?"

"Yes, dear, but you know the church is important to me."

She sighed. "Okay." She got out of bed. "Let me get dressed, and I'll go with you."

"No, baby, I want you well rested. It shouldn't take me long," Samson said.

"But you don't know that. You said the person was suicidal."

"I've handled plenty of situations like this. Sometimes they only want to know someone cares."

She picked up the sheer robe and slipped it on. "Okay, well, if you need me, call me."

"I will, sweetheart. I'll be back soon." Samson kissed her on the lips.

He hated lying to Julia, but she would never understand this need for him to comfort Delilah. How could she when he didn't seem to understand it himself?

Chapter 35

Delilah made sure her hair looked a little disheveled. She blotted a wet towel to her eyes, and it smeared her mascara. The doorbell rang. "Perfect timing," she said out loud, then answered the door. "Oh, Samson." Delilah threw herself in his arms as soon as he walked in the door.

Samson held her up and led her to the sofa. "Let's pray." He reached for her hand.

Delilah watched Samson as he prayed for her mental healing. He was praying in vain because in Delilah's opinion, she was perfectly sane. Samson released her hand, and she smiled to appease him. "Thank you. I feel better already," Delilah sniffed.

"I have a friend who's a doctor. I'll call him tomorrow so he can maybe prescribe something for the anxiety you've been feeling lately."

"I have some medicine. I just don't like taking it because it increases my appetite, and I sure don't need to gain any more weight."

Samson didn't agree or disagree verbally, but his eyes let her know that he didn't think anything was wrong with her weight. She recalled the kiss from earlier. It took her all evening to devise the plan to get him to her house so they could finish where they'd left off. Now that he was here, she wouldn't be satisfied until he gave her what she wanted.

"Samson, do you think it's possible for a person to mean well, even if the end result turns out to be bad?"

"It depends. Can you elaborate?"

"I'm talking hypothetically."

"You can have good intentions. It happens to me sometimes. We all make mistakes; we just can't keep making the same ones."

"Do you think our kiss earlier was a mistake?" Delilah licked her lips.

"It shouldn't have happened."

"That's not what I asked you."

"I could have used better judgment."

"But I don't see anything wrong with what happened. We were two people caught up in the moment."

"That flies in the movies, Delilah, but in real life, no."

Delilah's hand found its way on top of Samson's thigh. She rubbed it. She expected him to move it, but he didn't. He swallowed out loud. "You seem a little tense," she said.

"I have a lot on my mind."

Delilah continued to rub his leg. "You can push my hand away. I won't be mad." She enjoyed teasing him.

He moved his leg. "It looks like you're all right now, so I'll be going." He jumped up. Delilah stood up, blocking his path.

She placed her hand on his chest. "I have a confession to make. I sort of lied to get you over here."

"These games need to stop." Samson's nostrils flared up.

"Don't be mad. You were so tense earlier, I just wanted you to get out and have a good time."

"I left my wife to come see about you."

"And it means a lot to me."

He placed his arm on her shoulders and attempted to nudge her to the side, but Delilah wouldn't move. Delilah felt like it was now or never. She got on her tiptoes and plastered a kiss on Samson's lips. At first he resisted, but before long he gave in and started kissing her back.

"Where are your cameras?" Samson asked.

"I got rid of them," Delilah responded.

Delilah led Samson to her bedroom and stripped for him. She smiled because, unlike with his wife, he didn't need a little pill to perform, and Samson put on a performance. She should have felt guilty sleeping with a married man—her pastor at that—but she didn't. She felt it was her duty as a member of the Pastor's Aide committee to help out the first lady.

If Samson weren't with her, he would find some other skank who would care only about the money, not the man. Yes, she was doing Samson, Julia, and Peaceful Rest a favor.

Moments later, Delilah watched Samson snore. He had been at her place for two hours. She didn't want him to leave, but she knew waking him up and sending him back to Julia was the right thing to do—for now, that is. Soon, Samson would realize she was the woman he should be with and serve Julia with divorce papers.

"Baby, you need to wake up." Delilah gently nudged Samson.

"Let me get one more hour," Samson said as he turned and cuddled her.

"No, baby, you got to go now."

When he came to his senses, he couldn't get out of Delilah's bed fast enough. "Lord, what have I done? I can't believe I did this. Why didn't you stop me?"

Delilah responded, "Because I wanted it just as much as you did."

"This can't happen again. Promise me, you won't tell anyone."

Delilah smiled. "It'll be our little secret."

Chapter 36

Samson burnt rubber getting out of Delilah's driveway and into his own. He checked his appearance several times before getting out of his truck and going into the house through the garage door. He had several missed calls on his cell phone from Julia, but guilt wouldn't allow him to return any of them.

All the lights were off. He took his time going up the stairs, careful not to make much noise. The sound of the television could be heard from the hallway. Julia's back was toward the door, so he didn't know if she was sleeping or awake. He tiptoed to the other side of the bed. He looked in her direction, and her eyes were closed.

He went to the master bathroom. He could still smell Delilah's scent on his body so there was no way he would get in the bed next to Julia. He would take his chances by showering first. He placed his dirty clothes in the hamper. A few minutes later, the hot water cascaded down his body as he thought about the events that led up to him cheating on his wife.

It was now official. His lustful thoughts had led him to act, and now he was an adulterer. As much as he wanted to blame Delilah for what had happened, he couldn't. He had the opportunity to walk away, but he didn't. Instead, after she said there were no cameras, he allowed his libido to control his actions. At no time did he think about the beautiful woman who now lay in his bed, the woman he vowed to be faithful to.

Although only two people knew about his affair, he was ashamed of himself. He was supposed to be better than the average man. He was a man of God. He was the leader of a flock—a flock that depended on him to be without blemish.

It didn't matter how long he stayed in the shower. The water could not wash away his sins. Samson closed his eyes and let the water flow down his body as he prayed. "Father God, I've given the enemy a front-row seat in my life. Cleanse me, Lord, so that I can serve you and be right in your eyes. Lord, forgive me for the sins that I committed. Please protect Julia so she won't find out her husband failed her."

Tears flowed down his face mixing with the water as he continued to pray. Afterward, he turned the water off, got out of the shower and dried off with a towel, not knowing how long he had been in the bathroom. When he re-entered the bedroom, Julia's back was now in the direction of the bathroom. He slipped underneath the covers and cuddled his wife. Her body stiffened, but she didn't move his arms. He held her close and they slept in that position most of the night.

Samson's arms flapped over an empty space in the bed the next morning. He shifted in bed. Julia, fully dressed, sat at the edge of the bed staring down at him. "What time is it?" he asked, as he sat up.

She ignored his question."What time did you get in last night?" she asked.

"It was after nine."

"More like after ten. I stayed up as long as I could, but I knew I had a long day today, so I went to bed."

"I'm sorry." Samson's eyes darted away.

"So what happened?"

"Baby, I can't go into details. I vowed I would keep their situation confidential." He wasn't completely telling a lie. Delilah's childhood trauma wasn't up for discussion. As a pastor, he had to make people feel confident that what they shared with him would remain with him and not be broadcast.

"But I'm your wife. Your mother told me that your dad would share things with her."

Samson's mom would be a thorn in their relationship. She needed to keep her comments to herself. "I'm not my dad."

"So are you saying you don't trust me to keep the information to myself?" Julia placed one of her hands on her hip.

"No, don't put words in my mouth."

"Then, Samson Judges, what are you saying?"

"You have enough on your plate being married to me. You don't need all this extra drama. People's problems can weigh you down."

Julia moved near him. "I'm your helpmate. Let me help ease some of the burden. Maybe you wouldn't be so tense." She rubbed his upper arm.

Samson felt bad because the only thing he wanted Julia to do was stop. He didn't want her touching him right now. The guilt from last night made him want to confess, but he knew it would be the wrong thing to do. Julia didn't deserve to be hurt that way, so he kept the affair to himself.

Samson held her hand in his. "Baby, I appreciate you offering, but I think I have everything covered."

"I'm here if you need me." The sincerity in her voice softened Samson's heart.

"Why don't we talk later about you taking a more active role in the ministry."

"Thanks." Julia hugged him.

Samson closed his eyes and held her tight. They kissed before releasing each other. "You sure smell good. What's that you're wearing?"

"It's called Heat. One of my sorors got it for me. It's a fragrance by Beyonce."

"I like it," Samson said.

"I hoped you would. I sprayed some on last night, but we know how that ended."

Samson broke their eye contact. If eyes were windows to the soul, he didn't want Julia to see the guilt that surfaced.

Chapter 37

Delilah felt no remorse for sleeping with Samson—well, a little—but the feeling passed through her quickly as she thought back to the moment Samson took the first move. Granted, she made it hard for him to resist her, but he could have walked away. He didn't, though. He didn't have to come over to her place, but he did.

She didn't lie to Samson when she told him that she didn't have any cameras hooked up. She didn't need them because she had a permanent video of them and their sexual encounter embedded in her head. She lay in bed most of the morning, hugging the pillow where Samson laid and replayed their time together the previous night over and over.

The phone ringing interrupted her daydream. "Hi, Samson. I'm so glad you called. I missed you too." Delilah was so excited to hear Samson's voice on the other end, she didn't give him a chance to talk.

"Delilah, I wanted to make sure things were cool between us."

Delilah sat up in bed. "More than cool. I got your back. You know it."

"Good. Then I don't have to worry about you telling anyone what happened last night, do I?"

Delilah knew she should be mad. He seemed to only

care about what others would think. She had to look at things from his point of view. He was the pastor and now a married man. "Samson, our little secret will remain between us, okay?"

"About our next session, maybe we should—"

Delilah didn't allow him to finish. "I need our session more than ever. You helped me get through that bleak moment."

"There won't be any repeats of last night."

Delilah laughed. She knew and he knew that what happened between them was only the beginning. If he wanted to pretend it didn't mean a thing, then she would play along with his charade. "Whatever you want, Samson."

"Thanks, Delilah. You have a good day now."

"I will now that I've heard from you."

Delilah hung up with Samson and quickly dialed Keisha's number. She blurted out what happened. Keisha repeated over and over: "You're going to burn in hell. Ooh. I can't believe you slept with him again. Girl, God is not going to let you get away with that."

Delilah listened as Keisha went on and on about why she thought Delilah was wrong. "Are you finished?" Delilah asked.

"You ain't got to worry about me. You need to be on your knees asking God to be easy on you."

"It's not like I made him sleep with me. He made the first move."

"Come on. You set the stage for it, playing the 'woe is me' role."

Delilah couldn't disagree with her. She knew exactly what she was doing the moment she dialed Samson's number and asked him—well, tricked him by faking emo-

tional distress—to come over. Delilah ended her call
with Keisha. Her phone beeped reminding her about
the Pastor's Aide committee meeting scheduled for
later that afternoon. The meeting was set about an hour
before Bible Study.

Delilah spent the rest of the day working on a report
she owed a coworker at Trusts Enterprise. She finished
the report and hit the send button in her e-mail. When
she was finished with that, she surfed the Internet. "I
wonder if Samson's online."

She attempted to send him an instant message, but
it wouldn't go through. She logged on to her Facebook
account and sent him a private message. She typed the
words: *I didn't say anything to give away what happened last night. I just said thank you for helping me.
If anyone wants to read more into it, then that's them.*
Once she hit the send button, she logged off her computer and headed to church.

Delilah arrived in the church parking lot at the same
time the Pastor's Aide meeting was scheduled to start.
She headed straight to the fellowship hall. She waited
outside the door until Dorothy finished praying. When
she heard Dorothy say amen, she walked into the room.

"What are you doing here?" Dorothy asked.

"This is a Pastor's Aide meeting, right?" Delilah stood
staring Dorothy straight in the eyes.

"Yes, it is."

"Then I'm in the right room."

"I thought you dropped out." Dorothy frowned.

"Well, you thought wrong." Delilah found an available seat and sat down around the table with the rest
of the women.

"Humph," Delilah heard someone say.

Delilah ignored her and retrieved her notepad and pen from her purse.

"Ladies, we only have an hour, so let's get straight to business," Michelle said.

Dorothy stopped rolling her eyes at Delilah and looked back at her notes. "As we all know, the pastor's anniversary is coming up, and unfortunately a few people can't participate in the program because of other commitments." Dorothy read off what roles were still needed to complete the program.

Delilah raised her hand along with the other women. Each was called on. Delilah was ignored. Delilah raised her hand again. No one else did. Dorothy had no choice but to acknowledge her. "I would like to recommend Keisha Green to do one of the solos. She's a great soloist. If you've ever been to First Baptist, then you've heard her sing."

Some of the ladies knew of Keisha and added, "She brings the Spirit with her. Not only can she sing, she can play the piano too."

Dorothy asked, "How do you know this Keisha?"

Delilah contemplated whether to reveal their friendship or keep it a secret. Since the other ladies could vouch for Keisha, she was proud to say, "She's one of my friends."

Marie said, "I say why not see if Keisha can do it. I mean, we did need one more soloist, and she is good."

To Dorothy's dismay, they voted to ask Keisha to perform a solo.

Delilah left and went into the hallway to call Keisha. "Guess what? I got you on to sing a solo at our pastor's anniversary program. Please tell me you can do it."

"When is it? Because I'm supposed to sing at this church down in Grand Cane in June on the second Sunday."

"It'll be the following week," Delilah assured her.

"I'll do it," Keisha responded.

Delighted, Delilah said, "Thank you, girl. I owe you one."

"And I will be collecting."

Delilah caught the tail end of Dorothy's speech when she re-entered the room. "Since nobody else is going to say it, I will. In light of how Delilah treats the first lady, I don't think she should be a part of Pastor's Aide."

Delilah looked Dorothy in the eyes. "I'm not resigning from the Pastor's Aide committee, so you might as well get used to it."

Dorothy said, "We all know you don't like First Lady Julia, so why do you want to be on the committee responsible for celebrating our pastor and his wife?"

"Has anyone in here ever heard me say that I disliked our first lady?" Delilah scanned the room. No one responded. Some dropped their heads. "Exactly. So please don't speculate. Now, we have less than an hour before Bible Study starts, so if we want our meeting to be over by then, I suggest we get back to it."

Delilah walked back to the table and took a seat. Dorothy looked annoyed, but didn't say anything else concerning Julia. The meeting continued until it was time to adjourn for Wednesday night Bible Study.

Chapter 38

Julia surprised Samson by bringing him dinner. "I knew today was one of your long days, so I wanted to bring you some food."

Julia was now acting like the woman he knew before he got married. "Thank you, baby," Samson said.

"I'm going out there to talk to Elaine for a minute, so eat up."

Samson watched Julia walk out of his office. His entire day up until this point had been rough. He couldn't concentrate because he kept remembering his actions the night before. He had been so busy putting out little fires, he didn't have time to meditate. Julia stopping by early with dinner was the only bright spot of his day.

"Elaine said it was okay to come in," Michael said, peeking his head in the door.

"I was just eating this good food my wife brought me. Have a seat."

"Oh, I'm not staying long. Just wanted to let you know that I am leaving early. My wife's sister got admitted to the hospital, and I didn't want her driving herself to the hospital."

"Oh no, is there anything I can do?" Samson asked.

"Just pray for her, please."

"Call me later and give me an update." Samson stared at the doorway after Michael left his office.

Thirty minutes later, Samson and Julia entered the sanctuary to start Bible Study. The pews were not filled, but there was a big crowd for a Wednesday night. After one of the deacons led the congregation in prayer, Samson stood up to start teaching. "Tonight we're going to be talking about 'A Thorn in the Flesh.'"

Samson scanned the room. His eyes locked with Delilah's. She was seated on the third row to his right. She smiled. He didn't. He dropped his head and looked at his Bible. "Turn your Bibles to Second Corinthians, twelfth chapter. Is Paul talking about a physical ailment or is he talking about a stronghold? Let's discuss."

Samson took questions from members of the congregation during his lecture. "I hope our discussion tonight will help you on your daily walk with the Lord. Remember, you can't do it by yourself. You must put on the full armor of God each and every day. Let us pray."

When Bible Study ended, members of the congregation crowded around Samson. Delilah walked in his direction. Samson turned his back to her, hoping she would go the other way. He felt a tap on his shoulder. Samson took a deep breath ready to face Delilah. "Give me one minute," he said without looking over his shoulder.

"Oh, I just wanted to tell you I'll meet you at home," Julia said.

Samson, relieved, responded, "If you'll wait, I'll follow you."

"There's no need to," Julia assured him.

Julia and Samson hugged. With opened eyes, Samson saw Delilah standing near the front door. Their eyes met once again. She turned and walked out. Julia was the first to push away. "Wow. You act like I'm going away for a long time. I'll see you at home, okay?"

"I love you so much," Samson responded.

"I love you too. See you later." Julia walked away.

Samson remained behind to talk to some of the church members. An hour later, Samson pulled up in front of his house. The lights were off, and soft music greeted him as he made his way up the stairs. A floral fragrance filled the air in the candlelit room. He could hear the shower running, so he assumed Julia was in the shower.

Knowing Julia would expect another attempt tonight, Samson opened up his briefcase and removed a Viagra pill from the bottle and hid the container back in his briefcase. Samson headed to one of the other bathrooms to freshen up. He popped the pill in his mouth and prayed it worked. Julia was still in the bathroom when he entered the bedroom. He lay across the bed and waited for her. If he could sleep with Julia, it would erase the image of Delilah in his head.

Julia, a vision of loveliness, seemed to be gliding to the bed. "I see you made it." Her words purred with each enunciation.

"The only person missing from the party is you."

"Let's get this party started."

Samson and Julia kissed. The pill hadn't kicked in, but Samson was determined to make something happen tonight. He would not disappoint Julia again. Delilah's naked body popped in his head. He shook his head several times, attempting to make those images disappear. They wouldn't. Julia increased the intensity of her kiss. Samson's body responded; he couldn't honestly tell if it was due to Julia, the pill, or images of Delilah.

Regardless, the time they both had been waiting for was at hand. He whispered in Julia's ear, "Are you ready?"

"Yes," Julia answered, not trying to mask her excitement.

Their union was more than Samson could have imagined. Samson erased any thoughts of Delilah. For the first time he and his wife were together, he finally knew what it meant to make love. If he were writing a book, he would describe it as a miraculous, earth-shattering union of two souls.

Samson smiled as he saw the satisfied look on the face of his now-sleeping wife. "Thank you, Lord," he said before drifting into a sound sleep.

Chapter 39

"Just my luck." Delilah turned her back toward the oncoming car as she pumped gas into her car.

"Oh, you can't answer a brother's calls now?" Luther yelled out his car window.

"We have nothing to discuss," Delilah said, wishing the gas would flow into her car faster.

"You wrong for leaving me with the bill."

Delilah laughed as she continued to pump her gas. "Man, you need to get over yourself and move on."

"My sister tried to warn me about you, but I wouldn't listen."

Delilah placed the pump back on the lever and retrieved her receipt. She walked closer to Luther's car and said, "Don't get mad because the player got played. Find yourself another victim because I'm not the one."

"You better be glad you look good or else I would have to regulate."

"I have two best friends, Smith and Wesson, and they won't let anyone bother me."

"Ooh, you're a bad woman."

"No, I'm a player squasher, and I suggest you remember that before you step to me again." Delilah twisted as she walked away and got in her car.

Delilah heard Luther call her everything but a child

of God. She didn't care. She peeped Luther's game the moment she met him. He was a user, and she wasn't the one. He could find another victim because she was not going to be played with.

"Fooling around with him is about to make me late," Delilah said as she rushed to make her Thursday session with Samson.

Elaine wasn't at her desk when Delilah entered the office, so she walked right in. The back of Samson's chair was facing the window. "Sorry, I'm late. I got caught up in traffic on West Seventieth Street," Delilah said as she placed her keys on top of the desk.

The chair swiveled around. "Samson had another appointment, so he asked me to step in his place." Michael stared at her.

The smile on Delilah's face changed to a frown. She had not planned on talking to the associate minister. "I don't think I should be talking to you about my problems."

He tapped his pen on the desk. "You can just reschedule then because I'm all you've got." Michael flashed his pearly white teeth.

One thing about Peaceful Rest, the ministers were above-average-looking men. Michael, however, was not Delilah's type. He was too smug in her opinion. She didn't appreciate the judgmental tone he seemed to use whenever they held a conversation. It would be a cold day in hell before she revealed anything of her past to the likes of him.

"Tell Samson, I mean Pastor Judges, I'll call him to reschedule," Delilah said.

"Whatever suits you," Michael said. He dismissed her

without saying a word. He looked down at a book and never looked back up.

Delilah left the room disappointed she wouldn't be seeing Samson. She had been looking forward to their visit all day. She didn't realize she'd left her keys on Samson's desk until she got outside.

She rushed back inside. Delilah heard voices when she got near Samson's office. She stopped outside the door.

"Thanks for covering for me, man," she heard Samson say.

Michael responded, "She didn't seem too thrilled, but at least for now you don't have to worry about her."

Delilah was pissed. Samson had deliberately avoided her. He could have called to cancel, and she would have saved her time and energy. She took steps toward the office until she heard Julia's name.

"Only a woman could put a smile like that on your face," Michael said.

"Yes, Julia, man. I didn't know it could be that good being married."

"That's good to hear. I was worried about you for a minute. You seemed so tense."

"It's been an adjustment, but believe me, Julia and I are adjusting just fine."

"That's good to hear. We don't want y'all to be a statistic. We're relationship-builders, not destroyers."

Samson agreed. "I like that. You should talk about that at our next conference."

"Sounds like a plan to me. Let me get to my wife before she has a fit. Her car's not working, and if I'm late picking her up from work, I'll have to hear it all night."

"Well, you better go. We can't have that."

Delilah slipped out of the room and into one of the other offices. She peered around the corner and caught the sight of Michael's back as he walked down the hallway. She ran back to Samson's office. Elaine was still nowhere around. She walked in his office and slammed the door.

"Samson, we have a problem," Delilah said.

Samson stuttered, "I thought you were gone."

Delilah walked to where he sat. "I bet you did."

"What are you doing?"

Delilah sat on his desk and hiked her skirt up. "I don't like what I heard. So you and Ms. Prim and Proper are finally adjusting, huh?"

Samson pushed her leg out of the way. "What goes on between me and my wife is our business?"

"Aren't you curious about how I know you two are having problems in the bedroom?"

"Delilah, I'm warning you."

She leaned down. "Because, Samson, I saw the bottle of Viagra. You're only thirty and never—and I repeat, never—had a problem getting it up for me." Delilah leaned back and laughed. "So did you sleep with her to try to forget about me?"

"She's my wife, and I will not have you disrespect her anymore."

"You weren't concerned about your wife when you were lying in my bed."

Delilah's body shook from anger.

"What we did should have never happened. It was a mistake."

Delilah picked up the first thing she could and threw

it at him. Samson ducked. "I can't believe you. You took advantage of my weakness, and now you're saying it's a mistake."

"Delilah, calm down."

"I see why some women snap now—because of men like you."

"What's going on here?" Elaine asked with one hand still on the doorknob.

"Ask him," Delilah said, as she whisked out the door.

Elaine shut the door behind Delilah and stood in front of Samson's desk with both arms folded. "I've sat back and watched that woman prance in and out of this office."

Samson held his hand up in protest. "Don't."

"Don't what, Pastor? Have you forgotten you're not only a pastor but a married man? Delilah's up to no good, and you're too blind to see it."

"You mind your business and let me take care of mine." Samson hit his fist on his desk.

"Julia will be hearing about this."

Samson needed to do some damage control. Elaine had gotten beside herself. He stood up. "What goes on in our office is confidential, and if I hear about you telling my wife anything about Delilah or any other person—male or female—who needs counseling, you can hand in your resignation because you will be let go."

Elaine gasped. "I can't believe you're threatening to fire me."

Samson sat back down. "Look, I know you don't like Delilah, but that's something you'll have to ask the Lord to help you with. She can rub folks the wrong way, and as you heard she was rubbing me the wrong way."

"Samson—and yes I called you by your first name because you're not acting like a man of God right now. Delilah is going to be the death of you if you don't watch it."

"I got everything under control."

"It doesn't look like it to me."

"Elaine, we've known each other a long time. I love having you work for me, but I mean it—if I ever hear about anything that goes on in this office from Julia or anyone else, you can look for a new job."

"You're the boss." Elaine saluted him.

"It's not even like that. Every time you mention Delilah to Julia, I have to listen to her whine. My house is a happy home right now, and I don't need anyone from the outside trying to ruin it."

"Then I suggest you keep Delilah out of your personal space."

Samson couldn't win when it came to Elaine. "When—or if—she decides to reschedule her appointment, you will be cordial to her. Understood?" Samson couldn't let on that he and Delilah had something more personal going on.

"Whatever you say. I'm out for the day."

Samson hated to be harsh with Elaine, but he had to ensure she kept her mouth shut. He wasn't sure how much she'd overheard. He could not risk her calling Julia about his and Delilah's verbal altercation. Things at home were finally looking up, and he'd meant what he'd said—he would not let anyone destroy it.

Chapter 40

Now that Elaine was out of his office, Samson had another problem to deal with—Delilah. She flew out of there before they could iron out their differences. Samson thought of a quote by the poet and playwright William Congreve: "Heaven has no rage like love to hatred turned. Nor hell a fury like a woman scorned."

He turned off his computer and grabbed his briefcase. The phone rang as he exited the door. He debated whether to answer it or let it go. He opted to answer. He needed to redeem himself. It could be someone in need. Julia's voice rang from the other end of the phone. "Where are you?" she asked.

"I'm on my way home now," he snapped. He didn't mean to snap, but it came out that way before he could catch himself.

His call with Julia ended, and he left his office. On the way home, he stopped at an area grocery store and purchased a floral bouquet. Julia was in the den watching television when he got home. "Hi, sweetheart. Sorry about what happened earlier." Samson handed her the bouquet of flowers.

"These are beautiful." She greeted him with a kiss. "Thank you."

"I was thinking, why don't you put the food up you cooked today and we go out tonight for dinner instead?"

Julia held on to the flowers. "Works for me. Let me put everything away, and I'll go change."

"You look just fine to me."

Julia moved the hair from out of her face with her free hand. "Please, I've had this on all day."

An hour later, Julia and Samson were seated at the Olive Garden eating salad and pasta. "This has always been one of my favorite places for Italian food," Julia said. Samson had to strain to hear her because a group of women sitting at a nearby table were talking loud. "I like your lasagna better," Samson responded.

"Oh, you really are trying to butter me up, aren't you?"

The voices of the group of women sitting next to them got louder. "Our first lady has no idea that her husband has been laying hands on me, and, girl, his hands are big too," Samson heard the woman say.

All the women at the table laughed out loud. Samson sipped on his drink and hoped Julia wasn't paying them any attention. Another one of the women said, "You know you're wrong."

"He's the one married—not me," the cheating woman said.

"Aren't you afraid of what will happen to you if his wife finds out?"

Another person said, "She needs to be more concerned about how God is going to deal with her."

The cheating woman said: "Me and God have an understanding. I stay out of His way, and He stays out of mine."

"You're going to burn in hell," another woman at the table said.

"And you'll be right there with me, Ms. Sleeping With the Chairman of the Deacon Board."

Samson had heard enough. He had no idea what church the women went to, but to hear them go on and on about their adventures made him very uncomfortable.

"Good thing we don't have to worry about that at our church," Julia said, making it clear she had heard them as well.

Samson played it off. "Yes, our men might be a lot of things, but they are doing their best to honor their marital vows."

"Let's hope."

Samson didn't know if that was a personal jab at him or if his guilt made him feel as if it were. Either way, he was glad when the bill came so they could leave the gossiping women by themselves.

Chapter 41

Seething, Delilah slammed the phone down for the umpteenth time. "That cow won't put my calls through."

She had been trying to reach Samson all day, but Elaine kept saying he wasn't available. Samson wouldn't answer his cell phone either. Agitated, Delilah logged on to her computer to play a game of Bejeweled to help relax her mind.

Her instant message alerted her that Samson was online. "Got you now."

She typed in a few lines and sent the message. There was no response. The computer beeped and the words "offline" appeared near Samson's login name.

He was playing games with her—the ignore game. That was one game she didn't like to play. She got ignored when she tried to tell someone about the predators in her foster homes. She got ignored when she had to showcase her body on the stage for perverts. Men only saw her physical beauty; none were interested in knowing the woman within. No, being ignored was no fun, and she wasn't going to play it with Samson.

Satan seemed to know when to hit a person at her weakest moment. Delilah picked up her phone to call Samson again, but William was calling her at the same time. Instead of hearing Samson's voice, she heard William's on the other end of the phone. "You got something for me yet, darling."

"Maybe." Delilah gritted her teeth.

"It's either yes or no."

Delilah would give Samson one more chance. Samson loved his church and dear wife too much to allow their affair to be made public. If he didn't react the way she felt he should, then she would have no recourse but to give William what he wanted—the ammunition to use against Samson."He's coming around," Delilah responded.

"Buy more low-cut blouses, tighter dresses. Do whatever you have to do. I want that property."

Delilah dropped the phone. She swore the phone grew hot as she listened to William go on and on about the land he wanted. She was glad when he finally decided to end the call.

"Samson must have forgotten about the video," Delilah said as she typed a long e-mail to Samson reminding him.

The computer sounded. "You've got mail."

Delilah laughed. "I knew that would get your attention." Samson's login name showed in the "sender" section of her e-mail.

She read his words out loud. "I thought you destroyed it."

She opened up her instant message browser and typed, "My computer made a backup."

The computer beeped to alert Delilah of an incoming instant message. Samson responded, "Delete it."

"Why?"

"Because it's the right thing to do."

"Samson, Samson, Samson," she said out loud and

then typed. "Why have you been avoiding me?" Delilah hit the send button in the instant message box.

"I've been busy."

"Too busy to talk to the woman responsible for putting fire back into your marriage?"

"Don't say that."

"Don't deny it. I bet you think of me when you're making love to her."

"Are you going to destroy the video or what?"

"Maybe."

"Maybe?" He put several question marks at the end of his statement.

Delilah had Samson agonizing. He had no idea what she was going to do next, and that's exactly how she wanted it to be. "I need to see you this weekend," she said, as she typed those exact words.

"I will see you at church."

"That's not what I want and you know it."

"Fifteen minutes. I can stop by for fifteen minutes and then I have to get home to my wife."

"I'll be waiting." Delilah put a smiley face at the end of her sentence.

Regardless of Samson's motives for going over, Delilah had no intentions of giving him the only copy she had of their liaison. If he thought he could sweet talk her into handing over that piece of evidence, he would be making a wasted trip.

Delilah wrapped her pink satin robe around her and waited for Samson to stop by. While waiting, she placed a DVD in a case and set it on the table.

The doorbell rang alerting her to Samson's arrival. She rushed to the door. "Come in," she said as she moved to the side so he could enter.

"Where's the disk?"

"I know your mama taught you better manners than that. At least give a sister a hug."

Delilah moved in for a hug. Samson inched back. "We better keep our distance."

"I know I'm hard to resist." She tightened the belt of her robe and walked into the living room. She knew Samson wasn't far behind her.

"Delilah, I don't have time to play these games with you."

Just the mention of the word game set off a bell in her head. She stopped and turned around. "Oh, I know you're not talking about me playing games. I've been trying to reach you all day. Ain't nobody that doggone busy."

"You're not the only member I have."

"But still you could have called me back." Delilah picked up the disk from the table and waved it in the air. "If I wouldn't have mentioned this video, I would still be waiting to hear from you."

Samson reached for the disk. Delilah placed it behind her back."Not so fast. What happens after I give you the video?"

"Nothing."

"Then give me one good reason why I should give it to you."

Delilah sensed his frustration with her but wouldn't give up her antics. "I need the reassurance that no one else will see it. Julia wouldn't understand."

She placed the video beneath her robe near her chest. "If you want it, come get it."

"I'm not touching you."

"I guess you don't want it then."

"This is blackmail, and it's not right."

Delilah laughed. "You have options. Are you going to come and get it?"

Samson paused to walk away, but on second thought, turned around. "This is the last time."

Chapter 42

Samson scrambled to find his pants. "I've been here an hour. I told Julia I was on my way."

"You'll learn to stop lying to your wife." Delilah's laugh sounded sinister to Samson. It was as if she was mocking him for yielding to temptation once again.

"Where's the disk?"

"Oh it's blank, but you can have it." Delilah reached on the coffee table and held it out."

Samson threw his arms in the air. "I've got to get out of here."

"If I were you, I would shower first. You wouldn't want to go home smelling like another woman, would you?"

Samson thought about it. Delilah had a point. He followed her to her bathroom, removed his clothes, and took a quick shower.

Delilah was sitting on the sofa in her living room when Samson finished showering and getting dressed.

"I want that disk, Delilah," Samson demanded.

"There's no disk."

He didn't believe her but would drop it for now. He had to get home to Julia before she got suspicious. "We'll talk about this later."

"I betcha," she said.

Samson broke several traffic laws trying to make it home. He checked his cell phone but didn't have any calls from Julia, so that put him at ease. "What is she doing here?" he asked out loud when he saw his mother's car in his driveway.

Samson said a quick prayer before heading into the house. "Lord, please don't let me say something disrespectful to my mama."

Kelly greeted him at the door. "Here's my baby boy."

"Mom, I'm thirty years old and married, so don't you think it's time for you to stop calling me baby boy?"

She looped her arms through his. "I don't care how old you get. You'll always be my baby boy." They walked toward the dining room.

"Ain't he cute?" Julia teased.

"Oh, I see. Y'all going to double team me," Samson surmised.

"Just having a little fun with you. Lighten up, son," Kelly teased.

"I'm surprised to see you here," Samson said to his mother.

"If you would take the time to call me or come see me, I wouldn't have to make these impromptu visits."

Samson leaned down and kissed her on the cheek. "You're here now. Why don't you stay for dinner?"

"I'm meeting your father over at a friend's, but I did want to talk to you about something." She looked at Julia and then back at him. "Alone."

"Follow me." Samson led her to his study.

She took a seat. With her small frame, the black leather chair seemed to swallow her body. "My sources tell me that someone's been sweeping around your backdoor."

Samson sat in the chair next to her. "Translation please."

"Delilah has been seen coming to your office on several occasions. Now, I haven't said anything to Julia because I'm sure there's nothing to tell." Samson remained quiet. "There isn't anything to tell, right, son?" his mother asked for clarification.

"No, Mom," he lied. He couldn't look her in the eyes.

"Well, hypothetically speaking, if there were"—he felt she knew he was lying—"it would be in your best interest to either stop counseling her by yourself or have one of the associate pastors do it. Being seen alone with that woman is not good for your marriage."

"Delilah is not a problem."

"Anytime a woman acts as brazenly as she does around you, there's a problem. She acts like she's your woman, and that's not good for your image."

"So what all has Elaine told you?"

"Elaine's not the only person I talk to. I have eyes in many places. You best remember that."

Samson reached for her hand. "Delilah is not a threat to my marriage. And if you must know, Julia and I are doing just fine, and I know you know what I mean."

Kelly stood up. "In that case, my job here is done. You make sure things stay that way. And mark my words, Delilah is nothing but trouble."

"Wasn't it you who taught me not to judge people?" Samson asked as he walked her out of the room.

"I also taught you not to be a fool either."

"Touché."

Samson walked his mom to her car. "Remember what I said. Stay clear of that woman. She'll be your downfall if you don't."

"Yes, ma'am."

Samson turned to walk back in the house. Julia stood at the door waving at his mom. "So did you two have a nice visit?" she asked when Samson returned to the house.

Samson knew she wanted to know what was discussed, but he refused to let her know, so she could fish for information all she wanted. Over dinner, Julia discussed ideas she had for some of the church ministries.

"Now do you see why I need to quit my job?" Julia asked.

Samson saw how Julia's eyes lit up. He didn't want to disappoint her. Against Samson's better judgment, he responded, "Okay, give it until the end of the summer and put in your notice."

"Thank you, honey," Julia smiled.

Julia led Samson to the bedroom. She undressed him. "What's that?" she asked.

"What?"

"It's red." Julia rubbed the scratch on his shoulder. A mark that was placed on him by Delilah the last time they were intimate.

Samson's underarms perspired. "Something bit me." He looked at Julia, and since she didn't stop kissing him, he assumed she believed his lie. After another lovely night together, Julia fell into a sound sleep.

Sleep evaded Samson. He closed his eyes, but visions of fire and brimstone greeted him every time he drifted off. While Julia rested, Samson lay in torment, fighting his internal demons.

Chapter 43

The grocery store was crowded. It seemed others had the same idea as Delilah. She got out early with hopes of beating the Saturday shopping crowd. Delilah couldn't decide whether to get apple juice or orange juice. Although she made a good salary working for William and had the money he had given her for his special assignment, Delilah was a frugal shopper.

"I can't believe I ran into you," Kelly said.

Delilah looked up in her direction. Being coy, Delilah responded, "Hi, Mrs. Judges."

Kelly lashed out at Delilah."Don't speak to me, you home wrecker."

A few of the people standing near looked in their direction.

In a calm and controlled voice, Delilah said, "Ma'am, maybe we need to table this conversation for later." Delilah looked around, and some of the onlookers looked away.

Kelly moved her shopping cart beside Delilah's. "My son swears there's nothing going on between the two of you, but I'm a mother. I know when something's not right. You stay away from him, or you'll have me to deal with."

Delilah had to hand it to the petite woman—she had

spunk. If she wasn't Samson's mother, however, she would be lying on the floor of the grocery store. Delilah liked to remain low-key, so she would not be a participant in Kelly Judges' madness. She walked away.

Kelly yelled, "Don't walk away from me. If you can do the dirt, take it like a woman."

Delilah left her buggy and walked near Kelly. "For a former first lady, you're acting like a woman with no class. I suggest you take your issues home to your husband or Samson because they are no concern of mine. Have a good day."

Delilah turned around and walked to her shopping cart. She could hear Kelly mumbling something. She cut her shopping trip short and checked out with the groceries she already had in her basket.

As soon as she got in her car, Delilah dialed Samson's cell phone number. "You need to check your mama before I do," she said when he answered. "She just cornered me in the grocery store trying to put all of your business out in the streets."

"Say what?" Samson responded.

Delilah relayed what happened. "I didn't tell her anything. I tried to reason with her, but your mama is out of control."

"I'm glad you told me," Samson sighed. "I'll call her later."

"Oh, I don't get a thank-you for keeping your little secret. I'm feeling so unappreciated these days."

"Thank you, okay? Is that good enough for you?" he snapped.

"No need for an attitude. It's not my fault your mama is all up in your business. But you need to handle her before I do."

"Don't threaten my mama."

"Chill out. I wouldn't touch your mama. I'm saying, she's going around asking all these questions. She might get an answer she might not want to hear."

"We've talked about this. You agreed to keep what goes on between us between us." Samson's voice cracked.

"Mama's boy, haven't you heard a word I said? Your mama is the one putting your business out in the streets. Handle her, and your business will stay a secret; otherwise don't be surprised if everyone finds out about us." Delilah hung up the phone without waiting on Samson to respond.

Delilah weaved in and out of traffic on Youree Drive. She had only a few bags of groceries, so it didn't take her long to unload them once she got home.

During her final trip to the car, one of her male neighbors asked, "Hey, who is that guy in the black SUV that be coming through? He looks familiar."

"Mr. George, you sure are nosy."

"You keep turning a brother down, so I just wanted to know who my competition is."

Delilah laughed. Mr. George was old enough to be her grandfather. "Mr. George, you need to stop."

"Be careful. Some of these men are only out for one thing. Don't let him break your heart."

Too late. My heart is breaking every day because he's married to another woman. "I'll be all right. But thanks for looking out." Delilah smiled as she took the last bag into the house. Mr. George had been one of the first people to welcome her into the neighborhood. She mostly kept to herself, but on rare occasions she would stop and talk with him to find out the neighborhood gossip.

She thought about Kelly as she unpacked her groceries. She had some nerve stepping to her that way. Delilah was tired of women judging her because of her beauty. Kelly's disrespectful actions mirrored that of some of the other women she had encountered lately at church. Someone at church had been spreading rumors about her, and she had a feeling she knew who it was, and it was high time she did something about it.

Delilah changed clothes and got comfortable on her couch. She retrieved the phone from the coffee table and dialed a number. "Is this Elaine?" Delilah asked when someone picked up.

"Speaking. Who is this?"

"Your worst nightmare if you don't keep my name out of your mouth."

"Who is this?"

"The woman you can't seem to stop talking about. Ms. Delilah to you."

"I know exactly who you are. I just wanted to see if you were bold enough to tell me."

"Unlike you, I don't have to go behind people's backs and talk about them. Samson needs to watch who he has working for him."

"Now you're stepping into my business."

"The moment you start putting my name in your mouth, you put me in your business."

"I don't have to stay on the phone and listen to this."

"Then hang up. I just wanted you to know that I knew what you were up to. You probably want Samson for yourself, so that's why you're trying to cause confusion where there is none."

"I hope Samson wakes up and sees you for the woman you are," Elaine said.

"He needs to wake up and see what kind of person he has working for him. If you were so loyal, there would be no way you would be spreading false rumors about him."

"I praise Samson; you on the other hand are nothing but a piece of trash. I hope you leave Peaceful Rest and go back to the hole you crawled out from."

"Well, keep hoping because I'm not going anywhere." Delilah hung the phone up, saying to herself, "And that's a promise."

Chapter 44

"Mom, how could you?" Samson asked as he talked to her on the phone.

"Why is she calling you? You shouldn't be talking to her at all."

Samson paced the floor in his den. Julia had stepped out, and this was the first time he'd had a chance to contact his mom about her confrontation with Delilah earlier that day. "I told you yesterday there's nothing going on, so please drop it. If Julia hears of this, it'll start some unnecessary drama."

"Boy, don't talk to me like that."

"Mom, I didn't raise my voice. I'm just saying, you were in a public place discussing private issues. You could have been a little bit more discreet if you were going to confront her."

"I'll give you that. But seeing her standing right there on the juice aisle, I forgot all about being the saved woman that I am. She brought out the worldly side of me."

"Mom, you've always had a temper, so don't go blaming that on Delilah."

"I hope you take up for your wife as much as you take up for that Jezebel."

Samson listened to his mom rant about Delilah. She

talked about her lack of style and class and compared her indecency to the wholesomeness that Julia possessed. If it had been anybody but his mama, Samson would have hung up the phone.

Once Samson's mom got tired of talking about Delilah, she asked, "How's that lovely wife of yours anyway?"

"Oh, Julia's fine. She ran an errand, and I'm waiting on her to get back."

"Concentrate on your marriage and stop fraternizing with that woman."

"Julia and I are fine, and I'm sure you know that since you two call and talk to each other every day."

"If you must know, yes, Julia thinks so, but I've met plenty of women like Delilah, and I'm going to tell you like I tell Julia—I don't trust her and neither should you."

Samson's phone beeped. Elaine's number flashed across the screen. "Mom, this is Elaine. I'll talk to you later." He clicked over. "Elaine, what's going on? I normally don't hear from you on Saturdays."

"That woman almost made me forget I was saved for a minute."

Samson had a feeling he knew which woman she was talking about. Against his better judgment he asked, "Who? And what did she do?"

"Delilah Baker has gotten on my last nerve. She had the nerve to call my house accusing me of spreading rumors about her. Samson, I want you to know whatever that woman tells you is far from the truth."

"Calm down. I haven't talked to her, and I don't plan on doing so until our next session."

"Well, I just wanted you to know. I don't want you

thinking I'm out there bad-mouthing you, Pastor. It's her I can't stand."

"Elaine, you know God doesn't want us to be backbiting."

"Pastor, I try not to talk about anybody, but something about that woman brings out the worst in me."

"You need to pray and ask God to work with you on that. Don't allow those feelings to hinder your relationship with God."

"Oh no, Pastor. I read my scriptures every day, and I pray. I ask God to forgive me for the evil thoughts I have concerning Delilah—I really do." Elaine attempted to assure him.

Samson knew Elaine was serious, but she didn't need to convince him. She needed to take her issues directly to God. "I want you to read these scriptures and meditate on them." Samson recited verses from Psalms and Proverbs that spoke specifically about backbiting.

"As soon as I get off the phone with you, I'm going to read these. I promise."

Satisfied that Elaine had calmed down, Samson ended their call. He was unaware Julia had returned. She greeted him with a smile when he entered the kitchen. "Baby, why didn't you say something? I could have helped you bring the bags in," Samson said as he helped her unpack the groceries.

"Sounded like you were counseling someone, so I didn't want to interrupt."

"I don't want you to ever feel like you can't come talk to me, okay?" Samson said. Julia stopped what she was doing and looked at him. "Is there something you want to tell me, Samson?" she asked.

"No, baby. I just want to make sure we have open communication. If anything is bothering you, don't hesitate to let me know, and I'll do the same."

Julia continued to put away the groceries. "Now you know I've never had a problem telling you what's on my mind."

"I know our marriage started off a little rocky, so I just want to make sure we keep our relationship moving in a positive direction."

Julia stopped again and faced him. "Everything's moving right along."

Her response seemed too crisp. Samson had a suspicion she had heard some rumors concerning Delilah too. If she wanted to pretend the rumors didn't exist, so would he. He would not open up Pandora's box.

Chapter 45

Sunday morning found Delilah curled up in a ball. Her stomach felt like a twisted knot. The food she ate the night before didn't agree with her. By the time the ibuprofen she took earlier kicked in, church services were long under way. Now that she was a member of Peaceful Rest, she rarely watched the services on TV. This Sunday, she had no choice.

With her elbow propped up on a pillow, she watched as the choir sang a hymn. Samson and the congregation joined in as he took his place behind the podium. The camera scanned the church. Delilah wanted to knock the happy look off Julia's face as she sat on the front pew with her baby blue hat trimmed with gold and diamond-like studs. "That should be me," Delilah said out loud.

Samson had the congregation hyped. "Are you being faithful to God? Now don't answer that just yet. Turn your Bibles to the sixteenth chapter of Luke."

Delilah reached over to her nightstand and pulled her Bible out. She found the scripture and read it out loud. "He that is faithful in that which is least is faithful also in much: and he that is unjust in the least is unjust also in much."

"There was another topic I had planned to discuss with

y'all today, but the Lord had other plans. How can we be faithful to God when we're not faithful to the ones we love? Husbands must be faithful to their wives, wives to their husbands."

Samson got several amens. Delilah wished she was there so she could get a better feel for how people were responding to Samson's sermon. The cameras remained on Samson, but she wanted it to move around the congregation.

"You're such a hypocrite," Delilah yelled at the television.

At the closing of his sermon, he said, "So before we leave here today, I want each and every one of us to ask ourselves, Are we being faithful to God?"

The broadcast ended. By then, the medicine had kicked in, and Delilah's stomach no longer hurt. Physically Delilah felt fine, but the old Delilah—the one she tried to keep at bay most of the time—threatened to resurface. Delilah thought about what Keisha said about finding a new church home. The more she thought about it, the more that didn't seem like a bad idea after all.

Delilah spent the rest of the day channel surfing and on the Internet. She checked Samson's Facebook page for updates. She felt Julia should be monitoring his page because some of the pictures of the women leaving comments were provocative. Those same women knew by Samson's profile name that he was a reverend. Some hussies had no shame.

Delilah ignored the alert for private messages from guys she didn't really know but were on her friends list. "He must be crazy," she said out loud when she saw a friend request from Luther. She had to hand it to him, he was persistent—cute, dumb, and persistent.

Delilah was surprised to see Julia on Facebook too. Out of curiosity she clicked on the link. Because she wasn't a friend, she was not able to see the comments. She clicked the photos link. "I'm going to be sick again," Delilah said out loud as she clicked on the slideshow from Julia and Samson's wedding. Delilah was surprised to see herself in one of the pictures. It was when she had caught the bridal bouquet. Delilah and Julia both had fake smiles plastered on their faces.

As much as Delilah hated to admit it, Julia did make a lovely bride. It was too bad her happiness would be short-lived if Delilah had anything to do about it. She clicked off Julia's page and posted a question to her own page. "What would you do if you were in love with another woman's husband?"

The topic must have been hot because by the end of the night Delilah had fifty comments from different people on her friends list. Most of the people said they wouldn't act on it. A few said they would and even went into detail about how they would go about getting the man they wanted. Delilah shook her head. "Just scandalous."

Michelle sent her a private instant message. "You're a little bold putting your business out there."

Delilah responded, "Just because I ask a question doesn't make it personal."

"I know you better not be talking about the pastor."

Who does she think she is? The marriage patrol? Delilah thought. Delilah typed, "Are you guilty of thinking about someone else's husband?"

"It's hard having a civil conversation with someone uncivilized."

Delilah said out loud: "You contacted me. I didn't contact you." Delilah typed, "And you have a good day too, Sister Michelle."

Delilah laughed because she was sure Michelle was mad that Delilah wouldn't go back and forth with her on a subject that was none of her business. She needed to worry about that handsome husband of hers. Delilah didn't care how perfect their relationship seemed; she was sure if she wanted to she could break up their happy union.

Michelle's instant message image disappeared. "Don't back up now. Anybody else out there got something to say to me?"

Michelle needed to mind her own business as far as Delilah was concerned. She was lucky Delilah didn't have her heart set on Calvin.

Chapter 46

Two months had passed since Samson and Julia had said the words "I do." Married life for the Judges had done a one hundred eighty-degree turn. Julia's attitude was more pleasant, and Samson no longer needed Viagra to perform some of his husbandly duties. Life for Samson couldn't be better. It had been a week since he'd heard from Delilah. He should have been more concerned about a member of his flock, but under the circumstances, it was best that they kept their contact with each other at a minimum.

"Samson, I've been calling out for you," Julia said, as she stepped out of the walk-in closet holding one of his pin-striped suits.

"Just find me a suit that will match your dress."

"Can you wear this one?" she asked. Julia held up a dark brown suit.

"I should be able to. I haven't gained any weight."

Julia tilted her head. "Baby, you're still fine, but you have put on a few pounds."

"It's all that good cooking and loving you're giving me."

"Whatever." She went back to the closet and came out holding a black suit with lime green pin-stripes. "I like this one. I have the perfect dress to match."

"You'll look good in anything."

Julia smiled. "Samson, I don't know what's gotten into you, but I like it."

"Hurry up and put those clothes up and show me how much."

An hour later, Julia and Samson cuddled. "See, I told you being married to a minister wouldn't be boring."

"I wasn't too sure. My parents seemed so boring growing up. I just knew a preacher was the last man I would ever want to marry." She looked into Samson's eyes. "And then I met you."

Samson kissed her. "It was love at first sight for me too."

They kissed some more. Samson's cell phone rang in the background. "Aren't you going to get it?" Julia asked.

"They can wait." Samson went back to kissing Julia.

Julia used her hand to stop him. "It might be important."

Samson couldn't disagree with her. "Hold on. Don't move."

He sat up on the side of the bed and retrieved his cell phone. The call had gone to voice mail. He scrolled through his missed calls and dialed Delilah's number. "Hello." Silence on the other end. "Hello," he said again.

"Samson, why haven't I heard from you?"

Samson's entire demeanor changed. He got out of the bed and went out in the hallway. "Do you know what time it is?"

"Please, I need you," Delilah begged.

"Call the office tomorrow. I'll make sure Monroe's available to speak with you." Samson didn't wait for

Delilah to respond before he ended the call. His pleasant mood turned sour. Delilah called right back. He hit the ignore button and turned his phone off.

Julia was sitting straight up in the bed when he entered the bedroom. "Who was that?" she asked.

"Nobody important." Samson's forehead tensed up.

"Whoever it was must have pissed you off?"

"I'll be all right. Let's not talk about it. Where were we before we got interrupted?" Samson placed his phone on the nightstand and crawled into bed with Julia.

He woke up to an empty bed. He called out for Julia but didn't get an answer. He reached for his cell phone but didn't see it. "I swear I thought I put the phone on this side of the clock." He was surprised to find it on Julia's side of the bed.

Samson went in search for Julia, but she was nowhere in the house. He was disappointed she didn't wake him up before leaving. A piece of paper on the kitchen counter caught his attention. The note indicated that Julia had to leave for an early hair appointment. He tossed the note in the trash and then went upstairs to shower and dress.

Shortly afterward, he was back in the kitchen fixing himself a bowl of cereal. An hour later he was entering his office. Elaine put the person she had on the phone on hold and greeted him as soon as he walked through the door. Things between them had been tense since the day he went off on her about Delilah. Gradually, things were getting back to normal between them. There was one thing left he knew he had to do, something that weighed on his shoulders.

"Elaine, when you get off the phone, let me see you in my office."

He sat down and started preparing for his day, beginning with prayer. Elaine was standing at the door when he finished praying. "I didn't want to interrupt," she said.

"Come on in and have a seat," Samson invited her.

Elaine, humbled, sat down across from him. She remained quiet. "I wanted to apologize for the tone I used with you last week," Samson said.

"That's water under the bridge," Elaine assured him with the swish of her hand.

"I care for you as not only a church member, but I consider you a friend. I know you're only looking out for my best interest, and I appreciate it." Samson had let his guilt from messing around with Delilah cause him to be too abrupt with Elaine that day. But he was still adamant about her not disclosing information to other people outside of the office, especially his wife.

Elaine responded, "I'll try my best to keep my comments about certain people to myself."

Samson knew she was referring to Delilah. "It will cut down on confusion for everyone involved."

"Well, if there's nothing else, I need to finish the church programs for Sunday."

"That'll be all," Samson responded. As soon as Elaine was out of his office and shut the door, Samson let out a heavy sigh. Elaine didn't realize how close she was to being fired. He needed an assistant who could keep her mouth shut.

Chapter 47

Dorothy had done her best to keep Delilah out of the loop when it came to the duties of the Pastor's Aide committee for the pre-anniversary celebration they were having for Samson on Friday night. Fortunately for Delilah, not everybody on the committee had a personal vendetta against her. In fact, one of the other older women, Lora Stampley, didn't like the way Dorothy always wanted to have the final word on things.

"I'll see you at six," Lora said.

"Six?" Delilah asked.

"Yes, I thought somebody told you. Plus it was in the church bulletin."

"Ms. Lora, thank you for letting me know the time changed," Delilah said. She hadn't paid attention to the date change in the church bulletin, so she was glad Lora called her.

"No problem, dear. I'll see you there," Lora said before disconnecting the call.

The dinner for the pre-anniversary celebration had been moved up to six o'clock, so that meant Delilah had only thirty minutes to get ready. It seemed everyone else had been notified of this but her. Fortunately, she already had her clothes picked out. Delilah would show them. Since Dorothy and her buddies wanted to be ugly, she would arrive only in time for the dinner to start. She had planned on helping with decorations and anything else. See, God didn't like ugly, and as Ms. Shadows used to say, He wasn't too keen on cute either.

Satisfied she was dressed to impress, Delilah drove to the Holiday Inn, the place where the dinner was being held. She recognized church members in the parking lot.

Everybody wore their Sunday best on this Friday night. Some people greeted Delilah, while others turned their noses up. She never could understand church folks. Some of their attitudes were enough to turn away someone, but fortunately for her, she was secure.

She bypassed the long line and went to the registration desk. Two women from Pastor's Aide were checking people in. "Do y'all need some help?" Delilah asked.

One of the women looked up. The expression on her face let Delilah know she was surprised to see her. "No, uh, we got it covered," she stuttered.

"Fine. Then I'll just go on in."

There was assigned seating. The Pastor's Aide committee and their guests were supposed to sit near the pastor and other ministers. She hoped there was enough room for everyone because she was headed to take a seat at the table. She would not be without a seat.

Delilah reached the table and sat down. She had a good view of the front podium. "I see you made it," Dorothy said.

Delilah turned to look in her direction. "No thanks to you."

"I meant to call you, but I got busy." Dorothy's hands were full of programs.

"Sister Dorothy, no need to lie."

"I can't believe you're calling me a liar right here in my face." She took one of the programs and fanned.

"Would you rather me talk behind your back?"

Michelle, with Calvin by her side, walked up. "Ladies, everything all right here?"

All eyes were on Delilah. Delilah looked at Dorothy. "It's fine as far as I'm concerned."

"Dear, can you help me pass out these programs?" Dorothy turned and asked Michelle.

Michelle followed behind Dorothy. Calvin sat at the end of the table. "Don't let Ms. Dorothy get under your skin."

Delilah retrieved her compact mirror from her purse. "I've confronted worse."

Calvin said, "Luther, told me about your date."

"Don't get me started on your trifling brother-in-law." Delilah checked her reflection in the mirror and snapped it shut.

"I did tell him he was the one in the wrong."

Delilah and Calvin talked about Luther. Calvin confessed, "It was Michelle's idea. I should have used my better judgment and stayed out of it. Luther's not relationship material."

"You can say that again."

Most of the tables in the room were getting filled up. Delilah coughed a few times. "Calvin, make sure no one gets my seat. I'm going to go see if I can find a water fountain."

Delilah's cough didn't subside until she drank some water. She detoured to the restroom before returning to the banquet area. When she entered the bathroom, she came face-to-face with Julia, who stood in front of the mirror adjusting her lime green skirt.

Delilah stood and watched her for a few seconds before Julia looked up. Neither said a word. Delilah walked in and retrieved a tissue from the box on the sink's counter. She turned the water on, and it spurted out, splashing on Julia. "Sorry," Delilah said.

"Yeah right," Julia responded.

"Excuse me?" Delilah didn't like Julia's attitude.

"You heard me right the first time."

Delilah was steps away from reaching over and popping Peaceful Rest's first lady in the face, but the door opening saved her from making a step in Julia's direction. Both she and Julia turned to see who was entering.

The unknown woman went into a bathroom stall. Delilah looked directly at Julia. "Is there something you want to say to me?" Delilah asked

Julia seemed to retreat. "I have nothing to say to you."

"Then good luck with that water spot." Delilah turned and walked out of the bathroom.

Chapter 48

Julia's demeanor had changed since being back around Samson. He whispered, "What's wrong, baby?"

"I don't want to talk about it," Julia snapped.

He had to increase his pace to keep up with her as they walked to the banquet hall. Whatever was bothering her, he was glad she smiled and shook people's hands as they made their way to the front of the banquet hall.

Samson felt honored that his church members cared enough for him to do this. He was satisfied with being able to preach the Word at Peaceful Rest and on a live TV broadcast. He didn't need the extras. Julia's phone rang and she answered it, so Samson took the opportunity to look around the room. He smiled with joy as he scanned the smiling faces in the room. His facial expression changed the moment he saw Delilah enter the banquet hall. She seemed to be walking in slow motion. Ironically, she was wearing a shade of green. She demanded attention just by walking in the room, and he wasn't the only man who looked in her direction.

For a moment he thought she was headed to his table, and he raced to think of what to say. Then he saw her stop two tables back and take a seat. Relieved, he picked up the program someone had passed around to all the tables.

Julia hung up her phone. "Your parents won't be able to make it. They had a flat."

"Dad should have called. I could have gone by before coming here."

"Your mom said all is well. Your dad is just a little worn out from changing the tire. It seems he had quite a time."

Samson called his father, and when he was assured that Regis was fine, he got off the phone. The pre-anniversary celebration had begun. Samson squeezed Julia's hand. She no longer seemed tense. They stole hidden glances at each other and smiled. Samson and Julia held hands throughout the ceremony when they weren't clapping after a performance or eating.

Samson's heart was filled with gratitude as heads of some of the church auxiliaries presented him with tokens of appreciation. He couldn't imagine what they had in store for him on Sunday because they were adorning him with gifts now. Their empty plates had been removed from the table and filled with various gift bags.

Some of the men had to help Samson carry the items to his vehicle. "Happy pre-anniversary," Delilah said as he passed her in the hallway.

"Thanks," he responded. He looked up ahead and saw Julia standing in the banquet hall doorway. He didn't dare stop walking.

"What did she want?" Julia asked when Samson approached her.

"She just spoke." Samson led them back into the room, and they said their good-byes.

Silence filled the car for most of the trip to their house. Samson finally spoke. "What's wrong, honey bun?"

"Nothing," Julia snapped.

Samson dropped the subject until they were getting ready for bed. Julia got in the bed and turned her back toward him.

"You know we promised to not go to bed angry with each other," Samson reminded her as he placed his arm around her tense body.

"Why did you lie to me last night?" Julia asked.

Samson had to do a mental rewind. He couldn't remember lying about anything. "Baby, I'm not sure I know what you're talking about."

"Of course you're not."

Samson moved. "Let's sit up and talk."

"You're right because I want you to look me in my eyes and tell me why you lied about that call last night."

Samson had his *aha* moment. He knew he wasn't crazy. He had put his cell phone on the other side of his clock. He let out a few deep breaths. Julia had invaded his personal space by checking his cell phone without his knowledge.

"Are you going to answer me or not?" she asked.

"Julia, I'm in shock. I never took you for the insecure type. You don't see me going through your purse, do you?" Samson countered.

"This isn't about me. It's about you and the fact you got a call from Delilah and lied about it."

"Technically, I didn't lie. I never told you who it was because there was nothing to tell."

"Then why the secrets? What else are you hiding?"

"I need to be asking you since it seems you have all the answers," Samson said. "You're the one playing *CSI* when there's nothing to investigate."

"I'm sorry, okay?" Julia avoided eye contact with Samson. In a solemn voice, she said, "I just felt like you were lying, and when I saw that woman's number in your phone—it just burned me up."

Samson touched her chin and tilted her head toward him. "Who am I in bed with? Who do I wake up with? I'm with you, so there's no reason for you to question my loyalty." Samson hoped his words were enough to ease Julia's mind.

Chapter 49

Delilah missed service last Sunday, but she was determined to be there this week no matter what. She applied her makeup to match her suit. She decided to wear a lilac-colored knee-length suit she had purchased from Dillard's department store. Keisha had done her hair the day before, so all she had to do was remove her hair net and watch the long, cascading curls fall loosely. She ran her hand over a few loose strands. *The first lady wouldn't be the only one looking good today*, she thought.

Keisha had assured her she would be there to perform for the anniversary program. She sure hoped so because she was counting on her to show up and show out. Listening to a local gospel radio station, Delilah eased into a parking place near the front of the church. The parking lot wasn't as full as it normally was. On days when there were two services, some members would opt not to come to the first morning service.

Delilah didn't plan on missing any of the services. She waited in her car until she knew it was time for church to start. The usher at the door handed her a program and directed her to sit to her left side. Delilah wanted to sit on the right side, so she moved past him and started walking toward the pew she preferred. She heard the usher call her name, but she ignored him and sat where she wanted to. If the service hadn't already started, she was sure he would have tried to make her move.

Associate Minister Monroe preached the first service. Afterward, Delilah caught up with Michelle to see if she needed her to do anything. "We got it covered," Michelle assured her.

"Don't say I didn't offer my services," Delilah said.

"I'm sure I wasn't the only one who turned them down," Michelle said before walking away.

There was an hour break before the second service started. Delilah didn't have a reason to go back home, so she wandered the halls. She passed by Samson's office a few times. His door was open so she could see a few people going in and out. As soon as he was in the office alone, she slipped inside.

"Happy anniversary, Pastor," Delilah said.

Samson looked up. He didn't look too happy to see her. "Delilah, I don't have time to talk to you today."

"Now, what kind of greeting is that for one of your die-hard supporters?" Delilah stood in front of his desk.

"Julia will be here any minute, so I suggest you save whatever you have to say for later."

"I don't get a happy anniversary? It's been one year this month since I joined Peaceful Rest. Don't I get some congrats or something?" Delilah asked. She eased her way around his desk.

Samson moved his chair farther from Delilah. "I'm happy that you joined Peaceful Rest, okay?"

"So can I get a hug?" she asked.

Delilah saw the sweat drip from his forehead. She got a tissue and wiped it for him. He grabbed her wrist. "Don't."

She dropped the tissue, and it landed in his lap. Delilah's cell phone rang. Keisha's special ring tone played. "That's my friend. We'll continue this later."

Delilah left Samson's office and ran right into Elaine. "Oops, sorry," Delilah said.

"Ms. Dorothy is looking for you." Elaine looked like she wanted to say something else, but she didn't.

"Thanks." Delilah smiled, turned on her heels, and twisted down the hall.

She found Dorothy talking to another one of the women on the Pastor's Aide committee.

"Elaine said you were looking for me."

"Yes, your friend who's doing the solo is here." Dorothy handed her a lilac-and-white corsage. "Make sure she puts this on." Dorothy reached down and got another one. "And this is for you."

"This is pretty. Thanks." Delilah was truly surprised by Dorothy's kind gesture.

She went inside the sanctuary and noticed the seats were filling up. She looked around to see if she could locate Keisha. "Boo," Keisha said from behind her.

"Girl, don't sneak up on me like that no more."

Keisha and Delilah hugged. "We'll be sitting near the front. Tell our musician what song you're going to sing, and he'll do your music so you won't have to play the piano and sing," Delilah said as she led her to where the minister of music sat. "Victor, this is my friend Keisha. She's on to sing a solo today."

Victor asked in his high-pitched voice, "Do you know what song you want to sing yet or are you just going to let the Spirit move you?"

Keisha responded, "I'll be singing 'The Battle Is The Lord's.'"

"Let me hear you sing the first verse so I can get your key," Victor said.

Delilah listened to the lyrics of the song Keisha was singing and thought about Samson. She wondered if she was fighting a losing battle concerning him.

Chapter 50

"How do I look?" Julia asked Samson for the umpteenth time. They were in his office doing last-minute preparations before the anniversary program started.

Samson responded, "If you looked any better, I would have to keep you hidden in my office."

"You sure? This dress looks a little too short." Julia turned around and viewed herself in the mirror hanging on the wall.

"Baby, you look perfect, okay? Stop stressing."

She picked up the lilac purse that matched her suit. "This is my first anniversary as first lady. I want to make a good impression."

"I'm honored to have you on my arm."

Someone knocked on the door. Kelly was standing on the other side when Samson opened it. "You two ready? The guests are here, so we're ready to start."

"After you two," Samson said. He held out his arm and allowed Julia to exit the office behind his mother.

Samson's parents were escorted in first and took their seats on the first pew. Two seats decorated in lilac and white were situated at the front of the church facing the pulpit. Calvin and Michelle were on program to escort the pastor and first lady. Everyone stood up as Calvin escorted Julia and Michelle escorted Samson into the sanctuary.

Samson wasn't flashy and didn't like a lot of fanfare, but he appreciated all that his congregation and other ministers in the community were doing for him.

Julia whispered, "You are loved by so many people."

That was the best part about the program. He could feel the love, and he didn't want to ever lose the people's affection or respect. A soloist brought tears to Samson's eyes as she sang, "No matter what you're going through the battle is not yours, it's the Lord's." He glanced at his program and saw the name Keisha Green listed. The Spirit hit him, and he jumped on his feet. He wasn't alone; other members of the congregation were also standing and waving their hands in the air.

Someone shouted, "Yes, Lord. It's yours."

The guest minister, Reverend Jonas J. Johnson, stood up after Keisha's solo. "Y'all want to have some church up in here today, I see. Let the Lord use you."

Keisha was handed the microphone again, and she sang a few more stanzas. The Spirit of the Lord was in the sanctuary during the entire service. Reverend Johnson's sermon struck Samson close to the heart. "We're here to celebrate a great man of God. My sermon today has been about the duties of a good pastor. I'm not going to keep y'all much longer, but I have a few more words I need to share with my brother. As a pastor, you should have good moral character."

Samson nodded his head in agreement as he listened to Reverend Johnson go over the duties of a pastor. "The pastor is accountable to God for how he treats the church. How can a pastor lead God's flock if he's doing the same thing the people of the world are doing? See, I know this man we're honoring today. He's a good man. I've known him since he was a little boy. When the rest of us wanted to run out and chase women, Samson was chasing the Word of God. So Samson"—Reverend Johnson looked directly at Samson—"keep your eyes focused on the Lord and ministering to His flock."

Before he took his seat, Reverend Johnson said: "Samson, I know I speak for everyone assembled here today. We love you, we respect you, and we're honored to be able to celebrate your anniversary with you today. So, great man of God, keep preaching God's Word." Amens were heard throughout the room.

Samson reached over and squeezed Julia's hand. During the presentations, Julia couldn't control her emotions. She cried the tears that Samson held bottled up inside; he felt such joy for all the things the church and their friends in the ministry did for them. After the service, Samson and Julia tried to thank everyone personally for their contributions to the day's event.

"Jonas, you brought it home," Samson said as he hugged him.

"I'm just a messenger boy," Reverend Johnson responded.

"I want you to meet my lovely bride." Samson introduced Julia to him and other people standing around who hadn't met her.

They made their way to the fellowship hall, where the members had prepared a feast. After Samson blessed the food, the crowd lined up to get plates and drinks.

Julia said, "There goes the soloist. Come on, I want to tell her how much I enjoyed that song."

Samson followed Julia as they made their way through the crowd. "We wanted to tell you how much we enjoyed the song," Samson told Keisha when they approached her.

"Thank you, Pastor Judges." Keisha extended her hand to shake his.

"I wish I could sing like you," Julia said.

Keisha reached to shake her hand. "Don't I know you from somewhere?" she asked.

Julia squinted her eyes. "We may have seen each other around."

"What high school did you go to?" Keisha asked.

"Huntington."

"That's where I know you from. We were in gym together."

Julia said, "That was so long ago. I'm sorry, I don't remember you."

"I see you've met my best friend," Delilah walked up and said. She continued, while looking at Samson, "I'm responsible for getting her to sing at your anniversary. She did a great job, didn't she?" Delilah smiled as she looped her arm through Keisha's.

Samson felt the room getting smaller. "Great. Keisha, thank you for blessing us with your voice." Samson then turned his attention toward Julia. "Dear, we'd better go take our seats so Ms. Dorothy can stop giving us the evil eye."

Samson placed his hand on Julia's arm and led her to their table. Two hours later, Samson and Julia were headed home. "It wasn't as bad as you thought it would be, now was it?" Samson asked.

"This whole day was wonderful. I don't know why I was nervous in the first place." Julia squeezed his hand.

Samson smiled as he drove. His church family adored him, and he had the love and respect of his wife. Life couldn't be more perfect.

Chapter 51

Delilah helped clean up the fellowship hall after everyone left. To Delilah's surprise, Keisha stayed around and helped too. The other women on the Pastor's Aide committee couldn't stop talking about how good Keisha was. Before they walked to their cars, Keisha had invitations to sing for other programs.

"Thank you for helping out," Delilah told her friend.

"No problem. I wanted to tell you something, but I changed my mind."

"Don't do me like that," Delilah pleaded.

By now they were standing near Delilah's car. Keisha scrunched up her nose and looked off in the distance. "It's nothing."

No matter how much Delilah begged, Keisha wouldn't say anything before she drove off. Delilah wondered what was on Keisha's mind and called her once she got home. "You're going to tell me eventually, so you might as well spit it out now," Delilah said.

"Delilah, it's probably best I keep my comments to myself. We've had a joyous time in the Lord today; let's not spoil it."

"You're right. It's been a good day overall and there's no need to spoil it. I'm going to run me some bath water and then relax for the rest of the night."

Delilah hung up with Keisha and did just that. After a long bubble bath, she went to bed early. The sound of someone beating on her door woke her up the following morning.

"Hold on," she yelled as she tripped over her shoes in search of her robe. She found the robe, put it on, and tightened the belt around her. "Coming." Delilah was prepared to go off on whoever was standing on the other end of the door. She looked out her peephole. "It figures."

She opened the door and in walked William. "Early bird catches the worm," he said in a cheerful voice.

"Or a bullet," Delilah said under her breath.

"Dear, you're looking kind of rough."

Delilah's hand flew to her head. She hadn't bothered to tie it down last night. She glanced at her appearance when she passed the mirror. With the nighttime sweat, her curly hair had frizzed up. She wasn't too concerned because William wasn't anyone she was trying to impress.

William leaned on his cane. "I just came to check on my investment."

"You could learn to come at a more decent hour," Delilah snapped.

"If you were coming into the office like the rest of my employees, you would be up already."

He did have a point. It was after seven, but she had planned on sleeping until at least nine today. "I don't have any updates on Samson, so you made a wasted trip."

Delilah noticed William retrieving something from his pocket. He handed it to her. "How would you feel if I left this on the cars of everybody at your church?"

Her fingers gripped the picture showing her naked with several men standing around her. She couldn't even remember who they were. It was probably a bachelor party. She had done many private shows, and this was evidence from those days. She wouldn't be able to show her face around church anymore.

She could see Dorothy, Michelle, and Elaine now getting a thrill out of her embarrassment. Nope, that wasn't going to happen. She tore the picture up and let the pieces fall to the floor.

"Don't worry; that wasn't the only copy." William sat on the sofa and patted the space next to him. "Talk to me."

The time was at hand to pay the price for making a deal with the devil. The devil was asking for his due. Delilah sat next to William, and as if on cue she gave William the ammunition he needed against Samson. William drooled as she gave him details about her and Samson's last rendezvous.

"I got him now," William said. He pulled out his cell phone and dialed a number. "Move on to stage two."

"Who was that?" Delilah asked William after he'd hung up the phone.

"It doesn't concern you. Do you have video footage, pictures, or anything else that I can use against Samson?"

"No, just my word," Delilah lied. Although the video footage was from before Samson married Julia, she knew William wouldn't care. She promised Samson she wouldn't show the video to anyone else, and she planned on keeping that promise. She would prove her loyalty.

"Mr. Judges will be pushing to sell that land now. Dear, you've earned yourself another bonus." William reached into his pocket and handed her an envelope. "Good job. And once he signs over the deed to that land, there's more coming to you."

"You can keep your money."

"No, you've earned it." William let the envelope drop on the coffee table. "I've got to go. I'm meeting the mayor for breakfast."

Delilah remained seated as William let himself out. She felt a burning sensation inside the pit of her stomach. *Lord, what have I done? Samson doesn't deserve this. I have to warn him.*

Chapter 52

Samson sat behind the desk in his office and leaned back in his chair as he thought about the events of the previous night. Julia showed him a side of herself that made him a very happy man. He reached in his briefcase and retrieved the bottle of Viagra. He threw it in the trash because he was more than positive that he would no longer have any use for it.

Elaine walked in. "Delilah's outside, and she insists on seeing you."

"Tell her I'm tied up for the rest of the day."

"I swear that woman won't give it up. I owe you an apology because now I realize you've been innocent, and she's the one who won't give up her quest to get next to you."

"Apology accepted. Now do whatever you have to do to get rid of her."

"I got your back, Pastor." Elaine left his office.

A few seconds later, Samson could hear Delilah shout, but shortly thereafter he heard the other door slam. To his relief, Elaine accomplished her mission. Elaine said, as she walked back in Samson's office, "She asked me to have you call her at your earliest convenience."

"That would be never," Samson stated under his breath as Elaine left to finish doing her tasks.

Samson turned his chair around and peeped through the blinds. He saw Delilah get in her car and speed out the parking lot. "Delilah, you have to let this go," he said out loud.

Samson returned phone calls and e-mails most of the morning. Before he realized it, it was close to noon. "Elaine, you can go to lunch now if you want. I'll man the phones."

"You sure? Because after your anniversary program yesterday, I've been fielding calls for speaking engagements throughout the city."

"I got the phones. You go ahead and go. Take as much time as you need."

Elaine grabbed her purse. "You don't have to tell me twice. I'm out of here."

Samson turned up the volume on his computer as he listened to some gospel tunes. His singing was interrupted by a sinister laugh. He turned to face the enemy. William strolled into Samson's office with his gold-tipped cane, holding a manila folder. He took a seat without waiting for an invitation. "I would have knocked, but I didn't want to interrupt your mini-concert."

"You can leave because we have nothing to talk about."

"But, Reverend Judges, that's where you're wrong. We have a lot to discuss. This is for you." William handed Samson the folder.

Pictures of Delilah in various naked poses with and without men in them stared Samson in the face. He didn't know what to make of it all. He dropped the folder down. "Now, do you want your congregation to know the kind of woman their great pastor has been lounging around with?" William asked.

"The Delilah I know would not do something like this."

"There's a lot about that woman you don't know. But since I like you, I thought you would want to know."

Samson shouldn't have been shocked at the pictures, but they caught him off guard. As Delilah's pastor, he would do his best to make sure the information didn't get out to the general congregation. "William, this is a private matter. I will talk to Delilah about it. Now that you've delivered this, you can go."

"Not too fast, preacher man."

"I don't have time to play games with you." Samson stared straight into the eyes of the enemy. William didn't flinch. His cold, black eyes stared back at Samson.

"Delilah told me about your affair. I know about the two of you sleeping together." Samson opened his mouth to speak, but William interrupted him. "And before you say it happened before you got married, I know for a fact it was before and afterward, so don't try to deny it."

William gave Samson details of his last interaction with Delilah—information that had been given to him by Delilah. Samson knew William was no longer bluffing.

Samson slammed his fist on the table. Some of the items on the desk jumped a few inches high. "Satan, get thee behind me."

William laughed. "I've been called worse. I'll give you twenty-four hours."

"Get out of my office," Samson stood up and said.

William got up and walked toward the door. He stood in the entranceway. "Since I'm such a generous person, I'll give you forty-eight hours. Forty-eight hours, Reverend, to let me know you're signing over the land

to me or"—William picked up a picture of Julia on the
stand next to the door—"your little wife will be finding
out about your indiscretions, and you won't be able to
talk yourself out if it either." William left Samson alone
with his thoughts.

Samson picked up the pictures of Delilah. "How could
you?" Samson cried out to the photos as if Delilah was
standing in the room with him. "You said you loved me."

Everyone tried to warn him about her. Delilah's telling William about their affair was the ultimate betrayal.
He could not lose his wife—not because of his few minutes of weakness. He had to do something—and fast.

Chapter 53

For the second time that day, Delilah felt like going off on someone for beating on her front door. She opened the door without looking through the peephole. The sight of Samson standing on the other side surprised her. He walked in and threw a folder at her. Pictures fell on the floor. "How could you, Delilah? How could you betray me like you have?"

"Samson—" she stuttered as she reached down to pick up the pictures. Photos of herself in her birthday suit were not what she expected to see. "Where did you get these?" She already knew the answer before he responded.

"Your boss made a personal delivery. I should have known you two were working together when you told me you worked at Trusts Enterprise. I mean, you're the only person I know who has a job but was hardly ever at the office."

"It's not what you think, Samson." Delilah closed the front door. She didn't want to give her neighbors any new gossip for the week. "Come have a seat."

"I think I'll stand."

"Suit yourself, but I'm going to sit down." Delilah left and went to the living room.

Samson stood in the doorway.

"You can sit next to me. I won't bite."

"Delilah, I don't have all day. I want to know why you told William Trusts about our affair."

Delilah started to lie, but knew it wouldn't do any good. "You left me no choice."

"You could have kept the information to yourself like you promised me." Samson shortened the distance between them. He now stood near the couch.

Delilah held up a few of the pictures. "And risk him showing these to people?"

"So you sold me out to the devil himself."

Delilah tried to lighten the situation with a laugh. "Come on, he's not that bad," she lied.

"He's threatened to tell Julia unless I sign over the church's land."

"Then do it. What's the big deal? It's not like the church won't benefit from it financially. From what I know, the offer is triple the market value."

By now Samson had taken a seat at the other end of the couch. "Even if I wanted to, I would have to get the board's approval."

"Then do it. This isn't as bad as you think," Delilah said.

"I've been real adamant about holding on to the land. People will start looking at me suspiciously if all of a sudden I say I want to sell."

"People are allowed to change their minds. Do it and don't let William hold it over your head."

"I'm real disappointed in you, Delilah. I trusted you."

Delilah couldn't believe what she was hearing. She had kept their little secret from his wife. She had dealt with him ignoring her. She didn't like it, but she understood his first allegiance was to his wife. She didn't betray him; he betrayed her. He shouldn't have slept with her and given her a false sense of hope—hope that eventually they would be together.

For the first time, she recognized that the man sitting in front of her was selfish. He was only concerned about Samson and could care less about how his actions hurt other people. If he did, he wouldn't be accusing her of betrayal. The pain in her eyes spilled out into words. "I've done everything you've asked of me. I never thought you could be so selfish."

Samson stood up, anger seeping from his pores. "Because of you I might lose my wife. I hate the day I ever let you talk me into sleeping with you."

"You've got to be kidding." Delilah stood up at this point. "You slept with me because you wanted to, not because I made you. In fact, you initiated the doggone kiss, so go tell your little wife that."

"Julia's not like you. She wouldn't understand how I could sleep with the likes of you."

Delilah put her hands on her hips. "So what are you saying, Samson?"

"I'm not saying you're a harlot, but come on now, Delilah. Those pictures say a thousand words."

Delilah picked up one of the couch pillows and threw it at him, hitting him on the arm. "Get out. Get out of my house now!" Samson used his arms to block the blows Delilah began to throw. "You already have William as an enemy. Now you have me. Get out of my house now."

Samson rushed out of her house. Delilah's feet felt lifeless. She slid down, and the couch caught her. She grabbed a pillow, buried her face in it, and cried like she had never cried before. Her life was in ruins. Would Samson ever forgive her for telling William everything? Most importantly, she thought, *God, will you ever forgive me for allowing the enemy to take over my life?*

Delilah felt all alone—like no one cared about her. But a still, small voice said, "You have Me." Delilah knew it had to be a word from God and immediately felt a sense of peace. But just how long would that peace last?

Chapter 54

Samson drove around for hours after leaving Delilah's house. He went out to the lake and watched the ducks. He picked up a few rocks and threw them in the water. He couldn't believe the situation he found himself in. How could he have been so stupid as to get involved with Delilah?

Several scriptures came to mind, most notably the forty-first verse of the twenty-sixth chapter of Matthew— "Watch and pray, that ye enter not into temptation: the spirit indeed is willing, but the flesh is weak."

Samson had to admit that praying was the last thing on his mind when he opted to sleep with Delilah. If it had happened one time since his marriage, he may have gotten away with calling it a mistake, but it happened more than once. Delilah was temptation in heels. She demanded attention just from entering a room.

His ego got in the way of him resisting her. He knew she could have any man, but she wanted him. His ego overruled his right judgment. His wrong decision now had his back up against the wall.

A man like William didn't make idle threats. If Samson didn't do what he wanted, he had no doubt that William would tell Julia everything. Granted, it would be William's words against his, but in light of how Delilah boldly came to his office time after time, Julia would side with William.

He loved his wife and wanted to make sure they had a long life together. He had to do whatever he could to protect his family. Samson sat on the bench and shook his head. His parents would be disappointed. He could hear his mom chastising him now for allowing himself to be caught up in an affair. What-ifs floated through his mind. Would his congregation forgive him? Maybe he should tell Julia about it because he was not going to let William have leverage over him for the rest of his life. His mind filled with endless possible outcomes of his selling or not selling the land. None would result in a happy ending for him.

As much as he hated to give in to William's request, he had no choice. He had to convince the board to sell. Now he had to think of the right words to say to convince everyone else that it was a good idea.

Samson dialed Calvin's number. "I need to see you as soon as possible. It's about the church land." Samson and Calvin made plans to meet at his house for dinner.

When he hung up with Calvin, Samson called Julia. "Hi, baby. Add two more names to the pot. I've invited Calvin and Michelle over for dinner. Calvin and I need to discuss some church business."

A few hours later, Calvin and Samson were seated in his study with the door closed. "I know I've been adamant against it in the past, but now I feel we should sell our land to Trusts Enterprise."

Calvin had a shocked look on his face. "Man to man, what does William have on you?"

"Nothing," Samson lied.

"I never saw why we couldn't sell in the first place, but you're our church leader, so you know I'm going to go along with whatever you think we should do."

Samson rehearsed what he would say earlier and repeated it verbatim. "I figured we should not turn away
the blessing. We're being offered three times what the
property is worth. We have enough land here to ex-
pand and build the community action center right in
our own backyard."

"True. But I know William. He's known for doing some
underhanded things."

Samson looked Calvin straight in the eyes, hoping
Calvin wouldn't be able to read between his lies. "He's
not my favorite person, but in the end I must do what's
best for the church. Selling the land would be in our
best interest."

Calvin stood up. "If you think it will be, then, Samson,
you will have my vote. We can call a special board meeting and get this thing rolling."

Samson shook Calvin's hand. "I knew I could count
on you to have my back."

"That's what friends and lawyers are for." Calvin chuckled.

Later that night, while in bed, Julia said, "You and
Calvin sure had a lot to talk about. What's going on?"

"You're going to find out about it soon enough, so I
might as well tell you. The land that Trusts Enterprise
has been looking to buy, well, we're going to sell it."

Julia curled her body into her husband's. "But you
said the Lord had told you not to sell."

"I'm a man. I can change my mind."

"And y'all want to talk about women."

Samson wasn't in the mood to be intimate with his
wife, so he just held her as she slept. Sleep evaded
him, however, as he thought about something Delilah

said—she accused him of being selfish. A small voice inside confirmed her words. Selling the land to Trusts Enterprise would allow him to keep the life he wanted—a loving wife by his side and a devoted church following.

Chapter 55

Delilah hadn't had a drink since joining Peaceful Rest Missionary Baptist Church a year ago. Now she was sitting in a restaurant with Keisha drinking her third daiquiri. "Girl, he had the nerve to compare me to his holier-than-thou wife, like he was appalled that he ever laid hands on me." She motioned for the waiter.

"Oh no, you need to slow down on those," Keisha said. She turned toward the waiter who was approaching them. "We're fine."

"No, I want another drink," Delilah insisted.

The waiter looked from one to the other because he didn't know whose cues to follow.

Keisha asked, "Do you want to be responsible for her getting in an accident?"

"No, of course not," the waiter replied.

"Then I suggest you not bring her another drink."

After the waiter left the table, Delilah said, "I didn't drive. You did."

"I know, and I'm too cute to be dragging out a slush. If you drink any more double barrel daiquiris, that's exactly what I will be doing."

Delilah raised her glass in the air and moved it from side to side. "I had stopped drinking and now look at me."

Keisha picked up one of her chicken wings and took a bite. "You're wrong, and he was wrong."

"This is payback for my life in the fast lane," Delilah slurred.

"Girl, God doesn't operate like that. If He did, we all would be dead. Now, don't get me wrong, the Bible says you reap what you sow, but this here, what you're going through, you brought on yourself."

Delilah couldn't disagree with her. "Samson made me sound like some whore."

Keisha stopped eating. She looked around the restaurant and then back at Delilah. "What I'm about to say must stay between us, okay?" Delilah shook her head in agreement. Keisha went on to say, "The only reason why I'm telling you this is because I'm tired of you having a pity party."

"That's why you're my best friend." Delilah had a half smile on her face.

"Julia and I used to go to Huntington together. Let's put it like this, she's like that Hurricane Chris song says, 'Loose as a goose.'"

"No, not Ms. Sanctified and Filled With the Holy Ghost Julia." Delilah held her hand up and then placed it on her chest.

"Every boy on the football team hit it, and when we were sixteen she had a baby. She got sent to 'school away from school' and came back to Huntington the following year. Nobody ever knew what happened to the baby. Someone said she lost it, but I heard her cousin tell someone that she had to give the baby up for adoption because she didn't know who the baby's daddy was."

Delilah sobered up as Keisha spilled the gossip on

Julia. Delilah had done some things in her life she wasn't too proud of. She would feel uneasy sometimes when people like Julia and her clique looked down at her because they didn't think she was of their caliber. Learning that Julia had been pregnant at sixteen and didn't know who the baby's daddy was shocked Delilah. Never again would she let Julia turn her nose up at her.

"Thanks for letting me know. If Samson only knew, he wouldn't have married her."

"Oh no, you don't. What I told you is not for you to go run tell Samson. If she wants him to know, let her be the one to share the information with him. Understood?"

"Yes, Keisha." She wouldn't tell Samson, but if Julia stepped to her the wrong way one more time, she wouldn't hesitate telling her a thing or two about herself.

The waiter brought the check. Keisha reached for it, but Delilah snatched it. "I got this. That's the least I can do for you hearing me whine about Samson."

"I'm used to it. My title should be beautician/counselor because I'm telling people how to run their lives and styling their hair all at the price for one. I need to up my prices."

They both laughed as Delilah paid the bill and the two headed out the door. Keisha dropped Delilah off at home. Delilah felt better after talking with Keisha. She fumbled for her keys and made it inside her home just in time to catch her ringing phone.

"Your boy has agreed to meet with me tomorrow. You did it, baby girl. And your bonus will be on hand as soon as he signs those papers."

"William, I'm glad you got what you wanted," Delilah said dryly.

"Cheer up. You can still get your man. Blackmail always works for me," William laughed.

Delilah hung the phone up while William was still laughing in her ear. What Delilah needed now was to talk to Samson. She needed to be assured he was doing okay. She knew they both said some bad things to each other, but they were spoken in the heat of anger. She still loved Samson, and she wanted him to know it. Delilah picked up the phone and dialed Samson's number.

Samson answered, "What do you want?"

"I wanted to apologize for earlier. I understand your frustration, but William threatened to send pictures of me to everyone in the congregation."

"Because of you, I now have to sell the church land."

"Samson, I'm sorry. I really am." Her words were met with a dial tone.

Delilah was tempted to call Samson back but thought twice about it. Samson needed time to cool down, and she would give it to him. Once he did, Delilah knew he would understand why she did what she did—at least that's what she hoped.

Chapter 56

Samson and Calvin sat in the church conference room the following morning. Elaine had been directed to bring William and his attorney to the room when they arrived. "Let me do most of the talking," Calvin told Samson.

"They're right in here," Elaine said as she opened the door.

William wasn't dressed in a flashy suit, nor was he carrying his customary cane. His attorney extended his hand. "Thank you, gentlemen, for meeting with us today."

After the obligatory greetings, Calvin got straight to business. "My client, Peaceful Rest Missionary Baptist Church board, will be meeting to take an official vote. We wanted you to know that although Samson Judges has the right to sign over the land, he cannot do so without the board's approval. Saying all of that, an emergency board meeting has been called." Calvin handed William's attorney a legal document.

William's attorney reviewed it. "This looks to be in order."

William asked, "What is it?"

"This is an intent to sell, pending the board's approval," Calvin answered.

William's attorney's cell phone rang, and he took a

quick look at the display screen. "Gentlemen, I must take this call. I'll be right back."

Once he was out of earshot, William said, "You two aren't trying to pull the okie doke on me, are you?"

Samson looked at Calvin. Calvin shook his head to indicate it was okay to speak. "William, I gave you my word; now I hope you'll keep your word."

Samson and William had a staring match. "What we discussed will stay between us," William assured him.

"Good. Then as soon as your attorney approves the document, we can go on to the next step, right, Calvin?"

"Correct," Calvin nodded.

Less than thirty minutes later, Samson sat alone in the conference room. He held on to one of the copies of the pending sale. "Lord, please forgive me. I know you told me not to sell the land, but I had no choice."

"Good. There you are. Now I don't have to argue with Elaine to let me in to see you," Delilah said as she came in and shut the door.

Samson didn't have the strength to fight Delilah. He let her talk.

"Can you forgive me?" Delilah asked.

"Delilah, it's a done deal. Now if you'll excuse me, I've got things to do so I can get home to my wife." Samson started packing up his stuff so he could leave.

"It's only noon."

"Bye, Delilah."

Delilah blocked the door. "Hear me out first."

Samson looked down in Delilah's face. The desire he once felt for her had dissipated. When he saw her now, he saw doom. He saw the manipulation, the reasons he was selling the land God had told him not to sell. He grabbed hold of Delilah's shoulder.

"Ouch," she said.

"Sorry." He didn't mean to hold her so tight. He released his grip. She moved out of the way. He felt guilty for playing with her emotions just so she wouldn't tell Julia about their affair, so he stayed to listen to her. "You have five minutes," he said.

"I haven't slept since this happened. I need to know where all of this leaves us."

Frustrated, Samson threw his hands up in the air. "There is no us. There will never be an us, so get over it and move on."

Delilah's cheeks turned red. "I've tried to move on. Do you think I like feeling this way about you? Do you think I like spending my nights alone wondering what you and your wife are doing?" She laughed. "You're the reason why I'm like this."

Samson hung his head down and shook it from side to side. "I know I'm going to regret this, but tell me. How am I responsible for your delusional state of mind?"

"Are you calling me crazy?" Delilah asked. Samson looked at her and didn't say a word. "Well are you?" she asked again.

Samson tapped on his watch. "Your time's running out, sweetheart, so I suggest you hurry it up."

Delilah blurted out, "If you hadn't slept with me, then I wouldn't be feeling like this."

"I've never given you any reason to think it was more than what it was—two people comforting each other during a time of need."

Delilah's eyes darkened. "You're a cold-hearted S.O.B. I can't believe I fell in love with you. I might just tell your wife myself."

Samson grabbed Delilah's arms again, and this time he didn't loosen his grip. "If I catch you near my wife, you'll regret it." He pushed her away and watched her stumble.

Samson left the conference room and didn't breathe easily until he reached his office. He looked at the mirror. He didn't like the man staring back at him. His anger had gotten the best of him, and he hoped and prayed that he would not live to regret it.

Chapter 57

Delilah couldn't stop pacing the floor. After the incident at church with Samson, she could not think straight. Keisha was on the other end of the phone trying to calm her down. "I can't believe he grabbed you. Are you sure that's what happened?"

"I wouldn't say it if it wasn't true. I think I was more in shock than anything else."

"Well, don't do anything without thinking things through," Keisha said.

"I should march over to his house and tell Julia all about us."

"Don't do that. It might make you feel better right now, but tomorrow you'll regret it." Keisha attempted to be the voice of reason.

"I would feel better if I hadn't let myself fall in love. He's just like every other man I've met."

"Don't fault the man. You're the one who put him on a pedestal."

"But he's my pastor. He's supposed to do better than the men in the streets."

"Delilah, you're not looking at your part in all of this. You purposely set out to seduce the man. He's a man, not God. All men have their Achilles' heel, and apparently you were his."

Delilah agreed with Keisha on that fact. If she tried, she was sure she could seduce him again. Yes, that's it. She would get him to see that he still wanted her. All she had to do now was get him over to her place.

"Keisha, I've got to go. I need to make a phone call," Delilah said.

"Remember, don't act right now. Let things simmer down."

"Yeah, okay." Delilah ended the call with Keisha and then dialed Samson's number. When he answered, she said, "You owe me for hurting me."

Samson apologized for his actions earlier but didn't agree to come see her. Frustrated, Delilah used her ace in the hole. "Either you come see me or I'll meet you at your house."

Samson used a few curse words, words Delilah didn't know he knew. "I'll take that as an 'I will see you later.'"

"Yes, I'll be there in thirty minutes," Samson responded.

Delilah took a quick shower and sprayed her favorite perfume over her body. She dressed in a long spring halter dress. "Perfect timing," she said when she heard the doorbell ring. "Glad you could make it," she answered the door.

Samson stormed in. "What is it, Delilah? These games need to stop now!"

Delilah didn't waste any time. She threw herself into his arms and started kissing him. As much as he tried to protest at first, Samson took the lead and passionately kissed Delilah back. An hour later, Samson was pushing Delilah off him and looking for his clothes.

Delilah watched with a huge grin on her face. "Now

that we've made up, can we start back up my counseling sessions?"

Samson pulled on his pants and looked at her. "You just don't get it, do you?"

Delilah pulled the cover up over her chest. "As much as you act like you're the one in control, Samson, I'm the one who holds all the chips. See, I have nothing to lose. You, on the other hand, could lose it all."

"I knew I shouldn't have come over here." Samson scrambled and looked around for his keys.

"Payback is something else."

"Vengeance is Mine, said the Lord," Samson said.

"The Lord also said thou shall not commit adultery, but you don't seem to have a problem doing it over and over again, now do you?" Delilah couldn't help but sneer at him.

"You're an evil woman, Delilah. I'm glad I finally see you for what you are." Samson was upset with himself for allowing his flesh to overrule his sound judgment. If he hadn't been messing with Delilah, he would not be in this predicament.

"Oh, baby, you should have thought of that before you put your hands on me."

"I apologized for it earlier," Samson said while standing in the doorway.

"I'm not your wife. She might believe you're all of that, but mister, the veil has been lifted from over my eyes."

"Bye, Delilah. I think it's best you find yourself another church home."

"Oh, I'm not going anywhere. I like Peaceful Rest."

"But—" Samson stuttered.

"Every time you walk through the church doors, just know I'll be sitting right there. I'll be right there watching you and watching your wife. I dare you to try to have me removed because not only will your wife know about us, I'll let the entire congregation know about how their pastor likes to get his freak on."

Samson stormed out of the house, and Delilah plotted her next move.

Chapter 58

"Father God, forgive me for I've sinned against you, my wife, and your people. My lust has set up a chain of events that have spiraled out of control. I need you to direct my steps, oh Lord. I confess I got too cocky. I thought I was untouchable. I thought my years of studying your Word would keep the enemy at bay.

"When the enemy attacked, I fell like an amateur, and I'm supposed to be mature in my walk with you, Lord. Show me where I went wrong so that I will not faint or falter the next time he attempts to attack me."

Samson was in deep prayer and meditation in the den and didn't know Julia was in the room until she touched him, alerting him to her presence. "Baby, I can tell something has been bothering you. If you want to talk, I'm here," Julia assured him.

"I appreciate it, but this is something the Lord has to handle."

"If you're this distraught about selling the church land, then maybe you shouldn't do it."

Samson remained silent while Julia massaged his shoulders. Tension in his body disappeared. "You always seem to know what I need when I need it."

"I'm in tune with my man."

Later on that night, the two discussed the state of

their relationship. "Julia, thank you for sticking by me through the down period."

"I apologize if I made you feel pressured to consummate our marriage, but I wasn't expecting us to have those types of problems so early in our marriage. It made me feel less than a woman," Julia admitted.

"I didn't know that." If Samson hadn't been so wrapped up in his own issues and lusting after Delilah, he would have known how their not being intimate affected his wife. He faulted himself for neglecting her in more ways than one. Samson cradled his wife in his arms as they slept.

Samson enjoyed the peace within his home and at church. As soon as Calvin assured him that the church land had been sold and he had William out of his hair, he would feel a whole lot better.

Calvin had been able to put off William and his attorneys until the board meeting. Less than two weeks after his pastor's anniversary, the board met for an emergency meeting.

Samson gave them the same speech he'd given Calvin two weeks before. "As you can tell from the paper Elaine passed out, we'll get three times more than what the land is worth." Samson made sure he held eye contact with each board member.

"If they want it that bad, ask them for $4 million, and they have a deal," Michael said.

Some of the other board members agreed. Calvin was writing down notes. "I'll make the amendment."

The chairman of the board called for a vote. Seventy-five percent of the board voted to sell the land. After the meeting, Calvin said, "I'll review the papers from

Trusts Enterprise one last time and then get the appropriate signatures. I'm sure as much as they wanted this land, they won't have a problem paying the $4 million."

"That's more than enough to get the community center built," Michael said.

"I agree," Samson said. "Thank you all for supporting it."

One of the elderly deacons said, "Samson, I wasn't too sure about your pastoring us at your young age, but now I see you were the best man for the job. I'm glad I listened to the Holy Spirit and voted you in."

Samson shook his hand. "I'm glad you did too, Papa Ray."

"Do you want me to call William or will you do the honors?" Calvin asked Samson.

"Let me be the one."

Once the room cleared, Samson called William. "The board approved it. Calvin will be bringing over the paperwork next week. You should be happy; you got what you wanted."

"Samson, you did the right thing. One piece of advice before I go—if I were you, I wouldn't worry about Delilah. Concentrate on your wife and let Delilah take care of herself."

Their call ended. Samson wondered if Delilah told him about their last encounter. He had no intentions of sleeping with her again; he only wanted to apologize for manhandling her. Little did he know they would end up in bed together. The tension between them excited him so much it made him block out everything else. He didn't come to his senses until after the fact.

He wanted her to find another church home. It was

selfish, he knew. It would make his life so much easier. William would now be out of his hair; if only he could get Delilah to see that moving her membership would benefit them both, then he would be able to rest. Right now his soul was in turmoil wondering if or when Delilah would try to drop the bombshell about their indiscretions.

Samson didn't like anyone having this much control over his life. Mission: Get Rid of Delilah was in full effect. He stomped one devil and now had to deal with another one—Delilah.

Chapter 59

"If Samson thinks he can get rid of me that easily, he has another thing coming," Delilah said out loud as she rushed to park her car in the church lot.

She eased her way inside the sanctuary. The first Sunday morning service had already started. She had planned to get there earlier, but she hadn't been sleeping well, so when she finally did go to sleep, she didn't hear her alarm clock go off.

Most of the good seats were taken, so she was forced to sit at the back. Delilah knew her being there would be a surprise to Samson. Seeing the smug look on his face as he stood in the pulpit made her want to slap him.

Samson stood behind the podium and swayed from side to side as the minister of music sang the last words of the song "I Shall Wear a Crown."

"God is good," Samson said.

The congregation responded, "Amen."

Samson opened his Bible and had the congregation turn to the sixteenth chapter of Judges. Delilah was more than familiar with the passage. She flipped her Bible to it.

After Samson read several scriptures, he said, "Today, I'm going to preach on, 'Every Man Has a Weakness.' Ushers, you can be seated."

Delilah closed her Bible. She tuned out the chatter around her and gave Samson her undivided attention.

"Some of you are probably wondering why I chose to talk about Samson this morning. Well, children of God, I must be obedient. God told me that some of us are walking around here like we think we're untouchable. Some of us have been in the Word"—Samson held up his Bible—"since Dino was a pup. But guess what? Just because you know the Word, just because you pray every day, just because you come to church every Sunday, it doesn't mean the enemy is not going to attack you. You best believe that joker knows your every weakness."

Delilah listened with interest. The congregation had no idea Samson was really preaching to himself.

"Samson didn't learn from his mistakes," Samson continued. "He kept falling into the same trap that some of us do. We think we can fight this battle by ourselves. But the Bible says what? Put on the whole armor of God each and every day. Don't put it on and then put it back down before the day is over with. When you do that, that's when the enemy can do a sneak attack. Say 'sneak attack.'"

The congregation yelled, "Sneak attack." Delilah remained quiet.

Samson went on to say, "And when the devil does a sneak attack on you, all you can do is fall on your knees"—Samson fell on his knees and looked up toward the high-vaulted ceiling—"and cry out to our Father in heaven." He stood back up. "Don't try to go through this life journey on your own. To fight the good fight, you must keep the armor of the Lord on at all times."

By the end of his sermon, ten new people joined church. Samson, Julia, and the other ministers stood in the receiving line to shake people's hands. Delilah got a thrill out of seeing Samson's face when he noticed her standing in line. She shook Julia's hand, although Julia hesitated.

"You look real lovely today First Lady Judges," Delilah complimented.

"Thank you, Delilah," Julia said with a half smile on her face.

"You preached today, Pastor," Delilah said to Samson, with an emphasis on the word "pastor."

"Why thank you, Delilah."

"For a moment, I thought you were talking about me. I was about to get up and run out of here," Delilah laughed.

Samson laughed, but she could tell he wasn't too thrilled. "Well, sister, I just deliver the Word the way God gives it to me," Samson clarified.

Delilah heard Julia clear her throat. She responded, "I'm holding up the line. I'm so sorry, y'all."

Delilah could really care less, but she wanted to be a dutiful church member. Her bladder was not going to let her make it to her house, so when she left the receiving line, she went straight to the bathroom.

After using the restroom, Delilah turned on the faucet and waited a few minutes for the cold water to turn warm. She hummed a song the choir sang earlier. The door to the bathroom flew open. "Thought you were gone," Julia said as she stood in front of the sink next to Delilah.

"I had to go to the little ladies' room."

"Too bad you don't know much about being a lady," Julia said.

Delilah looked at Julia's reflection in the mirror. She

washed her hands and dried them off. "You know, I could say something, but I won't. But then again, let me leave you with this little tidbit. How would your husband feel if he knew his holier-than-thou wife was a football lover and, oh yeah, a mother too."

"I don't know what you're talking about." Julia's hands shook as she unzipped her purse.

"Well just because you had a baby doesn't make you a mother, so I do stand corrected. Have a good day. Now meditate on that." Delilah rushed out of the bathroom.

Chapter 60

Julia entered Samson's office and looked like she had seen a ghost. "Baby, what's wrong?" Samson asked her. "Everybody, I'll talk to y'all later."

The people gathered in the room left, and Samson got up and closed the door. He put his arm around Julia and led her to the chair. "Do you want some water?"

"No, I'm fine." She looked up into Samson's eyes. "Delilah needs to go."

Samson hoped Delilah didn't go open up her big mouth about them. "What happened?" He sat in the chair beside her and held on to her hand.

"I just don't like her negative spirit. I think she's hindering me from being a better first lady."

"Well, dear, I can't have anything upsetting you."

"So are you going to talk to her?"

"Huh. What?"

"Talk to her. Convince her that it's probably best for her to move her membership."

Samson said, "I can talk to her, but it's probably best one of the other ministers do it. I don't want you getting the wrong idea because you know how you are when it comes to Delilah."

"I'm confident in our marriage. I trust you wholeheartedly to not jeopardize it with the likes of her," Julia assured him.

"Since you insist, I'll have Elaine schedule a meeting with her for later on this week."

Julia let out a deep breath. "Thank you, baby."

Samson thought it was odd that Julia wanted him to confront Delilah all of a sudden. He wondered what had transpired. The only way he would know would be to ask Delilah because Julia didn't seem too eager to divulge any information.

The next day, Samson had Elaine contact Delilah. Before the end of the day he planned to be rid of her for once and for all. He smiled at the thought of being Delilah free.

"A penny for your thoughts," Julia said as she entered the office.

"Give me a dollar and I'll think about telling you." Samson stood up and greeted her with a kiss on the lips.

"I thought I would surprise you with lunch. I took half a day off."

He wrapped his arms around her waist. "So you're trying to prepare them for when you leave permanently."

"Yes, but you know I have to make them think they still need me in the meantime. Don't want them getting rid of me before I quit on them."

"Nobody would ever fire you. You're the best thing since Gates created Windows."

"Oh, you got jokes."

Samson released her and picked up a brochure off his desk. "I was going to surprise you at home later. I was thinking about using some of the money I got from my pastor's anniversary and treating us to a trip to Hawaii.

Julia jumped up and down. "You know I've always wanted to go to Maui." She took the brochure and hugged him. "When do we leave?"

"I haven't made the reservations yet. I wanted to talk it over with you first." Samson loved seeing her excited.

"Stop talking and start dialing." Julia picked up the phone receiver and handed it to him.

Thirty minutes later, they were looking at a printout of their itinerary for their Hawaiian trip.

"Michelle's going to be jealous," Julia surmised. "We were just talking the other day about places we both wanted to go. I can't wait to tell her."

Julia kissed Samson on the cheek. Julia was so excited when she left Samson's office. He overheard her tell Elaine about their upcoming trip. He smiled. Now if only the rest of his day could go like his morning. He spent the afternoon responding to e-mails and reading. Elaine buzzed him over the intercom. "Your two o'clock is here."

"Send her in," he responded.

"Keisha, thank you for stopping by. I understand you're a busy woman, so I won't keep you long," Samson said.

"Pastor Judges, no problem."

"Would you like something to drink? Soda? Bottled water?" Samson asked from behind his desk.

"No, I'm fine." Keisha sat in the chair across from his desk.

"Keisha, I might as well get straight to the point. You know Delilah better than anyone, and as her friend I know you want the best for her. It's in my humble opinion that she needs to find herself another church home. You seem to be a good Christian lady, so I was hoping you could convince her to move her membership. Maybe even to your church."

When he finished, Keisha said: "No disrespect, Pastor Judges, but Delilah's told me all about you. I actually agree with you because she's not going to be able to spiritually grow under your leadership."

Samson couldn't believe his leadership abilities were being questioned. "So will you talk to Delilah or not?"

"Delilah's a grown woman, and she's going to do what she wants to do, so no. I'm not even going to waste my breath talking to her about it."

"It's in Delilah's best interest that you do." Samson tried to keep his voice at an even keel.

Keisha moved to the edge of her seat. "That's not a threat is it?"

"No, of course not," Samson stuttered. Samson's plan to have Keisha assist him in getting rid of Delilah had backfired. He hoped he hadn't made the situation worse.

Chapter 61

"Pastor, I tried to stop her," Elaine said, on the heels of Delilah.

"Keisha, I've been trying to call you."

Keisha twisted around in her seat. "You've found me," Keisha responded.

"In my pastor's study nevertheless. So tell me, what's going on here?"

Samson said, "Elaine, I got this. You can go back to your desk."

Elaine stood for a few more seconds before leaving. "And close the door behind you."

"Your pastor and I were discussing you and how important you were to both of us," Keisha said.

"Is that true, Samson?" Delilah asked. Delilah, at this point, was the only one standing.

"Something told me to drop by early; now I'm glad I did. Are you trying to push up on my friend?"

"Girl, please. Don't nobody want him," Keisha frowned.

"Ladies, can you hold it down?" Samson interrupted.

Keisha and Delilah both turned and looked at Samson. The look on their faces said it all. He remained quiet.

"Samson, we'll be right back," Delilah said. Delilah and Keisha left the room, and as they passed Elaine's desk, she said to Keisha, "Come on. That heifer there is nosy."

Keisha followed Delilah to the bathroom. Delilah didn't waste any time getting straight to the point. "Spit it out," Delilah demanded once they were totally alone.

"He called me because he wanted me to ask you to change your church membership."

"I'm going to tell you like I told him. I'm not going anywhere until I'm good and ready."

Keisha attempted to calm her down. "Delilah, look at you." Keisha used her hands to turn her toward the mirror. "Do you really like the woman you see looking back at you?"

Delilah couldn't deny it. Instead of her drawing closer to God, it seemed as if she was in a maze of confusion. Her entire life seemed to be spiraling out of control. William had given her enough money to quit her job and get her mind right for a minute, but it didn't bring any form of happiness. She was miserable, and her soul felt heavy.

Delilah started crying. "What am I supposed to do? Samson used me. He needs to pay for what he did to me."

Keisha patted her on the back. "He didn't use you. You knew the score going in. So many of my clients cry the same tune, but when you mess with a man that's already in a relationship, you can't be surprised if you get burned."

"But—" Delilah protested. "But he didn't have to sleep with me."

"No, he didn't, but you didn't have to offer it to him either. Come on. Pull yourself together and let's go."

"You go ahead. I'll call you later."

"You sure? Because I can have one of the other stylists take care of my appointments."

"Keisha, thanks for being a good friend, but I'm okay."

Keisha left Delilah alone in the bathroom. With all of the excitement, Delilah had left her purse in Samson's office near his desk. She wiped her face. She was calm when she returned to his office. Samson's back was toward her. He was looking out the window. "Where's your gatekeeper?" Delilah asked.

"Elaine's somewhere around here."

"Oh. Keisha told me what you two were talking about. You hate me that much that you want me to leave?"

Samson turned around. "Delilah, I don't hate you. You're not one of my favorite persons right now, but I don't hate you."

"I really do like Peaceful Rest. This has become my second home. I don't know how I'll fit in somewhere else."

"Be honest. The only reason you're here is because of me. I'm just a man, Delilah. A man who unfortunately got caught up in the flesh, and I do not want to hinder your walk any more. I'm already having to pay for what I've done. Move not just for my sake, but for yours."

Samson's phone rang. He answered it. He scrambled to get the phone off speaker but couldn't. Julia's voice echoed through the room. "Did you convince her to leave?"

Samson finally got the speaker off.

Upset, Delilah blurted out, "Tell her that would be a negative."

Delilah patted her feet as she waited for him to end his call with Julia. "I get it. You want me to leave because the wifey wants it. Well, you and she both can look at my face every Wednesday night and Sunday morning until I get good and ready to leave."

"Let's pray," Samson said, reaching for her hand.

He caught her off guard. Delilah responded, "I'll pray when I get home because right now I don't think your prayers will get through."

Chapter 62

Samson felt like he would have been able to convince Delilah to move her membership if only Julia hadn't called and interrupted them.

"What can we do to get rid of her? She's like a thorn in my side," Julia said that night over dinner.

"She's not bad," Samson said, avoiding eye contact with Julia.

"Humph. You just don't know." Julia threw her fork down on her plate.

Samson felt something else was going on, and Julia just wasn't telling him. "Enlighten me."

"Everybody knows she doesn't like me. She practically kisses the bottom of your feet. The list goes on and on."

"Sweetheart, we've talked about this before. You can't let the spirit of jealousy cloud your judgment."

"Samson, I know you're a preacher, but you and I both know jealousy has nothing to do with why I don't like Delilah. That woman wants my husband. I'm supposed to sit back and pretend like I don't know it? Enough is enough."

Julia finished eating her food and left Samson at the table alone to ponder his thoughts. He no longer had an appetite, so he ended up throwing the remainder of the food in the garbage disposal.

The following morning, Samson decided to stop by his parents' house before going to the church. His mom greeted him with a kiss. "The prodigal son has come home, Regis," Kelly said.

"Stop teasing the boy before he turns around and leaves," Regis replied.

Samson missed his mom's home cooking. She prepared a breakfast for him and filled his plate with his favorites. His spirit was more at ease as he relaxed with them around the dining room table.

"If I'd known you were coming, I would have told the fellows I wouldn't be able to make the golf course today," Regis stated.

"Dad, don't let me stop you. We'll talk later," Samson replied.

"You sure everything is okay? You've been heavily on my mind, but the Spirit told me to wait and let you come to me."

"Dad, I'm fine."

"Kelly, don't interrogate him too much when I leave," Regis said before leaving the room.

"That man knows me too well," Kelly laughed.

Samson would have laughed along with her, but he knew as soon as his dad was out of earshot he would be badgered with questions. "Mom, don't even start."

Kelly ignored his request. "Your wife wants Delilah gone, and you should respect her wishes."

"Since you're all up in my business, did Julia tell you that she refuses to leave? I've asked her to move her membership. What else do you want me to do?"

"Something else is going on and, son, you need to tell me what it is right now," Kelly insisted.

"There's nothing going on." Samson did his best to say it with a straight face. He was lying, and his mother knew it, although she didn't let on any. An hour later, Samson left and went for a long ride.

"Look who finally decided to stroll in," Elaine said when Samson showed up at church after noon.

"Hello to you too, Elaine. Did I get any calls?"

"You sure did. Your wife called and so did you-know-who."

"Well, whatever you do, please don't put any of Delilah's calls through."

"I would say I told you so, but that wouldn't be the Christian thing to say, so I'll just keep my mouth shut."

Samson went into his office and called Julia. He spoke with her for a few minutes. Next, he logged on to his computer. He responded to e-mails from people in various parts of the world. He had made friends with other ministers while taking missionary journeys, and some people were contacting him because they watched his sermons on the Internet. Samson felt blessed to be able to share God's Word with so many people.

His inbox was filled with Facebook messages. He tried to respond to them all by clicking on the links. Delilah had sent him several. He clicked on those as well. In the first few e-mails, she was apologetic, but her messages started getting harsher and harsher. Instead of deleting the messages, he decided to save them just in case he needed them for evidence later. He dialed Calvin's number. "Man, I hate to bother you, but I have a little situation."

"What do you need, Pastor?" Calvin asked.

"This must stay confidential," Samson said.

"It won't go any further than the phone," Calvin assured him.

Samson paused and took a deep breath before saying, "It's Delilah. She's harassing me."

Calvin waited for Samson to give him details. "What do you need me to do?"

Samson responded, "I want to get a restraining order, one where she can't come anywhere near me or the church."

"Are you sure you want me to do it because I can have it done today?"

Samson should have felt guilty about embellishing Delilah's actions, but he didn't. "The sooner, the better," Samson responded.

Chapter 63

Delilah spent most of the week filling out job applications. Although William begged her to stay at Trusts Enterprise, Delilah had given him her written resignation. In return, he gave her a nice nest egg to tide her over until another job came along. She wanted to repair her relationship with God, and cutting ties with William and his company was one way to start.

It was a beautiful Friday morning, so she gathered up her laptop and decided to sit on her porch to surf the Internet for a job. An unfamiliar car pulled up in front of her house. A man dressed in a police uniform strode up her walkway. She immediately put her laptop down on the side and stood up. "May I help you?"

"Are you Delilah Baker?" he asked.

"Yes," she responded.

The man handed her a sheet of paper. "You've been served."

Delilah looked down at the paper. "What in the world? What's this?"

"Ma'am, the information is on the paper."

Delilah read the paper, and before she finished, the process server was back in his car. "Ain't this a blip?" Delilah retrieved her cell phone from her purse and called Keisha. "You're never going to believe this. Samson has filed a restraining order against me and has banned me from coming to the church."

Even Keisha was caught off guard. "Delilah, I don't know what to tell you. Leave them people alone. You're always welcome to come to my church."

"It's that wife of his. I bet she's behind this."

"Now, Delilah, don't go doing anything crazy."

"Oh, he ain't seen crazy yet." Delilah ended the call with Keisha. She could no longer concentrate on looking for a new job. She picked up the laptop and the paper she had just gotten from the process server and went into her house.

Later that evening, Delilah drove by the church. She saw Samson's car in the parking lot and kept driving. She drove to his house. Julia's car was parked outside. Delilah laughed out loud at the thought of how Samson had tried to outsmart her but failed. The restraining order required Delilah to stay clear of the church, but Julia's name wasn't mentioned in the document.

Delilah pulled off her sunshades and placed them on the dashboard. She exited her car like a woman on a mission. She rang the doorbell and waited, purposely turning her back toward the peephole.

"May I help you?" Julia answered the door.

Delilah slowly turned around. "Me and you have something to talk about."

"You're not supposed to be here." Julia blocked the entranceway.

"I already know Samson's not here. I saw his SUV at the church."

"Well, he'll be here any minute. I just got off the phone with him."

"Then it's to your advantage that we hurry up and talk."

"Delilah, I don't have all day to play with you."

"Oh, you think this is a game. Whose idea was it to put a restraining order out against me?"

Julia smiled. She folded up her arms. "It was my baby's. I wished I would have come up with the idea though, and we would have been rid of you long before now."

"Go ahead and smile now, but don't forget that I know a little secret, a secret neither one of you would want to get out."

Delilah turned to walk away. "Wait!" Julia said.

Smiling, Delilah turned back around. "So can I come in? These heels weren't meant for standing."

Julia moved from the entranceway and Delilah walked in. She followed Julia to the kitchen. "I was cooking. You talk. I'll cook."

Delilah sat down and watched what could have easily been a good friend, but Julia had determined the state of their relationship the moment she told Samson she would marry him. "What happened to the baby you had when you were sixteen?" Delilah asked.

"Frankly, it's none of your business."

Delilah crossed her arms and leaned back in her chair. "Does Samson know about this baby? I can wait around, and we can tell him together," Delilah threatened.

"If it'll get you out of here, fine. I'll tell you."

"I knew we could work together."

In a monotone voice, Julia explained her past. "I was too young. My parents thought it was best."

"You've been selfish all your life. Just like your husband."

Julia slammed the oven mitt down on the counter. "Don't go judging me."

"I'm not like you, Julia. I never judged you in the sense that you judged me. You and your buddies always tried to make me feel inferior, like you were all that and here I was a measly sinner without hope for redemption. But thank Jesus I know about His grace and mercy and that in His eyes we've all sinned and fallen short."

"Now that you've had your come-to-Jesus moment, you can leave." Julia put back on the oven mitt and removed a pan covered with foil from the oven.

"I wonder what would happen if you accidentally burned yourself."

Julia looked at Delilah. Delilah laughed. "You're crazy, you know that."

"No, Julia. You haven't seen crazy yet." Delilah winked her eye. She stood up and said before leaving, "Tell your husband I stopped by. And your secret"—she paused—"it's safe with me—for now."

Chapter 64

Samson sped home after getting Julia's frantic call. He called Calvin while on the way. "She showed up at my house, man. I thought the restraining order was supposed to cover that."

"It does. If she stops by again, you or Julia need to call the police."

"Samson, man, you can tell me. You hit it again, didn't you? And it's been since you and Julia were married?"

"Man, you know me better than that." Samson would never confess to sleeping with Delilah since marrying Julia to anyone.

"Well, whatever it is, Baby Girl has some serious issues."

Samson dodged Calvin's questions and then headed home. Julia fell into his arms as soon as he walked through the door. "I'm scared, Samson. What if she comes back with a gun or something?" Julia asked.

Samson thought Julia was being overly dramatic, but he appeased her. "Calvin assured me that if she stops by again, we should call the police and let them handle her."

Later that night while Julia was sleeping, Samson slipped out of bed and went down to his study. He called Delilah. "This thing is between us; leave my wife out of it."

Delilah responded, "There's something you don't know about your holier-than-thou wife. You thought you picked the right woman, but think again. Check your e-mail."

Delilah hung up on him. Curious to see what Delilah meant, Samson logged on to his home computer. He searched for an e-mail from Delilah. "Bingo," he said. He clicked on Delilah's e-mail. It read: "You think you know your wife. Ask her about the child she had when she was sixteen years old. Ask her if she knows her baby girl ended up being placed in a foster home just like me because her adoptive parents were killed in a car accident. You and I both know what can happen to a young girl in foster care." Samson scrolled down and saw a picture of a teenager who looked just like Julia.

Samson couldn't believe Julia had been carrying around that secret. They were not to have secrets between them. Here he was feeling guilty about Delilah, yet the wife he thought he knew was not who Samson thought she was. Samson didn't have any kids, and he thought that Julia didn't either. Snapshots of the birth certificate and adoption papers stared back at him on the screen. He continued to scroll down.

Delilah wrote: "Do you want to know why the name of the father says unknown? Well, the woman you thought was so pure used to be the 'go-to' woman for the entire football team, if you can read between the lines." Delilah followed up her comment with a smiley face.

If what Delilah had revealed in the e-mail was true, Samson didn't know Julia like he thought he did. His mind was on overload. He couldn't compute everything disclosed in the e-mail. He laid his head on the desk, and that was the way Julia found him the next morning.

"Baby, how long have you been up?" Julia asked.

Samson lifted his head. His eyes were bloodshot. "I slept down here."

"You and that computer again. That Bejeweled game will get you hooked."

Samson didn't know where to begin, his sweet, innocent Julia. "I want you to see something." He moved the computer monitor so that Julia could see the screen.

If Samson hadn't caught her, Julia would have hit the floor. Julia got her balance. "I never meant for you to find out about it like this." Tears started flowing down Julia's face. "I'm so sorry. I should have told you," Julia said over and over.

"Why didn't you?" Samson asked.

"Because it was a part of my life I was trying to forget. I didn't want to give up my baby girl, but my parents wouldn't hear anything else about it. It was either give her away or be kicked out. They didn't want me disgracing the Rivers name."

"But didn't everybody know you were pregnant?"

"No, because they sent me to my grandparents' house in the country."

"Still, this wasn't the sixties. There were plenty of sixteen-year-olds having kids."

"I didn't tell you because I closed that chapter of my life." Julia's demeanor changed. Filled with rage, she said, "I should have known she was going to tell you."

"So you knew Delilah knew?"

Julia hung her head down low. "Yes. That's another reason why I wanted her kicked out of the church. Samson, will you ever forgive me?"

He embraced Julia. "You know I love you, but this is a lot to take in."

"I know, and I promise to never keep a secret from you again."

Samson felt like a hypocrite. Julia wasn't the only one with secrets.

Chapter 65

Delilah should have felt some type of relief from exposing Julia, but she didn't. Maybe if she could see Samson's expression when he read her e-mail she would have felt better, but since she wasn't privileged to know what transpired after the revelation she was left feeling a void.

Delilah logged on to her e-mail account to see if Samson had responded. The e-mail she thought was from Samson was actually from Julia. The message contained vile words. In her message, Julia called Delilah every name but a child of God. All of a sudden, Delilah started feeling better. With Julia's attitude, the guilt Delilah felt for exposing her disappeared.

Someone was outside Delilah's door banging on it real hard. "Who is that banging on my door?" Delilah yelled. She needed to put a sign up alerting people that her doorbell did work, if only they would use it. "What?" she asked as she opened the door.

She stared into the bloodshot eyes of Julia. No words were exchanged. She held the door open wider, and Julia walked in. Delilah looked behind Julia to see if she was alone. She closed the door behind her as they now stood face-to-face.

"I take it Samson read the e-mail," Delilah said with a smug look on her face.

"You had no right doing what you did," Julia yelled.

"This is a free country, so I can do whatever I please."

"How did you get that information?"

"Let's just say for twenty-nine dollars and ninety-five cents, you can find out a lot of information on people."

"Have you seen my daughter? Tell me. How did you get the picture?"

"Calm down. One question at a time. No, I've never met her, but because I was able to look up what school she last attended, I pulled the picture from their yearbook website."

"Resourceful aren't you?"

"I can be." Delilah tapped her foot.

"Do you hate me that much that you had to go dig up information on me?" Julia asked with disbelief on her face.

"Hate is such a strong word. Let's just say you're not one of my most favorite people in the world." Delilah laughed.

"This is my life. This is not a game. You're messing with my life," Julia yelled.

"The moment you and your friends decided to try to ruin my name at Peaceful Rest is the day we became enemies."

"Oh, you're smiling now, but don't think you're going to get away with it."

Delilah put one hand on her hips. She held out her other hand. "Look at me. I'm scared now."

"Oh, you don't have to be scared of me. God fights my battles for me."

Delilah rested her arm to her side. "I'm a child of God too, and I'm sick and tired of people like you trying to make me feel like I'm not."

"Good thing God pities fools because you're one of the biggest ones if you actually think you can have my husband."

Delilah was tempted to tell her that she'd had her husband several times but kept her mouth shut. Instead she said, "You like to look down your nose at me as if I'm not worthy to be in your presence, when you're the one not worthy to be in mine."

"Delilah, you got it all twisted."

"No, I don't think so. I know all about your open-door policy when you were in high school. Your parents might have let you keep the baby if you had known who the baby's daddy was."

"How dare you judge me? You can't judge me."

"Oh, now you got a problem with judging. I'm just speaking the truth. The truth shall set you free—or send you to divorce court." Delilah couldn't help but chuckle.

"You're spiteful and mean. I hate the day you walked through the doors of Peaceful Rest."

Delilah had had enough of Julia's rant. "You need to be at home talking to your husband about your bastard child."

"How dare you?" Julia reached her hand out to slap Delilah.

Delilah caught her arm before she could make contact and held it. "I suggest you leave before I forget that I'm saved. Yes, I'm saved, sanctified and filled with the Holy Ghost, but no, I'm not perfect, and now, Miss Thing, Samson knows neither are you."

Julia jerked her arm away. "I'm leaving, but I'm going to say this: You want my husband so bad that you tried to ruin me by revealing a part of my past that I long buried. But guess what? It didn't work. Samson and I are together, and we're going to remain together in spite of anything you can do."

"Are you sure about that?" Delilah asked. She crossed her arms.

"Positive. Stay away from Samson and please stay away from me."

Julia practically ran out of Delilah's house. Delilah's blood pressure skyrocketed. Sweat poured out of her pores as she paced the floor trying to decide her next move.

Chapter 66

Samson flipped the stations on the television. He wasn't really paying attention; he just needed a distraction from the feelings of despair that had him in a depressed state of mind. Julia had lied to him. Having a child and putting her up for adoption was not something a wife should withhold from her husband.

He was glad when Julia stormed out. He couldn't stand to look at her as she spurted out words of hate about Delilah. Not once did Julia take ownership. Yes, she said she was sorry, but sorry for what? Sorry he found out about her secret child? Sorry he found out about her past? Sorry she pretended to be one way but was in fact another? Was she any better than Delilah?

Those thoughts and more spun around in Samson's head. He didn't know how long he had been sitting there staring at the TV screen. He heard the door slam. Julia walked in the room. She appeared to be more upset now than when she had left. "I just got back from Delilah's house, and I want to know one thing."

Samson didn't like her attitude. He responded with an attitude of his own. "What?"

"Are you having an affair with that woman?"

Samson thought for a quick second. Since he wasn't technically having an affair with Delilah, he could answer her honestly. He responded, "No."

"That's all I need to know. I'll be in the bedroom when you're ready to talk," she said. She stood and waited a few seconds.

Samson didn't say a word. He watched her leave the room. He should have said something, but he was still angry at her. He knew he didn't have a right, especially after the secret he had been carrying around about Delilah. The house phone began to ring off the hook. If Julia weren't going to answer, neither was he. He didn't want to talk with anyone at this point. He needed some clarity to his situation, and he went to the only source that would give it to him.

Samson left the den and went into his study. He left the light off, and with the blinds closed it was dark in the room. Samson kneeled down near his desk.

"Lord, I come to you, meek and humble as I know how. I ask you, Father, to lead me and guide me so I will make the right choice as I deal with Julia's news. Father God, I ask that you watch over and protect the innocent child brought into this world. Lord, please forgive Delilah, for she has no idea that she's being used by the enemy to destroy your people.

"Lord, please don't forsake me. Without you, oh Lord, I don't know what I'll do. I know I have no right judging my wife for keeping secrets when I've been keeping one myself. Please soften my heart, so I can still see the woman you purposely sent across my path."

Samson didn't know how long he was on his knees praying, but when he finished he felt like the world had been lifted off his shoulder. He headed to his bedroom to speak with Julia. He paused outside the door when he heard Julia discussing with someone on the phone the information he'd just found out. Samson felt like he was the last person to know that Julia's child existed.

Despite his long, sincere prayer, it was obvious Samson still needed to work out his feelings about Julia's secret child. He decided not to interrupt her phone call and headed back down the stairs.

Samson needed to speak with a voice of reason, so he called his father. After their usual pleasantries, Samson told his father about his discovery, leaving out the fact that Delilah sent the information.

"Son, you need to talk to your wife. This is something she probably hid from herself. You say it happened when she was sixteen, right?"

"Yes, sir."

"That was her past. You can't hold it against her."

"But she lied to me. I never expected it from her."

"She didn't lie to you. She omitted the information," Kelly said.

"Mom, I didn't know you were on the line."

"I just got off the phone with your wife. She told me everything. Son, you need to march to your bedroom and make things right. Right now."

Regis interjected, "Kelly, maybe we should stay out of it."

"No such thing. Samson's my only son, and I am not going to let him ruin his life over his ego."

"Son, we'll talk to you later," Regis interjected.

Samson heard his father take the phone from Kelly, and the call was dropped.

Was his ego stopping him from accepting the fact that Julia made a mistake? Like him, she too was not perfect. They were two imperfect people with secrets between them—but only one of their secrets had been exposed.

Chapter 67

Delilah became obsessed with checking her e-mail. After Julia left, she called Samson, but he wouldn't answer. She logged on to her computer and sent him a few e-mails, but still no response.

She logged on to her Facebook account. *Ding*, the computer sounded, alerting her to which of her Facebook friends were online. "You can't avoid me now," Delilah said out loud when she scanned the list and saw RevSamJudges highlighted. Delilah typed a message then clicked on the send button. She waited at least five minutes, but Samson never responded.

Delilah thought that maybe he was away from his computer. "There's one way to find out."

Delilah left a message on his Facebook wall. She typed: "Hi. Just checking on you."

Delilah was about to log off Facebook when she received an e-mail alerting her to a new message. She clicked on the link, and it took her straight to Samson's wall. RevSamJudges' message read, "Stop messaging me."

Delilah felt like Samson was putting her on a public display. Since he wanted to go there with her, she would let it all hang out. She typed as she spoke out loud. "You didn't say stop last week when you were in my bed."

A few seconds later, she got a response from Samson. "That was a mistake."

Delilah couldn't be sure, but it dawned on her that Samson probably didn't realize their wall messages could be seen by other people. The things he said to publicly humiliate her infuriated her so much that she didn't hesitate to put their business on display.

"Since you and your wife were playing confessions, did you confess about us?"

"There is no us." Samson ended his remarks with several exclamation points.

"Let's see. We've slept together how many times since you said I do?"

"It was just sex, so get over it. Go find another man to harass."

"I'm way over it. You're not worth my time."

"Good, so now maybe you'll move on and leave me and my wife alone."

Delilah was fuming mad. She typed, "Consider yourself forgotten."

She wasn't sure if he saw her last message because according to her online alert, Samson had signed off.

Delilah leaned back in her chair and smiled. If they weren't on bad terms, Delilah would have called Samson and advised him to delete the log of their conversation from his Facebook wall. Now, thanks to Samson's not paying attention to where he posted his messages to Delilah, the world would know about their affair. Samson had no one else to blame but himself.

Delilah's e-mail started filling up with messages from Peaceful Rest church members and some people she had never heard of telling her off. She responded to all of them by simply cutting and pasting the words, "Mind your own business."

Let's see Samson talk his way out of this, she thought

Delilah's phone rang. She saw Calvin and Michelle's number on the caller ID. "Hello."

Michelle blurted out, "I knew you were no good. Stay away from Peaceful Rest. We don't want you there anymore."

"Your husband hasn't told you? I won't be coming back anyway. I got kicked out." Delilah hung the phone up. She would let Michelle wonder about her husband. Delilah's phone rang off the hook from various members. Most she had never spoken to before. She had no idea that news of her and Samson's affair would go viral on the Internet and cause such a ruckus. She couldn't believe that some people were blaming her—and her alone—for the affair.

Delilah laughed out loud because she could picture Julia dropping the bourgeois act and going straight hood on Samson. Yes, life in the Judges house would be filled with drama on this day.

A couple of hours later, Delilah was enjoying a Lifetime movie when she received a call from Keisha. "You know you ain't right, don't you?" Keisha said.

"What? I didn't do anything," she said, faking innocence.

"Girl, everybody—and I do mean everybody—who's come in this shop has been talking about this preacher and this woman having an affair and it being exposed on Facebook. I had no idea it was you until one of my clients told me who the preacher was. I almost dropped the curling iron on her."

"Don't blame me if she would have kicked your behind."

"How did this get on Facebook?" Keisha asked.

Delilah gave her blow-by-blow details of what had
transpired in the last twenty-four hours. "Samson put
it out there. I was just responding to his messages. I
didn't realize everybody would see them until I started
getting all of these calls," she lied.

"You a hot mess. I know we're not Catholic, but you
better be saying some Hail Marys along with them
prayers."

"Oops, somebody's at the door. Got to go," Delilah
lied and ended the call.

Keisha was right. She had a lot to atone for. She could
no longer blame her actions on William. She alone was
the guilty party. Revenge filled her spirit and tarnished
her soul.

Chapter 68

Samson had been giving Julia the cold shoulder most of the day. He had planned on letting her know he understood why she didn't tell him about her daughter, but the exchange with Delilah had put him in a foul mood.

His phone had been ringing off the hook all day, but he allowed all of the calls to go to voice mail. Today he decided to take a mental break from everything. Samson picked up the television remote and watched ESPN. Eventually, he dozed off. Julia's screaming voice woke him out of his light sleep.

"How could you?" Julia shouted as tears streamed down her face.

It took him a moment to register where he was. "Baby, what?" he said as he woke up.

In a calm voice, Julia said: "I've been praying to God most of the day, asking Him to soften your heart to forgive me from keeping that secret from you." The volume in her voice increased as the tears returned. "I feel like the biggest fool."

"Julia, I don't know what you're talking about."

"Delilah." Julia stormed away.

Samson jumped off the couch and went after Julia. "I don't know what she told you, but she's lying."

He followed Julia to the computer. "I didn't want

to believe it when my soror called me, so I decided to check for myself. Here it is for the whole world to see."

She rotated the computer screen, and Samson was at a loss for words. He thought the conversation with Delilah was private. He had no idea he'd hit the wrong button on Facebook. "Baby, I'm sorry."

Julia used her arms and wiped his desk, and everything in her arms' path hit the floor. "You told me I was paranoid for thinking something was going on between you two. You chastised me for checking your phone." She started beating him on his chest. He felt like he deserved it. He didn't stop her. She ranted. "Something in my gut told me you were sleeping with her, but I just didn't want to believe it. No, not my Samson. Not the man who promised to love and be faithful to me. Not the man who has been ignoring me all day."

Samson stood and took the beating to his chest. Julia got tired of hitting him and collapsed in his arms. He held her. When she stopped crying, she pushed him away. "I would tell you to get out, but this is your house, so I'm leaving."

"Julia, don't leave me. We can work through this."

"Once a cheater, always a cheater. I'm not going to be like my aunt. She stayed with a habitual cheater, and by the time she decided to do something about it, guess what? She'd contracted HIV and eventually died. No, that's not going to be me." Julia left Samson standing there and headed to the bedroom.

Samson followed her. Every time Julia would reach for a suitcase, he would move it. "Fine," she said. She grabbed a few items and put them in a duffel bag. She grabbed her purse and duffel bag and headed for the stairs.

"Julia, you're still my wife, and you're not going any-where," Samson said.

Julia removed her wedding ring and threw it at him. "This belongs to you. I'll be back later to get the rest of my stuff."

"Julia!" Samson called her name several times as she walked out of the house. He followed her outside. Some of the neighbors were outside. "Please don't go," he begged.

Julia threw her stuff in the car and got in. She rolled down her window after starting the engine. "I suggest you move or your feet will be run over." She laughed. "Then again, stay right there."

She revved the engine. Samson jumped back as she put the car in reverse and pulled out quickly. She was inches away from running over his foot. That pain would have been better than the ache Samson felt in his soul.

He dragged himself back in the house. The phone was ringing. He rushed to answer it.

"I've been trying to reach you all day. Open the door."

"Mama, now is not a good time."

"Samson, we're pulling up right now, so open the door." The tone in his mother's voice let him know that she was not to be played with.

Samson went to the door and let his parents in the house. They whisked past him without saying a word and went straight to his living room. He followed them. The look on his parents' faces let him know they had heard about the Facebook mishap. They were now seat-ed across from one another in the living room. "Son, we're very disappointed in you," Regis said.

Samson had never heard his father say those words to him. It cut him deep.

"You're a disgrace, and I'm ashamed to call you my son," Kelly added.

"Dear, we agreed to be easy on him," Regis said in Samson's defense.

"I warned him about Delilah. I knew she was trouble the first time I met her. But no, he didn't want to listen to me." Kelly's face turned beat red. "Now you've disgraced your family and, worst of all, you've disgraced your church."

Samson covered his face with his hands and cried. Neither his father nor mother tried to comfort him. Samson felt truly alone for the first time in all his years of living. "I'm so sorry."

Samson didn't know how long he sat there in his own misery. His father touched him on the shoulder. "We're going to give you some time to yourself. Pull yourself together. Tomorrow you must come clean with the congregation and pray that they forgive you."

"Mama," Samson cried out.

Kelly stood behind her husband. Without uttering a word, she held up her hand and followed Regis out the door.

Samson stared at the closed door as if in a trance. With a heavy heart, he laid down on the couch. Every time he closed his eyes, he could see the pain etched on Julia's face. The phone rang bringing him out of his stupor. He hoped it was Julia but was disappointed when he heard Calvin's voice on the other end. Calvin informed him of Julia's whereabouts. "If you wouldn't have lied to me about Delilah, I could have done damage control. People want you to resign. I have to admit, I don't blame them."

"I just got caught up."

"You were the man. I wondered how you could resist temptation in an area many of us men fail in. Little did I know you weren't resisting; you were a willing participant."

"Can you ask Julia to come to church tomorrow?"

"I'll see what I can do."

"I owe you all a public apology." Samson's voice drifted off.

"We're supposed to be boys. I asked you if you were sleeping with her, but you told me no. I would have helped you deal with Delilah."

"I just couldn't. Marriage is sacred, and I didn't want you to know I didn't keep my marriage vows."

"Well, I'm the last one you need to worry about. You have a woman in there whose heart is broken in two because of what you've done."

"If it takes me a lifetime to make it up to her—I will."

"Good luck," Calvin responded before ending the call.

It hurt Samson to know that Calvin was disappointed in him. He'd let everyone down. Samson prayed he didn't feel the full wrath of God.

Chapter 69

The aroma of revenge in the air didn't have a sweet smell. Delilah's phone wouldn't stop ringing, and she got tired of telling people off. She decided to let the rest of the incoming calls go to voice mail. Soon people wouldn't be able to leave messages because her inbox would be full.

As much as Delilah tried to relax, her mind wouldn't allow her to. Feeling remorseful, she did something she should have done prior to exposing Samson on Facebook—she fell down on her knees and prayed.

"My love for Samson overruled my senses, and I wanted him by any means necessary. I've destroyed a marriage because of my selfishness. I thought Samson would come running to me when both his and his wife's sins were exposed. It just recently dawned on me that nothing good will come out of spitefulness. Lord, help me to come to terms with the things that I have done.

"Lord, I need you to purge the old me and renew my soul. I tried it my way, and I ended up back in a dark place. This time, Father, I'm willing to do it your way. I promise to change my ways so that people can see Christ in me. I'm praying for your grace and mercy for the times that I've purposely set out to hurt your children. I pray that they will soon find it in their hearts to forgive me."

Tears were streaming down Delilah's face as she prayed a sincere prayer. The burden had been lifted from her shoulders. She stood up straight, and for the first time all day she had an appetite.

Keisha called her while she was fixing herself something to eat. "You sound much better," Keisha said.

"I feel better. I know I was wrong for my part in everything that went down."

"You live, you learn and try not to repeat the same mistakes."

"It'll be a while before I think about trying to get with another man." Delilah still had feelings for Samson, although she had come to terms with the fact that they would never be together.

"This new guy I'm with might have a friend for you."

"Oh, no. I remember the last guy you tried to fix me up with. He was a borderline stalker."

"Samson could say the same thing about you," Keisha said.

"You got jokes now. Comic relief you're not."

Delilah listened to Keisha talk about her new guy. Keisha sounded really happy, and Delilah felt glad for her. At least one of them had something positive going on.

A loud thud could be heard outside Delilah's front door. She looked out the peephole and saw Dorothy and Kelly standing on her front porch. "Keisha, let me call you back. I got visitors at my door."

"Maybe you shouldn't answer it with all that's been going on."

"I can handle two old busybodies. Trust me. I got this."

"Don't do nothing crazy."

"It depends on them," she said as she clicked off her phone and answered the door. "Well, hello ladies. Come on in."

They sped past her, and Kelly spoke first. "We came over to tell you that you are no longer welcome at Peaceful Rest."

Dorothy said, "It's best that you find another church home."

"Ladies, who made y'all the official dismissal party?" Delilah asked.

"I've tolerated you long enough. This last stunt you pulled with my son was it." Kelly started shaking.

"Calm down," Dorothy said, trying to comfort her friend.

"Don't go and have a heart attack in my house. If there's nothing else you ladies have to say, you can leave." Delilah held the front door open.

Dorothy wrapped her arm around Kelly's shoulder. "Come on. You've let her upset you enough."

"My baby's life is destroyed because of you," Kelly yelled as Dorothy led her out of the house.

Delilah tried to figure out the purpose of Kelly's visit. She came to the conclusion that Samson's entire family was crazy—all but his father, who seemed to be the only sane one in the bunch.

Earlier, Samson's phone rang off the hook. Now that he wanted to talk to people, he couldn't get anybody to pick up their phones. Calvin alerted him to an emergency board meeting to get rid of him. He wanted to be present, but Calvin thought under the circumstances, it would be best that he laid low.

"Lord, how can they make a decision about me if I'm not there to defend myself?" Samson said out loud after ending his call with Calvin.

Julia still refused to take his calls. He attempted to call his parents.

"Hello," Regis said on the other end of the phone.

"Finally," Samson said, relieved he got somebody. "Where's Mom?"

"She's out."

"Oh." Silence filled the phone lines.

"Anything else?" Regis snapped.

"I'm sorry. I'm truly sorry," Samson's voice trailed off.

"I'm not the one you need to be apologizing to. I suggest you go into your prayer closet and have a one-on-one talk with the Lord. He's the one you'll have to answer to come judgment day."

"I've asked God for forgiveness. Now I'm asking you."

"Son, I've addressed my concerns with you. I've prayed about it, and in due time this situation will be a distant memory. Let me deal with it, and we'll talk later, okay?"

Samson let out a sigh of relief. Maybe his father hadn't lost all respect for him after all. "Do you think you can talk to the board members? Calvin said there's an emergency meeting. If you leave now, you can catch it."

"Son, I refuse to do that. You must atone for the sins you committed."

Disappointed, Samson lashed out. "When did you become the judge and juror? Don't you think I deserve a second chance? We all make mistakes."

"Your mistake cost us our church land, son."

"How did you know?" Samson slid down in his chair.

"You're not the only one with a beeline to the Father. You forgot that He and I have a personal relationship. When your indiscretion got exposed, it was revealed to me. Son, you must repent for your sins."

"I have. I promise I have."

"There's a spirit of arrogance still within you. Humble yourself before the Lord before it's too late."

Samson got off the phone with his father. He thought about what Regis had advised. Samson had done everything his father said. He didn't know what more to do. He heard a still voice say, "Truly repent."

It was so crisp and clear, he looked behind him to see

if anyone else was standing there. Samson got down on his knees and closed his eyes. He said a prayer. With each word uttered, he felt the presence of the Holy Spirit. For the first time in a long time, Samson's spirit truly felt at peace.

After praying, he attempted to call Julia again. Michelle answered her cell phone. "She doesn't want to talk to you," Michelle said.

"Tell her I love her, and I really would like for her to be at church tomorrow because there's something I need to say to her, to you, and everybody."

"I'll tell her, but don't expect anything," Michelle snapped.

Samson hung up the phone and dialed Calvin's number. He didn't answer. He left a message. "Man, don't keep me in suspense. Call me."

Samson looked up toward the ceiling. "Lord, it's in your hands now. Whatever your will, I'll just have to accept it."

Samson had just dozed off when his phone rang. "Mama, I'm so glad you called."

"I just got off the phone with Julia. She might come to church tomorrow. I just called to tell you that," Kelly said in a sharp voice.

"Thank you, Mama. I owe you one."

"Just get your act together. That's what you do."

Their conversation ended. Although his mom acted like she was still mad at him, at least she'd called. That's all that mattered to Samson. His sincere prayers were already working. Now, if he could get his wife back. He prayed that she would find it in her heart to forgive him so they could move past this and build a life together as they had planned.

Samson had allowed his ego to get in the way of his sound judgment when he got involved with Delilah. As much as he wanted to blame it all on her, Samson knew the truth. He knew he was the one at fault. Now, once again, he needed to be in control. His life was depending on it—his life with Julia. Like his dad had said, he was in control of his own actions.

Chapter 70

Delilah was dying to know what was going on in the Judges household. She spent another restless night but got up in time to make a trip to the first service at Peaceful Rest Missionary Baptist Church. She pulled her hair back in a ponytail and dressed low-key so as not to draw attention to herself.

She slipped onto the back pew of the church after the choir made its entrance. Some people recognized her and stared. She tried to block them out. A few people started whispering. One of the older male ushers tapped guilty parties on the shoulder and used his finger to indicate he wanted people to be quiet. When everyone stood up for the inspirational song, Delilah looked for Julia in her normal spot on the front row. She wasn't there.

Samson sat behind the desk in his office for what could well be the last time. Calvin had delivered the bad news fifteen minutes ago. The board was asking for his resignation. He typed up something quickly and printed it out. He was reading over it when Julia entered.

She removed the shades revealing her puffy eyes. All Samson could say was, "I'm sorry, Julia."

"That you are. You better be glad I love your mama. She's the only reason I'm here."

"Thank you."

"Don't read more into it than there is. I'm only here

to let folks know that I am still standing. I'm not letting you or your tramp make me crawl into a hole."

"Delilah and I aren't a couple. Never were. It was something that just happened and hopefully one day we'll be able to get past this."

Samson got up and reached for her. Julia pushed him away. "Don't. Don't ever touch me again."

"Julia—please."

"You're pushing it."

Kelly entered. "Julia, can I talk to my son alone? We'll meet you near the entranceway."

Julia left the office abruptly. Kelly closed the door behind her. "Son, yes I'm disappointed in you, but you're still my son, and I love you. You see that woman who just left out of here?" Samson remained quiet. Kelly continued. "She loves you too. I'm a mother, so I'm mad right now and eventually I'll get over it, but Julia. . . . Baby boy, you messed up, and I don't blame her if she doesn't ever want to have anything to do with you again."

"But Mama—" Samson said.

Kelly held up her hand. "I don't want to hear any more of your lies. I'm going to leave you for a few minutes so you can get your thoughts together because you've got a whole lot of explaining to do."

Samson felt like a little boy after his mother chastised him. He walked to the window and looked out at the full parking lot. He said a silent prayer then reached for his robe out of habit. His hand dropped, and he left his office. Calvin was standing outside his office door.

"I think you'll want this," Samson said. He handed Calvin his resignation letter.

Samson watched Julia from a distance as he approached her. He was grateful Julia showed up. He whispered to her, "Thank you again for coming."

Julia remained quiet. The usher led them through the

door. Samson's heart skipped a beat. This would be a day he'd never forget.

The choir stopped singing, and the music stopped. To Delilah's surprise, Samson and Julia walked in the sanctuary together. A hush fell over the room. Samson was not wearing his customary black robe. Delilah wished she had been sitting closer, but from the distance Julia didn't look too happy. She could have sworn Julia jerked her arm when Samson tried to assist her to her seat.

Instead of going to the pulpit, Samson stood on the floor and grabbed the microphone from one of the podiums at the front of the church. The only sounds that could be heard were of a few babies crying. This was the day the parents should have taken their kids to children's church.

Delilah, along with everybody else, was mesmerized as Samson opened up his mouth to speak. "As I look around this room, I see many faces that just a few short weeks ago were singing my praises. Regrettably, I stand before you because of decisions I made that have caused my church family shame and my lovely bride pain."

Samson looked in Julia's direction. He continued. "I stand before you today to ask for your forgiveness. I know it's a lot to ask for. I'm not making any excuses for my actions. I am fully accountable for my participation in the affair. I ask that during this time, you respect my wife and allow her the space she needs to deal with this issue."

Delilah wouldn't dare look around. She could feel eyes on her. She listened as Samson continued his speech. "In light of everything that has happened, members of the board of directors have asked me to step down as pastor of Peaceful Rest Missionary Baptist Church. Although

I disagree with this decision, I do respect it and have turned in my written resignation. I've been told that Associate Minister Michael Monroe will step in and be your interim pastor until you've either decided to reinstate me or elected another pastor."

Someone shouted out, "Pastor Judges, why did you do it?"

Delilah's eyes were glued to the front as she waited for his response with everybody else.

Julia said, "Yes, why Samson?"

Samson looked at the hurt and despair on the face of his wife. He felt trapped as he glanced at the curious congregation. He responded, "My wife, like some of you, wants to know why. Well, I fell in Satan's trap. He used the other party to set a trap for me. I tried to resist, but she kept coming after me. The more I resisted, the more persistent she got."

Samson could see some people possibly swaying to his side. He continued. "Just like Satan used scripture to tempt Jesus, the other party used her body to tempt me. So I ask you to pray for me as I deal with the repercussions of allowing myself to be overcome with bad judgment. If she hadn't made me sleep with her, I wouldn't be standing before you today begging for your forgiveness."

"He's a liar and the truth isn't in him," Delilah yelled.

Samson looked up and saw Delilah walking down the aisle. She stopped near the middle. "Somebody get her!" Samson said frantically.

Nobody moved.

Delilah walked up to one of the other podiums at the front of the church and took the microphone. "Now that all eyes are on me, I have a few things I want to say."

Mumbling could be heard throughout the sanctuary.

Samson wanted to do something, but what could he do? None of the ushers, ministers, or members moved. Samson felt trapped.

Delilah's laugh ricocheted through the room. "The good Reverend Samson Judges has it all twisted. Y'all need to know that I didn't make him fall into my bed. He was more than a willing participant. In fact, he's the one who initiated it. Isn't that right, Samson?"

Everybody was now looking in his direction. Samson said, "Delilah, you need to stop this nonsense."

Delilah held her microphone and started walking in his direction as she talked. "You called yourself confessing, so if you're going to tell the story, tell the whole story. Yes, I loved you. And the operative word is loved, but I woke up."

"Are y'all going to let her talk to me like that?" Samson asked his congregation.

Julia yelled, "Let her talk. I want to hear what else she has to say."

Samson leaned on the podium to hold himself up as Delilah continued.

"For those of you calling and threatening me because I had an affair with the pastor, your energy has been misdirected. I didn't seduce him; he seduced me. I'm just as much a victim in all of this as his wife." Delilah dropped the microphone and took a seat in the nearest pew.

With his head dropped down, Samson moved away from the podium. The congregation began to mumble amongst themselves, and judging by the looks on the members' faces, Samson felt like his life was over. Delilah had just ruined any chances he had of making restitution. Samson's main concern at this point was his wife, but before he could reach her side, he watched Julia rush out of the sanctuary. Samson moved at record speed behind her, but Calvin blocked the door and soon Julia was out of his eyesight.

"I need to talk to my wife. She can't leave me like this," Samson said.

Calvin, without moving from the doorway, said: "Man, you need to chill out. Give her a little time. Right now, everything is too fresh."

"I'm losing everything, and I can't lose Julia too." Samson was distraught. Calvin must have felt sorry for him because he gave him a brotherly hug and then led him out of the sanctuary.

There would be no preaching at Peaceful Rest Missionary Baptist Church on this Sunday. People's minds weren't on worshiping the Lord; they were more concerned about what was going on in the Judges household.

Chapter 71

Delilah got caught up in the crowd of people and now stood face-to-face with Elaine. "You got a lot of nerve showing up here today," Elaine said.

"If you'll move, I'll be on my way," Delilah responded.

"Oh no, you're coming with me." Elaine grabbed Delilah by the arm and attempted to drag her to the side.

Delilah jerked her arm away. "We might be in church, but I'll still kick your behind."

"Ladies, this is a house of worship," one of the ushers interrupted.

Delilah rushed out the doors. "Now what?" she asked out loud when she saw that she had a flat tire. She had a feeling this was no accident. No one who passed bothered to ask if she needed assistance. She got in her car and sat behind the wheel. She dialed Keisha's number. "My tire's on flat. Can you and your friend come change my tire?"

Keisha asked, "Where are you?"

"At Peaceful Rest."

"Girl, now you know better. One of the members probably put your tire on flat."

"I wouldn't doubt it. So are you coming or not?"

"You're lucky I'm out of church. Steven just dropped me off and went to the store. As soon as he comes back, we'll be over."

Delilah wanted to get away from Peaceful Rest as soon as she could. She retrieved her spare tire from the trunk and without success attempted to change her tire. She was leaning on the car, minding her own business, when Samson stopped his SUV near where she was.

"If I were you, I wouldn't get caught talking to me. Someone might flatten your tire too," Delilah joked, although she was far from being in a joking mood.

"Seeing you stranded is like poetic justice. You get what you get," Samson said as he sped out of the parking lot."

Samson had tainted the love Delilah had for him with the way he talked to her and about her.

Calvin's car stopped by. "I would help you, but my wife would kill me. You do have someone coming, don't you?"

"I'm fine," Delilah said.

Calvin sped away. She wasn't familiar with the next car that stopped. The tinted windows rolled down to reveal a clear view of Julia. She was sitting in the passenger side. Michelle was in the driver's seat.

"You've ruined my life," Julia yelled.

"Save that for someone who cares," Delilah responded.

"Don't let me catch you off church grounds," Julia threatened.

"Does it look like I'm scared?" Delilah crossed her arms and leaned on her car.

Delilah heard Michelle say, "Come on Julia, she's not even worth it."

Julia yelled before she left, "Watch out for karma."

"Vengeance is mine, said the Lord," Delilah shouted back.

The church parking lot had thinned out by the time Keisha and Steven arrived. "Delilah, this is Steven. Steven, Delilah," Keisha said as she and Steven got out of his car.

While Steven changed Delilah's flat tire, Keisha and Delilah stood on the side of the car and talked. It didn't take Steven long to finish. "Thanks, Steven," Delilah said. "What do I owe you?" she asked.

"Thanks is all the payment I need," Steven assured her.

Keisha chastised Delilah right before getting in the passenger seat of Steven's car. "Next time, you'll stay your butt at home."

"I'm headed home now," Delilah said.

Keisha and Steven followed Delilah out of the parking lot. When they reached the main entrance, Delilah turned right. Keisha and Steven went in the opposite direction.

Delilah thought about Samson's appeal to the congregation for forgiveness as she drove home. As much as she loved going to Peaceful Rest Missionary Baptist Church, she knew this Sunday would be her last one attending. Samson wouldn't have had to resign if he hadn't pretended that she didn't matter to him. If only he would have treated her with a little more respect, Samson and Julia could have still been living the good life. As far as Delilah was concerned, Samson was the cause of his own downfall, not her.

Delilah was so busy thinking about Samson's misfortunes, she never saw the bullet coming. The driver's side glass scattered throughout the car, and Delilah's body slumped over.

Before blacking out, Delilah heard a voice recite Galatians the sixth chapter, seventh verse—"*Be not deceived; God is not mocked: for whatsoever a man soweth, that shall he also reap.*"

Delilah

Reading Group Guide

1. Delilah preferred to go by her birth name versus the nickname she had been given. Do you think there are hidden meanings in names?

2. Samson wanted to blame Delilah for all of his problems. Do you feel he was justified in doing so? Why or why not?

3. Kelly, Samson's mother, recognized Delilah was up to no good. Is there something she could have done to help Samson get rid of Delilah before the situation escalated to the point that it did?

4. Do you think Julia knew something was going on between Samson and Delilah before she married him? Why or why not?

5. Dorothy, the head of the Pastor's Aide committee, was a little bossy, so her and Delilah's personalities clashed. Do you have a Dorothy in your midst?

6. According to William Trusts, everybody has an Achilles' heel. Do you agree or disagree?

7. Samson knew how Delilah felt about him. Why do you think he didn't stop their one-on-one counseling sessions?

8. Do you think Delilah's past made her latch on to Samson the way she did?

9. Keisha tried to be the voice of reason, but Delilah wouldn't listen. If you see your friend making wrong decisions, do you discuss it with her or do you stay out of it?

10. In the end, Samson was the one responsible for losing his church and wife. Why do some people try to blame others for their problems?

ABOUT THE AUTHOR

Shelia M. Goss is the *Essence* magazine and Black Expressions Book Club bestselling author of *My Invisible Husband, Roses Are Thorns, Paige's Web, Double Platinum, His Invisible Wife, Hollywood Deception* and the teen series *The Lip Gloss Chronicles. Delilah* is her tenth novel and first work of Christian fiction. Goss, a freelance writer, is also the recipient of three *Shades of Romance* magazine Readers' Choice Multi-Cultural awards and was honored as a Literary Diva: The Top 100 Most Admired African American Women in Literature. To learn more, visit her Web sites:

www.sheliagoss.com,
www.myspace.com/sheliagoss,
or follow her on Twitter at
http://twitter.com/sheliamgoss.